# Rebel's Son

## Changed Heart Series #2

Michelle Janene

# Rebel's Son

## Changed Heart Series #2

Michelle Janene

STRONG TOWER
PRESS

Sacramento

Strong Tower Press

Sacramento, CA USA

strongtowerpress.com


**Publishers note:** This is a work of fiction.
Names, characters, places and incidents are either products of the author's imagination or used factiously. All characters are fictional, and any similarity to people living or dead is entirely coincidental.

**Cover art:** by D's Concepts and Designs

breaks: Lighted Sword: image # 42422439 idimair,

Map Font Underworld by hmeneses

Cover Images: NEstudio/Shutterstock.com, wavebreakmedia/ Shutterstock.com, Patryk Kosmider/Shutterstock.com, Shaiith/ Shutterstock.com

Font: MacHumaine by Bill Horton


Scripture quoted or paraphrased from Geneva Bible ©1599

*I am profoundly blessed by the support of family and my writing sisters. Without God's inspiration, their help, support, and love, I would never have become an author.*

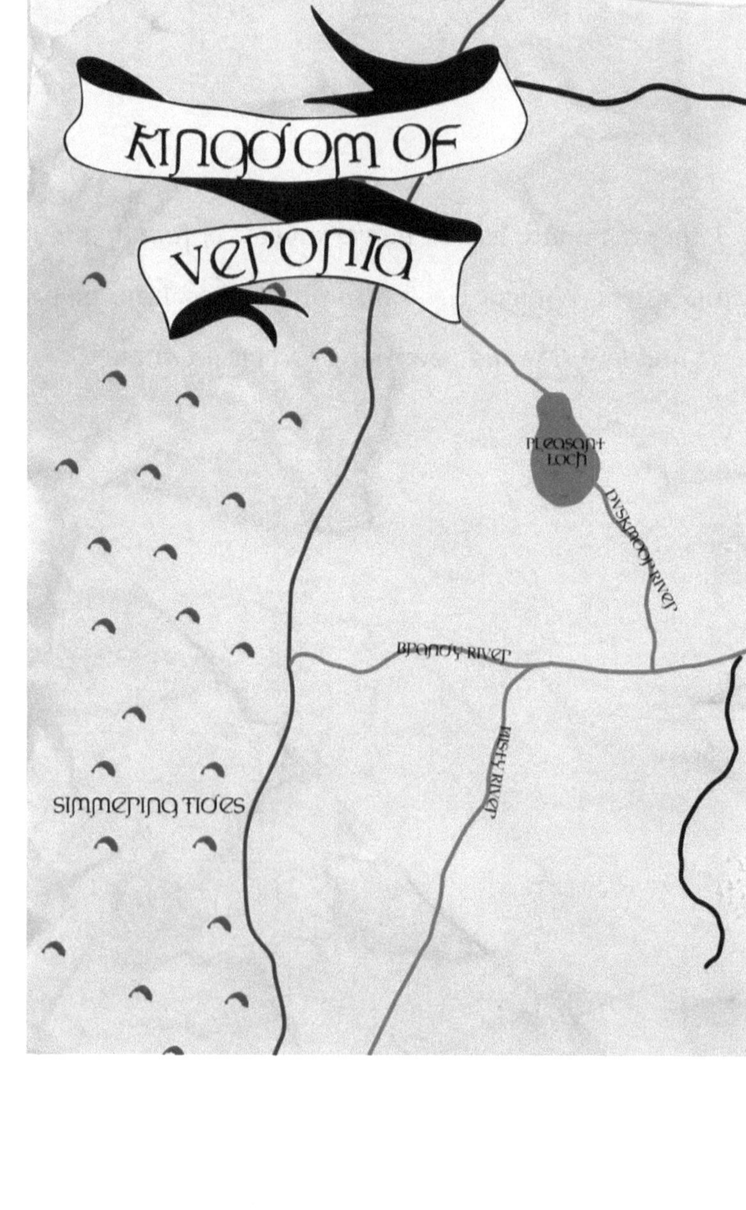

KINGDOM OF
VERONIA
PLEASANT LOCH
DUSKMOOR RIVER
BRANDY RIVER
MISTY RIVER
SIMMERING TIDES

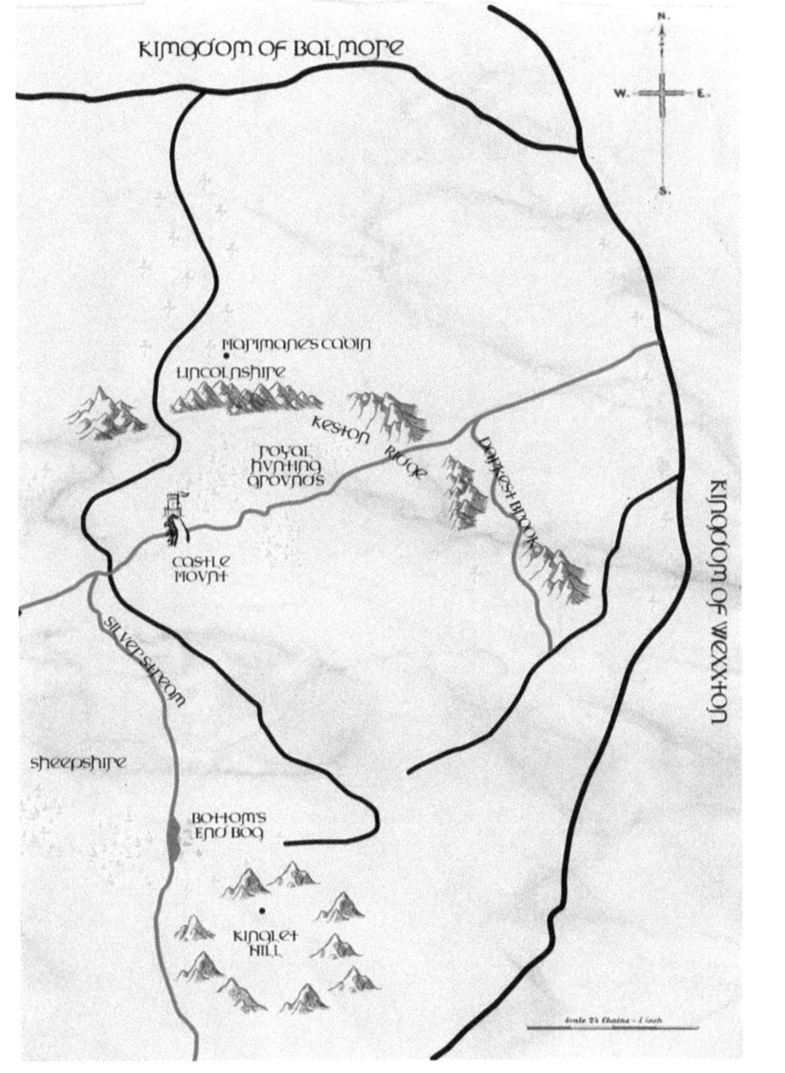

KINGDOM OF BALMORE
N.
W. E.
S.
Marimane's Cabin
Lincolnshire
Keston Ridge
Royal Hunting Grounds
Darkest Brook
Kingdom of Wexxton
Castle Mount
Silverstream
Sheepshire
Bottom's End Bog
Kinglet Hill
Scale 24 Chains = 1 inch

# *Chapter 1*

Shane slid his fingers unchallenged through his wavy hair as he strolled with quickening breaths. Merriment bubbled like one of Cook's rich stews hanging over a flame. He cleared his throat to suppress it. A stable boy passed him. The boy's steps accelerated, his gaze darting about. He wrung his hands together.

Shane slowed his exit from the ward to watch his masterpiece unfold. His heart quickened, and his breaths came in shallow puffs.

The youth cracked open the stable doors, searching the darkness before stepping inside. He glanced once more over his shoulder at Shane, his lips drawn in a harsh line. Shane tossed his head and waved at Ethan stomping toward him through the inner gate.

The stable boy opened the doors further. A scrape groaned above his head.

Shane became stone in midstride, riveted by the action unfolding.

A bucket toppled on the youth, covering him in sticky syrup.

"Your Highness!" Ethan snapped.

The lad stumbled back, and Ethan veered aside to give aid.

Shane grasped his childhood companion, pulling him to his side. "No, 'tis better yet. Watch."

The boy staggered and bumped the other door open. A bag of feathers rained on him.

Shane roared with laughter as the boy slumped to his knees in tears.

Ethan jerked free. "Is this what you have been about this day, Highness? Torturing innocent lads? Training with Sir Griff commenced hours ago."

Shane remained doubled over. "Is it not the funniest thing you have ever beheld? I must tell the royal jester." He wiped a tear from his cheek. "I amaze myself."

"What—by all that is holy—is the matter with you?" Ethan said as he reached the teary, crumpled, sticky lump.

Shane bristled and straightened. "Nothing is the matter with me." He tossed his head and threw his chin in the air. "I *am* my mother's son."

"The queen's name may mean 'rebellious' but never has she behaved other than a godly upright woman."

Shane shrugged off the reproof and left the curmudgeon. Ethan always dampened his merriment. Ethan remained to clean up after him. 'Twas just punishment for stealing his joy. With slow, meandering steps, Shane moved from the ward into the large bailey. What should he do next? He scanned the castle inhabitants for his next victim. Chuckling laughter toyed with him once more, raising a smirk to his lips. But it faded as quick as it sprang to life.

He tried to shake his spirit free of Ethan's chastisement. He was the crown prince. He skirted the chapel in the center of the crowded space as a dark humor filled him. *What right does that lowly would-be knight have to judge his lord?* The hallowed building towered over him, the windows, door, and steps forming a profound scowl of holy disapproval. Shane turned his back on the reproof.

The hollow clank of wasters of the other men-at-arms and knights training vied for his attention. He ducked into the tavern before ol'

Griff could require his presence.

Shaking his head to clear it of all unwanted notions, he took long purposeful strides into the dimly lit room. Glancing down his up turned nose at the few gathered within, he sighed and his muscles relaxed as each underling slipped from their bench and took a knee as he passed. His chin rose higher still. He straightened his jerkin. His chest filled until the toggles threatened to break free.

With only steps left in his regal parade, a twinge of guilt dared to prick him. Like some flighty maid with a needle, it pierced him for a moment but caused no lasting injury. The annoyance of guilt came, as he knew well of his father's disapproval of such abject observance. Shane brushed off the momentary stab. He had secretly decreed to all within the castle walls that he required such submission whenever the king was not present.

Shane plopped against the wall and put one foot on the seat beside him. No one moved. They dared not until a mug rested in his hand. He slammed his fist on the table, rattling it against the stone floor. A tankard shuddered into place.

"You are slow this day, keeper."

"Forgive me, Yer Highness," the gray-haired man inched his bent body to the floor.

"If this cup stays filled, mayhaps I will consider it." Shane dismissed him with a wave at the entire room and laid his head against the stone wall. He needed a new distraction. The owner's daughter brought her father a pitcher. She could prove promising. Recently coming into her womanhood, she could be plucked with little effort.

The tavern owner placed the ale on Shane's table, blocking his view of the lithe woman. "Our finest for His Highness." The man bowed again, though not to the floor.

"Being as 'tis the only tavern on this high lump of rock, your claim says little."

The old man bit his lip.

"You expect not for me to pour it myself? Send your wench to attend my needs."

The tavern owner's eyes narrowed. "Ye knows well, Highness, Rachel bes no wench. She bes me precious daughter."

The maid trembled.

"Precious indeed. She will serve me."

The owner opened his mouth, but Shane spoke first.

"I wonder the actions of the king when told of your disrespect for his son, the crown prince, ol' man."

"I've done naught—"

"Exactly! You stand there allowing my cup to remain empty as I languish without any amiable companionship." He winked at the tasty morsel.

The girl placed her hand on her father's shoulder. "I've finished much of me duties, Father. I can attend the prince. Fret not."

Her father frowned, but Shane shooed him away. The girl stood, hands clasped in front of her, on the opposite side of his table.

Shane straddled the bench and patted the seat beside him.

"I can see to yer needs better from 'ere, Highness." Her words were calm, her gaze appropriately lowered. She filled his cup.

"You know naught of my needs, girl." He slapped the bench. "What would your father do if he no longer owned this pathetic little hovel?"

Her knuckles whitened, but she moved to the far end of his bench. Shane admired the contour of her profile for a moment before he leaned forward, slipped his fingers in her apron strings, and pulled her along the bench. She came to rest between his legs. He brushed the smooth skin of her jaw with the back of his fingers. "Now, this is better."

She swallowed hard as her breaths quickened.

He skimmed his fingers along the curve of her neck, noting her pounding heart. His blood boiled. He wanted to throw her down on the table and teach her a great many things.

"Your Highness!" Light flooded his sanctuary.

"Go away, Eth. The girl and I are getting acquainted."

Ethan stomped to the end of his table, arms crossed. "You *will* leave Rachel be and resume your training at once, or I will be forced to inform the king."

Shane sipped his ale, watching its dark amber swirl in the bottom of the cup as he considered his options. How much pleasure could he get from the girl before the rat informed his father and they dragged him to the training corral? Shane drained the tankard and thumped it on the boards. *Not nearly enough.*

"We shall finish this another time, my sweet." His hand brushed over her breast.

She recoiled with a yelp.

"Leave her be." Flames flickered in Ethan's eyes.

Shane rolled his shoulders. "I see naught the importance of my presence in training—this day or any other. You all train for the honor of being knighted. It is not as if any would refuse to give the crown prince his spurs."

A growl rumbled through his escort. "You set a right poor example. What man will ever follow you into battle?"

Shane laughed. "Who claims I would so risk the people losing such a glorious ruler by leading the charge into battle? What would the people do without me to guide them?"

"Celebrate wildly in the streets."

Without a moment's hesitation, Shane slammed his fist into the man's jaw. Ethan stumbled a single step. It was not the first time Ethan had been the recipient of his wrath. Shane smirked. He was such a smart lad, one would think he would learn to curb his tongue and save himself the humiliation. They stepped from the dark tavern into the glowing sunlight.

Ethan dabbed at the blood at the corner of his mouth with his tongue. His strides were angry as he escorted Shane to the training ring. "Your title alone saves you. Were you any other man—"

"Aye, but I am nay any other man. I am the crown prince. And no one—not even you, ol' friend—would dare lay a hand on me outside the training ring. Well, not even there really."

"You smug—"

"Highness, so good of you to join us at last," Griff said.

"I know my presence is a great honor to your little school, Griff." Shane sized up the men to find his next amusement.

# Chapter 2

As the others trained in earnest, Shane poked some in the ribs with the blunted tip of his waster. Others he slapped on the backside with the flat face of the useless wooden weapon. Turning to one noble son, Shane winked. "Here, boy." Shane slapped his shoulder, pushing the young man to the center of the practice arena. "Let me offer some guidance."

They squared off. The other man lunged first. Shane swatted the weapon aside like a fly. He patted the startled opponent on his cheek. "Lose a little more of this lard, boy, and you shall move faster." Shane roared, tweaking his chin.

Shane waved for him to try again. The red-faced victim lunged with a snarl. Shane sidestepped the charge like a bullfighter. The man staggered. Shane thrust his foot into his opponent's backside. The noble son landed on his belly, his face in the dirt.

Shane threw back his head his hands holding his middle. "Hey, Griff, the boy should rest. Look at the effort it takes the lad to heft his great bulk about."

"Ignore him, Oswin, you are twice the fighter of the spoiled prince," Ethan said, helping the man to his feet. Ethan dared shoot a rebuking glance at Shane.

"Twice the fighter. He is large, but hardly twice my weight. What have you been drinking, Eth?"

"You are the only one to indulge in such vice."

A smirk filled Shane's face. "I *am* my mother's son."

Oswin had his back to Shane as he gasped for air.

Shane narrowed his gaze with a sneer and slid his waster between Oswin's fat thighs. The man did not see the obstruction until he attempted to return to his training. Entangled, he stumbled. His ankle twisted. The man yelped and landed with his face in the dirt yet again.

Shane slapped his knee and roared. "Oh, aye, I see now the manner of this warrior. You are quite correct, Eth. I could never lack such grace. He is a much better buffoon than I."

The boy lumbered to his feet and lunged at Shane with a murderous roar. His injured ankle caused him to cry out in pain, but he charged undeterred. It took four warriors to hold him back.

"Forget him, Oswin. He is not worth the grief which would be visited upon you for hitting him."

"I wish not to hit him, sir. I aim to beat him until he never rises again."

Ethan stepped between the two, sparing Shane having to teach the oaf another lesson. He warned the man to silence. "Do not dare put voice to such threats against your prince, Lord Oswin. It dishonors you and lowers you to his juvenile behavior. Come, let us go see Sir Carrington. He will know how best to treat your injury."

Shane took a few swings at the man-at-arms nearest him. He passed the remainder of the day in half-hearted attempts at sparring with the lesser men he was forced to train beside.

At last, the bell in the chapel's steeple rang out the call to supper. Shane let his waster drop and strolled out before being dismissed.

His servant, Alden, changed Shane's shirt as he stood barely raising his arms to help in the efforts. Afterwards, Shane threw water on his face, swaggered down to the hall, and approached the high table where he ate with his father and his little brother, Jak.

His father, Edgar, wore a hard expression on his weathered face. His now almost entirely gray hair was one of the signs of his advanced age. *How much longer till the ol' man turns my kingdom over to me?*

Shane had once overheard a servant say, "The king once had such fine dark hair. The graying commenced as soon as Prince Shane could walk and spread faster once he learned to talk."

Shane could not be the cause of his father's aging. He tossed aside the notion as he threw off all unpleasant thoughts.

Queen Mariamne approached, carrying two large serving trays. She still served as a common servant in the king's hall each meal. Her long onyx hair, streaked with ribbons of silver was braided and wrapped at the base of her skull. Mother did not appear to have aged nearly as much as his father, therefore, he could not be the root of the problem.

"Evening, my son," she said, though her customary joy seemed to have melted away this night. Only a step beyond him, she stumbled as her toe caught in her hem.

Shane reached out, encircling her with a strong, steadying arm. He pulled his mother close. He felt her pounding heart bang against her ribs, and his own heart trembled.

"Are you well, Mother?" He whispered as he brushed his stubble-covered cheek against her reddening one.

"Aye, son. Much thanks to you, only a small portion fell."

"Damn the food, Mother. Are you to right? I could not bear to see you hurt."

A slim smile appeared. "Disturbing news weighs heavy on my heart. But, oh, how I cherish your concern, my son. I pray it is ever so." She slipped away to continue her work.

Shane shivered at the loss. "God's blessing be upon you, Mother." Though the words performed an odd jig on his tongue, he meant them with all his shallow heart. There were times her presence alone kept the dark humor from consuming him. His spirit fluttered with rare compassion only she could stir. He followed her. "Mother, speak of it, and I will do everything in my power to make it aright." His hand rested on her upper arm as he longed to embrace her again.

"I pray you will, my son." She moved to the furthest table to deliver her trays. Her odd plea rang in his spirit, shaking loose some of the darkness and shining a torch on his wickedness. As he followed her movements, Father waved him to his seat.

"Is Mother well?"

"You will come on a hunt tomorrow."

Shane groaned. A hunt with his father meant rising before the sun. "Father—"

"This will not be debated. You will be on your horse before first light." Edgar trapped his son in the heated rage of his glare. "You *will not* defy me."

Shane quaked as his mind carried him back to times in his childhood when he feared and respected this man. When was the last time he'd looked at his father so? Shane raised his chin. "If you require my assistance in the hunt so desperately, of course I will come and give you aid, Father."

Edgar's fist pounded, rattling the dinnerware. Jak jumped, and the murmur of the hall fell to a whisper, accompanied by covert glances. Shane felt the heat of his father's wrath. He picked at his food as his stomach twisted into a knot.

Before half the meal passed, Shane excused himself. "I will see you on the morrow, Father. Rest you well." He popped his little brother in the arm as he left.

"Ow!"

"Better toughen, Jak, or you will never advance from squire to knight."

Shane savored the cool air outside. He raked his hands through his hair, closing his eyes to the memory of disapproving stares from so many within his father's walls. He would be king someday—soon, he hoped. And when he sat on the throne, no one would hazard to even look at him.

A small whimper deep in his spirit reminded him if he but did right, he would be approved. Shane sneered. He enjoyed the rush of his antics far too much. His heart thrilled each time his mind commenced work on a new venture. Being the crown prince of all Veronia came with certain privileges—if not, what good was it?

He needed an adventure now to wash away the unspoken impending doom his father threatened. His eyes scanned the ward for ideas. A servant girl approached the well, but he had tasted of her before. The maid brought to mind the bar wench, though. His feet moved with a near skip as he sauntered to the tavern.

The dark room only held two patrons, and they left after giving proper observance. Shane's heart raced. "Keeper?" he shouted.

The old man came from the back room and bowed low—though not to the ground as Shane demanded. "Welcome, Yer Highness."

"Where is the wench?"

The frail man straightened to his full limited stature. His jaw set and his chin jutted out. "Rachel bes here no longer, Highness."

"Send for her at once."

"Rachel lives here no longer. She now resides with relatives—far out of your wicked reach," said a familiar voice behind him. Ethan swaggered up to the man two years his senior.

"If you fancied her too, Eth, you had only speak of it. I would gladly give you a turn with her when I am done."

Ethan grimaced and scowled at him.

"Now, where is she?" Shane added his own growl to punctuate his words.

Ethan crossed his arms. "As I said, somewhere you can do her no harm."

Shane licked his lips. "I wish her no harm, Eth. I mean to pleasure her."

"I know not how you could be of the same blood as King Edgar the Honorable and Queen Mariamne the Righteous. They love the Lord and His laws. They care for their people above their own selfish desires. Are you able to comprehend the profound disappointment and embarrassment you are to them?"

Shane swung at him again. But—for the first time—Ethan took not the hit. He blocked the blow, landing one of his own in Shane's ribs, driving out the air. Shane doubled over with a stunned gasp.

"Never will you hurt Rachel or another woman in this castle as long as I live." Ethan shoved Shane on his rump. "And the Lord curse me if ever I swear fidelity to a man the likes of you."

"Your Highness," the old man shuffled to Shane and bent to help him up. "My Lord." The man could not contain his approving smirk.

Shane smacked his wrinkled hands away. "Dare not to lay your peasant hands upon me." He brushed away the rushes and went to his room, vowing Ethan would rue the day he ever laid hands on his prince.

# *Chapter 3*

"Highness?"

"Fie! Leave me be," Shane cursed the man rousing him.

"But the hunt with thee sire, Highness …"

Shane allowed Alden to dress him. "There is no good reason to do anything at this ungodly hour."

"Highness, you are injured."

Shane dismissed the servant's mention of the bruise adorning his ribs. His first instinct had been to reveal Ethan's misconduct. But Shane knew too well his father—and Eth's father also. They would inquire on the entirety of the matter. Shane conceded his father would approve more of Eth's response than side with his own behavior. He was also loath to admit Eth had landed him on his arse with a single blow. He would find another way to reward the sanctimonious shite for the injury—both in flesh and soul—and soon.

Alden finished. With his eyes but half open, Shane lumbered to break the fast. Food would at least make the arduous early morning hunt a little tolerable.

King Edgar waited, arms crossed, tapping his foot in the rushes at the end of one of the boards.

Cy sat on a bench—nearby as always. The man was like part of the castle. He served as Father's thane; of course he was Ethan's father, and somewhere in their history he had come to be called a brother to Mother. Oft times Shane resented the man, for Cy behaved as another parent. This morn, his blond brows furrowed and his frowned deep. No others lolled about and Shane's heart quickened.

"Good morn to you, Father. Good morn, Sir Cynric." Mayhaps his genial greeting would soften them.

"You are late. Let us be off." Father stomped through the rushes.

"May I collect a bite—?"

Father shoved open the door. "Had you been on time, you could have eaten your fill. Come!"

Cy followed close on Shane's heels assuring he moved to join the king.

Shane quickened his steps to catch up. They mounted their horses as first light kissed the Kestron Ridge. The three of them traveled without guard or escort. Veronia had been at peace since months after his birth, but the king never took such chances as to travel without a contingent of personal guards. Shane's heart beat harder, drowning out the pounding of his mount's hooves as they trotted from the castle's perch.

The late spring day dawned warm, though Shane shivered from the chilled reception afforded him. "Father, if this is about my training —?"

"'Tis about a great many matters, which concern me most grievously!" Edgar kicked his mount to speed.

Shane raced after him, but they did not head for the royal hunting grounds. Father charged north, toward the ridge. They did not slow until they neared the narrow mountain pass.

Father led his horse off the road to a stream, allowing it a long drink. He turned to Shane "I will no longer tolerate your insolence and your wicked behavior."

"Sire," Cy said.

Father whirled. "I know well the lessons of the Bible, brother. I have read the punishments God casts on a kingdom whose leader does not discipline his own. I will nay allow my people to suffer for my inaction out of some misplaced love and hope for this ingrate." Father kicked his horse to a trot.

An unyielding lump grew in Shane's throat, making it difficult to breathe. What did Father aim to do? *I am the crown prince. He cannot plan to kill me and hope to cover it up.* Was not murder a greater sin than any of the trivial games he got about? *What discipline can he hope to find way out here?* A myriad of possibilities bombarded Shane as the day wore on and they traversed the high pass single file.

Father led the way and Cy followed—slumped and far too quiet. Father never spoke either. He sat like a broadsword had replaced his spine, eyes straight ahead, his lips drawn and thin. When was the last time Father and Cy went anywhere when they did not laugh, let alone converse with one another?

Shane's muscles cramped. He shoulders and neck were as stiff as if mortar had been poured in them. His breaths came in quick puffs.

They spent the night in a cave. Edgar refused to speak, and Shane curled on his bedroll. Sleep did not come, as dark shadows of his future danced on the walls. Every muscle ached. Even his heart struggled.

His father and Cy stirred before first light. "Come, Shane. Let us deal with you and your behavior."

"Father, I—"

"Speak not a word to me until you are prepared to be a different man." Edgar stared, an unmoving force without reason.

Shane clamped his mouth shut and mounted his horse. His father had moved beyond discussion. Best to let the matter proceed as Father intended, without disruption. Shane needed no more wrath than was already to be visited upon him.


With much of the day behind them, they increased their pace once more in the valley on the far side of the ridge. They formed up side by side, Edgar in the middle. They skirted Lincolnshire, following the curve of the valley to the east. Deep in the woods, filled with late afternoon shadows, Father drew his mount to a halt and jumped from the saddle.

"This is the place." Father handed his reigns to Cy with a melancholy smile. "I remember the joy of that day now as only a wishful dream."

"Sire, I beg you again …"

Father held up his hand. The weak smile faded and the wrath returned. "You are the nearest thing my precious wife has to a brother, uncle to my children, and my closest friend, but I will nay entertain another word from you on this matter. Be silent or be gone!"

Cy inclined his head and reached for Shane's reins.

He relinquished them and stood as Father whirled on him—finger wagging in the air. "This is the day, boy, where I draw a line on the forest floor and you comprehend in your degenerate head, I will accept not another single act of disrespect and wickedness from you."

Shane opened his mouth with a tremulous smirk.

Edgar struck him, driving him back a step. "Shut your smug mouth and be quick to listen. You will hear your king well, and understand."

Father spun away his light cloak swirling the leaf litter. He stomped two strides away whirled back and returned one step. "You will attend all your lessons and train with utmost diligence. You will afford Father Bartholomew the unwavering respect due him by the church and God Himself as your instructor. You will demonstrate like respect for Sir Griff as my appointed captain and the honor due him as a proven warrior—something you have far to achieve." Father's finger rose again, and his words ground between his clenched teeth. "You, Shane, royal of Veronia, will never again take a maiden to your bed— or anywhere else—to bring her shame and dishonor. If one more such wicked betrayal comes to my attention—so help me—I will take my dagger and remove your offending sword myself."

"Majesty!" Cy coughed.

"He dishonors me with his unholy treatment of the women under my roof. But more importantly, Cy, he dishonors his God. Are we not told, 'Wherefore, if thine hand or thy foot cause thee to offend, cut them off, and cast them from thee: it is better for thee to enter into life, halt, or maimed, than having two hands, or two feet, to be cast into everlasting fire.' If he will nay do it, as his father, and the king, it falls to me."

Shane tried to swallow his heart, which now sat firmly lodged behind his teeth. He trembled seeing his father as the authority over him as never before. Shane knew him to be a man of action and suffered sanctions before, but never did he truly fear his king—not until this day.

Turning his attention back to him, Father clasped his hands behind his back and paced. The crunching leaves and snapping twigs added an odd cadence to his words. The musty earth emitted a foul odor to accompany his father's message.

"Not one more life within my kingdom will be subject to your childish and cruel antics."

Hoping to lighten the mood consuming him, Shane tossed his head. "But I am my mother's son."

Father slapped him again, seized his shirt, lifted him off the ground, and brought him to the tip of his nose. Father's hot words burned his face. "Never again will you blame my precious wife, that most godly of women, for your evil behavior."

"Edgar, no!" Cy tried to pull him off.

"Furthermore—she is not your mother, nor are you blood of my blood."

# Chapter 4

Shane pulled from his father's grasp. He brushed his shirt straight. "I have heard well, Father, you wish me to behave. I will endeavor to do better. There is no need to spin wild yarns."

"King Edgar speaks truth." Cy said, his head hanging low. "The queen found you wailing here in this small clearing."

"And by the grace of God alone you came to live in my home. I can remove you from it with as much ease."

The forest spun. The ground heaved and his knees trembled—his legs unsteady and weak. A foul heat churned his belly, and cold sweat chilled his skin. Shock—greater than what he'd received when Ethan struck him—overwhelmed his senses. "How can it be so?"

"You have heard told many times how Queen Mariamne suffered an attack only months after coming to marry King Edgar. She fled in secret from the castle in the middle of the night." Cy waited for Shane to acknowledge the well-known story.

Shane remembered the times his mother—*or should he now say the queen?*—had told him the tale. Cy served as her personal guard and was tasked with going everywhere with her. But she fled that night and hurt him grievously. It was a regret the queen spoke of on dark days. Now that same pain lay mirrored on Cy's face.

"Queen Mariamne spent that harsh winter alone in a cabin, not far from here." Cy pointed through the trees further north. "When the snows cleared, King Edgar received a vision from the Lord as to where to find his love. We came and collected her. She did not have a child. Mariamne passed her isolation in communion with God—alone. She gave her heart to Him, and God led her to you on our return to the castle."

"I cradled you in my arms for the first time here." The king picked up the retelling. "Believing I could not sire children after suffering a childhood illness, I welcomed you with an open heart and named you Shane—Gift of God. More love I could not have given you. Upon our return a small group of knights, sent on errand by their snooping lords, were standing in my hall. They were tasked with demanding I remarry and sire an heir.

When they saw you and their returned queen, they bowed and accepted you as my true son. God never gave opportunity to convey the truth of your origins. The lords were satisfied, and they left me to rule in peace."

"And what would they say now if they knew you lied concerning me?" Anger colored Shane's threat as a growing darkness beleaguered his soul.

Edgar stepped close, wrath flashing white-hot in his eyes. "Are you such a fool? They would leap for joy and throw a celebration in the streets. To know you have no rightful claim to my throne and will never rule over them—the rejoicing would continue without end."

Cold sweat caused Shane's clothes to cling to him. He shuddered. "What do you aim to do Fath—My King?"

"My course of action depends wholly on you. Your fate rests squarely upon your own shoulders. If you become the man of honor I raised you to be, not one more word will be spoken on the matter. You will receive the crown of heir apparent, and you will serve your people with kindness and compassion."

"And if I fail to meet your approval?"

"I will confess to the nobility my profound mistake in bringing you into my home. The crown will be placed on Jak's head—as the true heir to the throne—and you will be forgotten."

"Your mother will nay forget you, Highness. She loves you most dearly," Cy said.

Shane looked at the thane; hurt, anger, pain, and uncertainty consumed him. "It would appear I know naught of my mother, sir." Shane staggered a few steps away and crumpled to his knees.

The king did not allow him to wallow long before they were back in the saddle headed home. The late hour forced them to camp partway up the ridge or risk falling to their deaths in the dark. Mayhaps that would have been preferable to the torment Shane now suffered.

A tentative rap sounded on his outer door. Shane groaned for the person to leave him be, but the door creaked open nonetheless. "My son, are you well?"

Shane righted his weary body on the divan he had not left in three days. Since returning from learning he belonged not in his place of honor, nor to the family in which he was raised, he dared not move. He remained motionless, consumed by the singular thought of losing all to the true son of the king.

His forearms rested on his knees, his hands dangled lifelessly between. His head hung as words were pulled from him. "Call me not your son, Majesty. The truth has been spoken, and your endearment is no longer warranted."

The swish of her satin gown filled the room. She knelt and

reached for his hands. "Oh, my heart—"

Shane leapt, almost upsetting her balance—and his own. "Majesty, I am unworthy …" He could not finish, choked by the burn in his throat and the sting in his eyes.

She rose with silent grace. "Shane, prince of Veronia, you are my son. I love you, and I will not entertain your wallowing."

He leaned near and glared. "I am no son of your flesh, Majesty. Yet now, I am forced to pretend to be a man I am not or be tossed out with the filth. How is such love?"

"The evil you do is not you, my son."

"Stop calling me that!"

"Be sober and watch: for your adversary the devil as a roaring lion walks about, seeking whom he may devour."

He clamped his hands over his ears and turned. "Quote not from the Holy Book. It condemns me enough." He clenched his eyes closed. *Stop—all of it, just stop.* He crumpled to the divan once more as Ethan's words thundered back. *I do not know how you could be the same blood as King Edgar and Queen Mariamne.*

Though his eyes were closed, his vision beheld the reality. Mariamne's name may mean "Rebel" but she lived surrendered to God. Not a rebellious or contrary bone could be found in her. In truth, only he behaved the rebel—though named "a gift from God." He was no gift—only a curse.

"You are not the man you are becoming," she said again. "Turn while there is yet time. Please, my—please Shane. Will you not do this for me?"

He loved her—like no other. If he were to change his ways it would only be for her—the woman who loved him unconditionally.

"I will try, My Queen. Pray there is still hope for me."

She sat beside him. Her radiant smile lit the dim room until it shown in his very soul. Her warm hand caressed his cheek, loosening the dark hold on his spirit. "My precious boy, I pray God's mercy and grace upon you every hour of every day." She pulled him close in a tender embrace. "You are my heart."

Shane allowed his arms to encircle her. He felt her love and belief filling him from the top of his head to the bottom of his heels. Here—in this moment—he believed he could do anything. If only he could hold to this hope and act upon it. But he feared the darkness tugging at his spirit would never allow such a change to be wrought in him.

# Chapter 5

Shane lay hidden behind his bed curtains, hoping not to disappoint his mother.

*She is not your mother,* a voice sneered deep in his spirit, stirring the darkness.

His bare feet landed on the thin tapestry. He searched, hoping to find a man in his chambers. Forcing his fingers through his tangled hair, he tried to shake off the unwanted feelings. He plodded to the bathing chamber and repeatedly splashed his face. The coolness provided relief to his flaming skin and eased his nausea. He scrutinized his reflection. "Who are you?"

*Nobody. You know naught because of their lies. They stole you. Hid you. Forced you to conform to their ways. Now you are nothing. Not one of them and not what you could have been.*

"They saved me," he muttered.

*Your entire life, they have lied. Chained you to their rules. You could be free. You could choose your destiny. You do not have to meet their expectations ..."*

"If I stay, I could still one day be king."

*You could be king—now.*

Shane shuddered at the cold claw gripping his heart. Images of his mother—of Queen Mariamne—filled his thoughts. She loved him.

This he knew to be true—no matter what the disembodied voice taunted.

"Alden!"

The old man shuffled into the room. "Aye, Your Highness?"

"I wish to go out."

"Good, good. Which do you prefer?" Alden swung open the wardrobe and swayed with the effort.

Shane threw out his arms waiting to be dressed. "Linen tunic, purple jerkin, and black breeches with the black boots."

"Is there a special occasion, Your Highness, to dress in your finest?"

"I am the crown prince, what other excuse do I need to dress to the station I was born?" The last words caught like a fishbone, and he struggle to clear them.

Alden glanced over his shoulder as he pulled the items into his arms.

Did he know the truth? The king, queen, and Cy knew, but did any other?

"Here we are, Highness. Do you wish a shave before you dress?"

*Highness? It should be Majesty. Only one lying charlatan stands in your way, my son.*

Shane rubbed his stubble-covered jaw ignoring, the swirling of hate-filled thoughts. "No, I wish it to grow."

"Very good, Highness." Alden helped Shane into his clothes, but after sitting on the floor to lace the boots, he struggled to stand. "Will you be desiring a warrior's knot today, Highness?"

"Just brush out the tangles, Alden. I nay have all day."

Shane descended the stairs two at a time hoping to outrun the darkness. The hall was deserted. He glanced at the angle of the sun through a high window. He judged the time to be well after first meal but still an hour or better before midday. The simmering rich stew taunted his grumbling stomach. He poked his head into the kitchen; many turned at the intrusion and again he wondered who else knew his true status.

Cook smiled at him and inclined her round head to the bowl of apples near the door. He snatched one before hurrying to the training corrals. As he passed from the inner ward into the outer bailey, a yelp drew his attention. His steps quickened as a succession of yelps followed. Shane rounded the corner to find two boys kicking at a young hound. In two strides he drew up behind the lads, seized them by the collars, and yanked them off the ground.

"By all that is holy, what do you think you are doing?"

The boys trembled. "Was but a bit of sport, sir. 'Tis no harm. 'Tis only a mutt," one said.

Shane threw them down in a heap across the narrow alleyway. "The same could be said of you." He raised his foot to deliver a blow.

The lads screamed as they curled into balls, covering their heads. "Highness, we're sorry," the second yelled.

"Aye, sore are, my lord."

"'Twill never happen again!"

"Never, we swear, never again."

Shane turned and scooped up the pup as it licked an injured paw. He cradled it under his chin and stroked it until the creature relaxed. Heading back to the main street, in the opposite direction of the training corral, Shane approached the kennels where the huntsman and his pages and grooms cared for the king's hounds.

"Take this pup and tend to his injuries," Shane said, placing the dog in the hands of a groom.

"Aye, yer Highness."

"He will be well tended. Am I understood?"

"Aye, Highness. He'll receive the best care. I swears it."

Shane nodded and continued on to the far side of the bailey and his training.

"Your Highness." Griff greeted him with a scowl. "Has your health returned?"

"What?"

"The king spoke of you suffering a fever after the hunt. He indicated you may be abed a few days."

Why would the king offer an excuse for him?

*He covers his own lies. They all lie. Lies on top of lies that require yet more lies.*

Shane threw off the darkness smothering his soul like a sodden blanket. "I am again myself, Gr—Sir Griff."

The captain's brow rose. Others turned from their training.

*They trust you not. They will give not the crown to you. You must take it—now.*

"Where do you wish me to begin, sir?"

Griff stared at him. At last he pointed to a group at the back of the last corral. "Start work with the spear, Highness. Should prove less taxing after your illness."

Shane nodded and moved quickly to attend the task given him. As he worked with diligence at his training, the dark humor continued to poke him. It stirred ugly notions he wished to flee. But they were a part of him. He could find no relief.

Over the long summer since he learned of the truth, Shane felt himself turn from an irreverent ne'er-do-well into a suspicious, anger-filled brute. The voice pecked away at his soul like a woodpecker drilling holes in a mighty oak. The voice left a riddled shadow of a man behind.

Shane lashed out like a snarling dog at anyone who looked upon him. He saw the judgment in each glance and stare. The malevolence tormenting him kept him from sleep and would allow neither focus on lessons nor training.

*You need not cow to their rules. Take the throne. Grab the crown. Be a man of your own choosing.*

In desperation, Shane staggered into the chapel late one afternoon and crumbled before the altar. "My God, keep me from killing my king." Tears stung as they washed his face.

His tormentor did not fall silent but spoke no more of murder. *Who are you? Who is your true mother? Find her, my son.*

Shane stumbled from bed, unable to sleep for the drumming pain. Dressed in an unadorned tunic, and worn breeches, he grabbed Alden's cloak as he slipped from his chamber in the middle of the night.

*Where do you go? Stop.*

"I will leave word of my intentions." Shane jerked a sheet of velum free and scribbled.

*They deserve no courtesy. Go. Do as you please.*

"I will cause no worry. Or reason to celebrate my absence."

*You are your own man. Stop conforming to their demands.*

Shane scribbled his signature and dropped the quill atop the note.

*Go. Be on your way.*

"I will return."

*Of course you will.*

He chose a common bay from the stable and a worn saddle. He led the animal to the outer gate. "Where do you go this hour, Highness?"

"I am your crown prince! I am free to go where I wish—whenever I so desire. I will tolerate not being questioned by the likes of you."

The guard, ten years his senior, cleared his throat. "Let me summon an escort—"

Shane's broadsword flew from its sheath with a hiss and came to rest at the man's throat. "Open. This. Gate. Or I shall drop you where you stand."

A younger guard, who served beside the first, put the key in the lock and threw open the door nestled within the larger gate. Shane led his horse through, mounted, and made his way down from the high peak with care in the faint moonlight.

He rode with naught of a thought to where he went nor what he should do when he came to journey's end. At dawn he realized he sat at the foot of the Kestron Ridge. Mother's—the queen's—cabin. He would head there. Queen Mariamne had found peace and safety within its walls—mayhaps he would as well.

The hovel lay in shambles. The roof had caved in and the door was detached from its hinges and lay on the disintegrating porch.

*You will find no peace here.*

"Lord, save me! By my sword—let me be!" Shane shouted.

Roosting birds took flight with a cacophony of shrieks. Then silence.

He trudged back to Lincolnshire and wandered into a tavern. He hid his face under the cowl of the borrowed cloak. Slumped in a dark corner, he drank himself into a stupor, his thoughts muddled by the continual flow of libations.

A man spoke to his companion at the next table. "I tell ya true, Widow Ena tells Lucsa was wit' child."

"Nay, fool. Lucsa's lived in Lincolnshire all 'er life. She ain't ne'er married."

"Exactly, she had 'erself a tryst. 'Tis what I's tellin' ya."

"I's been to 'er cabin for repairs many a time. She ain't got no child. Nor do she speak of one."

"Widow Ena says 'twas years ago. The child been long gone, or dead. I but give warnin'. Don't involve yarself with the trollop. Father Titus will have yar hide."

Shane lost interest in the conversation. His befuddled mind swirled with notions. Could he find this woman? Could she be his true blood mother? Even in his addled state, he had to laugh at the unlikelihood of this woman being in any way connected to him. The alcohol twisted even his muddled hopes.

*And what if she were your mother?*

His head throbbed with the liquid spirits and the endless questions. Unable to capture a single clear thought, he staggered across the way and rented a room for the night at a small inn. He dropped into the filthy bed and found a measure of peace in oblivion.

*But what if she is your mother?*

# Chapter 6

*Bang! Bang! Bang!*

The pounding on the door jarred Shane from his stupor as though some ogre beat upon his skull.

"What?" he demanded and regretted the shout.

"If ye plan on sleepin' all day, 'twill cost ye another shiny farthing."

Shane brought few coins. It would be unwise to linger—lest he be discovered and King Edgar disown him. "I leave soon," he muttered.

"Ye have half an hour, or ye'll pay for the day."

Footsteps receded from the door. Each step like a smithy's hammer driving a nail through his skull. Rising made his inners convulse. He wanted to retch. He doused his head from the basin. He didn't care that it soaked him—it eased the throbbing. He staggered down the stairs and out into the blinding light. Pulling the cowl further over his face, he stopped a young boy hurrying down the street.

"Boy, know you where the Widow Ena's house lies?"

The lad cocked his head at him. "Mister, why'd ya wish to visit the midwife?"

"That would be none of your concern. Do you know or not?" Shane moaned at the ache his own voice caused.

"Second street, take a right, down 'bout ten houses on the left."

The boy ran off.

It took near an hour to reach the door of a wattle-and-daub hut at the end of the narrow lane. A placard engraved with a birthing stool hung above the door. This must be the place. He tapped on the door and groaned.

"Who be calling?" A slender, bent, old woman, with long, unkempt gray hair stood in the open doorway.

Shane could not think clear enough to formulate a ruse. "Ethan," he muttered and cringed at his own words.

"Aye, then ye be needin' a remedy." She shuffled inside.

"Nay madam, I wished—"

"Come ye, sit. I will get thee what ye really be needin'."

Shane relished the dim coolness inside and plopped on a low three-legged stool.

The old woman rattled bottles, picking up one, holding it close to her squinting eyes, reading the name, and putting it back. "Hemlock— nay, wolvesbayne—nay, arnica—nay, cabbage—now thee might be needin' a little of that for the pain." She set it aside and kept looking. "Caraway—nay, monkhood—nay, almond—yes, yes. There is one. Quickgrass?" She stopped and looked back over her shoulder at him with a crooked smirk. "'Tis for the womenfolk—thee won't be needin' any of that." She laughed at her own joke and continued.

She rattled off herbs for an eternity before she retrieved one dark bottle from a bottom shelf. She leapt up—startling him at both her sudden movement and her agility. "Eel! There, now we can make a proper elixir for what ails thee."

Shane moaned and dropped his head on top of his arms, where they sat resting on the table. He must have dozed, for he would have sworn only moments passed before she sat a steaming cup of a foul-smelling brew next to him and insisted he drink every drop of it.

"This concoction is rank."

"Yes, yes, now drink thee it down."

"I thought healers were supposed to make their potions at least tolerable."

The widow's smile revealed missing teeth in its lopsided curve. "Oh I usually do, dearie. But when a man has no one to blame for his ills but his own self, I have no compulsion to make his treatment easy upon him." She put her hand under the swaying wooden cup and pushed it to his lips. "Drink thee, or my effort will all be for naught. I cannot heal thee if thee will not take thy medicine like a man. Thee be a man, now, do thee not?"

The noxious liquid festered across his tongue, stagnated in his throat, and soured in his belly. Shane dropped the cup with a hollow clunk, the rattle renewing the aching in his head. He braced his elbows on his knees, cradled his head, and prayed he would not retch on the hovel's dirt floor.

"I have no more for thee today," she put out her hand for payment. Shane sat motionless. "If thee do not find me remedy satisfactory, thee is welcomed to leave."

"I think you poisoned me, witch." He fell to his knees and crossed his arms over his middle as the brew churned.

She folded her arms and tapped her bare toes near his knee. "'Tis the drink that poisons, ungrateful youth. Ol' Ena would never harm a soul."

Her drumming foot added to the pounding in his head. The potion bubbled and whirled. Sour spurts touched the back of his throat and snaked across his tongue.

Ena kicked a bucket to him.

Seizing it with both hands, he buried his face in it. The heat came to his cheeks first, followed by a deep lurch of his stomach. He gagged as the hateful medicine and some of the excessive ale scorched his throat before it cascaded into the bucket so violently he feared some of it would splash back on his face. He repeated the horrid process nearly a dozen more times before all the contents of his belly were expelled. He dropped exhausted to the floor, hoping death might think it fitting to take him.

His eyes fluttered open as he shuddered. He lay in the same spot where he fell on the witch's floor—though a tattered blanket now covered him. The bucket was nowhere in sight—nor was the old crone. He moaned and pushed upright. His middle ached, but the worst of the pain within his belly and his head had abated. Standing, he ventured outside to a late midday sun.

"Thee lives," the woman said, looking up from where she knelt in the garden beside her home.

"No thanks to you, hag."

"Watch thy tongue, sprout. I'll not have thee sully me reputation."

Shane snarled and spun on his heel.

*Your mother?*

Could he learn about this Lucsa woman and the baby she may or may nay have had an unknown number of years past without the witch? His head throbbed again.

Ena had returned to her work and took no notice of him.

"Widow, I came seeking information—"

"As thee have nay paid for me healing, thee will get naught more."

Shane reached into his pouch and drew out a single shilling. He flipped it to her. Ena snatched it from the air and bit it with what few teeth remained. Shane did not know quite what to do when she tucked it down her tunic, placing it between her bosoms. He choked on a bit of startled laughter and started coughing.

"If thee is catching somethin' more, the coin will warrant ye another elixir."

Shane waved his hands. "I require no more of your potions, woman—only a morsel of information."

"Well, be about it, sprout. I'm be old woman."

"I heard some men speaking in the tavern—"

"Good Christian men do not indulge in gossipmongering."

Shane ignored her. "They spoke of a woman heavy with child but no child was ever known to live in her home."

Ena huffed and returned to tending her plants. "Many women have lost a babe in childbirth. 'Tis a common affliction."

"This would be a reclusive—if not shunned—woman named Lucsa."

The old woman stilled. She turned and narrowed her gaze. "What trouble do thee wish to cause this poor woman? She has seen far more than her share of pain. I'll not be helping thee to cause her more."

"Can you tell me, did her child die?"

"I know not. A dreadful winter befell the land that year. Many birthed their babes without me present, for I couldn't venture far from me home in the deep snow, which lay even here in the valley."

Shane's heart pounded and his breaths quickened. "This would be a winter about twenty years ago?"

Ena brushed her hand against her apron, staring off into the distance. "Well, let me be thinking. The miller's boy was born that winter, and the tanner's as well. One of them went off to be squired at the manor of Lord Thorne. I think I was told he would receive his spurs this next spring. Such knighting occurs in the twenty-first year— does it not?"

"Aye," Shane could barely choke out the single word. He cleared his throat and took a slow steady breath, yet he spoke with an excited squeak. "Did this Lucsa ever tell of what happened to her child or who the sire was?"

She shook her head, tossing her gray hair about her face in puffs. "Nay, she suffered great shame amongst the good townsfolk, and her father disowned her. She would never speak of it."

"Might you be so kind as to tell me where I could find her?"

Ena's gaze narrowed again.

"I wish her no ill, healer. I must speak with her. I believe it will be good news if I have figured aright."

Still sitting on her knees, she pointed a boney finger. "Thee hear me clear, sprout. I will serve thee a brew, not at all to your liking, if thee harm Lucsa."

Shane nodded.

Ena sighed, and it shuddered her entire old frame. "Back out to the main road through town, and head north." Ena pointed in the general direction. At the oak, which looks like a pitchfork, venture off the road to the east. Thee will walk four or five paces before thee finds a small trail among the trees. Follow it to the north, cross a stream, turn east at the boulder shaped like a turtle, and continue down the slope for another few paces. Near a clearing, ye will find a one-room wattle with a leather door. Lucsa dwells there."

Shane tried to keep the complex directions in his addled mind, tossed the old crone a farthing, and headed off to find the woman who could be his mother.

# Chapter 7

Rocks that looked like turtles, pitchfork-shaped trees—Shane wandered around the forest for the rest of the afternoon. As the sun set, he slumped down next to a lumpy black oak. What was he doing here? He was terribly lost. He would never find the main road again, let alone make his way back home. *Home?* Where was his home? Raised to be king by parents who loved him yet lied his whole life. Forced to live by a set of standards both rigid and uncompromising— was it all for naught?

His head dropped back against the tree. The malevolent voice remained silent. His eyes open, and straightened. When did he last hear its wicked taunt?

*Thud! Snap!* Shane was pulled from his musings. *Thwack! Thunk!* He stood, moving toward the sound. Clearing a rise, he spotted a wisp of smoke snaking through the alders and oaks. It clung to the tree trunks and hunched behind bushes like a sinister forest creature stalking its prey—him. Shane shuddered. Cold gripped him, filled him, consumed him.

"What evil be ya about?"

Shane whirled to see a woman—ax hefted high—glaring at him. "No evil, my lady."

"I be no lady, ya fool. What are ya doin' out 'ere?"

"Forgive me, madam, I … I was …" What should he say? He sought his mother? What really drew him here?

"Are ya an imbecile? Speak, fool."

A voice—no, it was more of a nudge—stirred within him. *Leave. Flee now!* He staggered back a step but couldn't move further. "I came to hunt a little game, but it would appear hunting in unfamiliar grounds is unwise. I have lost my bearings. Forgive my intrusion." Shane tried to turn to leave. An unexpected gust of wind caught his hood, pushing it back to his shoulders. The woman gasped, the ax dropped to the ground with a thud.

"Who are ya?" Her words wheezed through her tight lips as her trembling fingers touched to her mouth.

Shane stared. Her hazel eyes grew to the size of plums. Her hands covered her gaping mouth. "Who …"

"Do you know me, madam?"

The woman remained silent. The only sound in the deep woods was the soft rustle of her skirt against the leaf litter as she trembled.

"Please, what has distressed you so, madam?"

"Ya look like—ya remind me of a man I knew in my youth."

"A lover?"

Her eyes narrowed, and her hands dropped to rest below her throat. "If ya have come to be makin' sport of a beleaguered, mistreated woman—ya can turn tail and shoo, boy."

"What became of your child, Lucsa?"

"I've no child." She collected her skirt, retrieved the ax, and stomped down the hill toward the smoke.

Compelled to leave, yet unwilling to let the matter be, Shane stood rooted in indecision. Like the towering timber sentinels around him, he became a part of the forest—only his locks fluttered in the gentle breeze. Leave? Stay? Which would bring happiness? Could he find such an elusive emotion here in the woods? *Go!*

"Why'd ya ask after a child? What's it to ya?"

Shane blinked and released the breath he held. She stood only half a pace away, looking at him, one fist on her hip. "Please, tell me what you did?"

*Go!*

She pointed the ax at him. "Why do ya pester? What business is it of yars?"

He raised his hands in surrender.

*Run! Leave now!*

Shane pushed away the whispered warnings niggling his insides. So different from the malevolent voice, it was easier to ignore.

Lucsa's dark brown hair blended into the tree trunks behind her. Only the untwined end sat on her shoulder to contrast with her worn moss-green kirtle. It could have been his hair for how similar in color and shade it appeared. Her nose was long and slender like his. His eyes were a little greener—closer in shade to the queen's, but similar enough.

The ax wiggled, urging him to speak. Shane sighed as he moved closer. "As a babe, I was found abandoned in these woods, madam."

The ax fell to the ground again. This time it took a nick out of the toe of his boot. He jumped back.

Lucsa shook her head, her hands again covering her mouth. "Nay. Nay, ya cannot be he. Me boy is dead."

"You did have a son then, Lucsa?"

"How do ya know me name?"

"Widow Ena. And she told me how to find you. It is true, then? You bore a son. Are you sure he died? Were rights spoken over him?"

Lucsa's hands dropped, and her eyes narrowed again. "Do ya be thinkin' a man of God would dare lower himself to say kind words over an illegitimate babe? Or that the professed God-fearing man who put his seed in me, not his wife, would acknowledge his own blood? There be no mercy for such a one—or for his fallen mother." She spat on the ground. "I curse them all—the pious priest, the licentious man, and the God they serve!"

Shane sputtered at her audacious words. "Lucsa, take care—"

"I'll not!" She leaned in with a menacing snarl, curling her lips. "What care did any of them show me?"

Shane suffered a small shudder under her wrath and redirected the conversation. "So you buried your own son?"

"I took me boy to the woods. Couldn't support us—alone. I couldn't care for him. The sanctimonious townsfolk shunned me. I could find no work. Nay other choice remained. Unable to bear seeing me babe suffer and die, I took him to the woods—"

"East of Lincolnshire, at the foot of the Kestron Ridge?"

Lucsa nodded. "Aye, the clearing lay not far from me home." She stepped nearer still, examining him. "Ya look so very like he did then." She tossed her head, and her braid dislodged to swing behind her. "'Twas a bitter winter …"

"Snow lay on the ground in the valley quite deep for months."

Again she nodded. "Could it be?" Her voice floated like a dream. She reached out a hand and laid it flat over his heart. "Did me boy live?"

"It would appear so."

Lucsa stroked his face. A tear rolled down her cheek. "I loved ya from the first moment I knew ya grew within me. I wanted ya. Ya need know that. I wanted to keep ya, but the unbending, church-dictating world conspired to keep us apart."

"Mayhaps now God has brought us together."

"God hates sinners, boy," Lucsa all but shouted. "I am a sinner, and ya are my sin. If life has ever been kind to ya, finding me will destroy all yar happiness. It's the way of fallen people."

"God forgives—"

She stomped back, arm flaying angrily about her. "I make no contrition and will serve no penance for bringing such a fine child into this world from a union of love. Ya hear me? I loved the man, and he professed love to me. I'll not allow the church or any god to say me love was wrong." A smile inched across her face. A lovely, gentle smile revealing only lightly yellowed teeth.

Shane's heart pounded as if he feared he would be devoured. He tried to shake free of the irrational panic. But was it so absurd?

*Run!*

# Chapter 8

Lucsa waved him back to her tiny hovel. Rays from the setting sun peeked through the chipping mud. The hide-covered door and two widows did little to keep out the chill early autumn evening. Lucsa offered him the one rough chair and pulled a stool beside it. The fire sparked and popped as she added fresh logs. The warmth inched toward his toes and knees but never eased his discomfort.

She stared. "What do they call ya?"

Why could he not stop shaking? Something more than cold beset him. "Shane. The man who raised me believed me to be a gift from God."

"Believed? Is he dead? Or does he nay believe any longer?"

Shane watched the flames dance. Shame and defiance swirled within him, mixing into an unpalatable brew. "He still lives. He is a very powerful man."

Lucsa leaned into him. Her nearness brought more chill—a deep cold that threatened to freeze his soul. "Did he use this power against ya, my son? Did he force ya to labor for him?"

"No." Shane shuddered, freeing him of the false visions. "He loves me." He tossed his head and sat at his full height towering over her where she squatted on the stool. "He has not always approved of my choices nor my actions, but he loves me. Till a few months ago, I believed him my father, and as the eldest I was trained to take his place someday."

She placed a frigid stiff hand on his knee. "He threatened to reveal the truth of who ya are. Eldest or nay, if ya be not blood, he'll push ya aside for his own. He wishes to make ya like him." She allowed the words to sink deep and fester. "Ya are yar own man, with yar own destiny. Ya could be more than his dreams for ya."

"What is greater than being king?" The words tumbled across his lips with such ease and speed he could not catch them.

"King?" Lucsa leaned back considering him. Her hazel eyes swirled with a dark foreboding. "King? Prince Shane, heir to the throne of Veronia—eldest son of King Edgar the Noble and Queen Mariamne the Deliverer. This is who my son Slade bes." She stood, brushing his upper arm with her hand and curtsied low. "Your Highness," She annunciated the words carefully.

Shane loved those words—the title that set him apart from all others—save Jak. It spoke of his importance and great worth. Those rare words labeled him with greatness, grandeur, and demanded respect. But somehow, hearing the title cascade off his true mother's lips mocked him.

"How may I serve ya—you, my lord?"

"Please, sit."

"As you wish, Majesty."

"I am not king."

"Yet, my son." The darkness swirled even more in her eyes. The motion made him feel lightheaded. His stomach rolled with unease. A log shifted in the fire, spitting out another resting upon it to roll at Shane's feet, drawing his attention away. Staring at the smoldering log, the darkness lost its grip on his soul, and he breathed of the sulfur air. This was wrong—*evil*.

"Now that ya know the truth, and ya have found yar true mum, what be yar plan, my dearest?"

Shane kicked the log back into its place, safe within the hearth, as his mind tumbled about, groping for clarity. What should he do now?

She rose, slinked behind him with the smooth motion of a barn cat on the hunt. Her hands brushed across his shoulders.

He stifled a shudder.

Lucsa ran one hand over his hair with a tenderness he did not think she could possess. "My strong son, ya were raised for greatness. The entire kingdom lies before ya." She stroked his cheek with the back of one hand, leaned down, and cooed. "The power to control men's destiny be within yar grasp. No one could ever tell ya what to do or how to behave. They would grovel at yar feet, seeking ya to order them." Her hand moved to the base of his neck, and her fingers worked through his hair. "Women would swoon in yar presence and vie to warm yar bed. The most beautiful of the land would be yars to pluck without reproach." She moved in front of him and crouched, taking his hands. "These hands will hold the power of life and death in them, dear Slade. No one can stop ya—when ya are king."

Shane felt himself falling into the darkness, but her words stroked a need he could not quiet.

"I could show ya how to get all ya yearn for—every desire of yar heart."

His mind quickened. Light shone in the dark places of his soul at the words learned long ago. *Delight thyself in the Lord, and He shall give thee thine heart's desire.* Shane closed his eyes, his breaths quickening and heart pounding. He stood, almost upsetting Lucsa's balance. He turned from her and moved the few steps to the door. "The hour is late. I should be away."

She chuckled—a spiteful, manipulative snicker. Ripples of hate and fear coursed along his spine. "Boy, ya could nay find your way in the light of day. Ya have no hope in the dark."

She spoke truth, but he resented hearing it. *Leave. Leave now. The Lord will keep him, and preserve him alive: he shall be blessed upon the earth, and Thou wilt not deliver him unto the will of his enemies.*

"I will be fine. A knight does not fear the dark or getting lost. And I will not be afraid in my own kingdom, madam."

Lucsa moved near, stroking his arm. "Stay the night. What harm could it do? As ya are a knight, and I am yar mother, after all. Let me have the joy of caring for me boy—who I thought dead all these years—if only for one evening. Ya honor my humble home with yar presence, Highness. Truly, one night will nay matter."

What harm would it do to stay? His heart beat out a warning cry, as Lucsa stroked his ravenous ego.

"Ya're such a strong man. I'll be sleepin' well, knowin' my son protects me. My son. I never thought to say those words. They dance as pure delight in my mouth. My son. My son, the knight. My son, the crown prince. My son, the future king. Sounds good, does it not?"

Only one night. What could be the harm? *Therefore, to him that knoweth how to do well, and doeth it not, to him it is sin.* Shane trembled as the truth of the light within and the desire of the darkness waged war over his soul.

"Come, my son, I've smoked cod and have a few apples I can roast for ya."

Shane's stomach grumbled. When had he last eaten? He would stay for a meal. When Lucsa retired, he would leave—no matter the hour. But surely he could not leave without food. A full belly would sustain him until he returned to Lincolnshire. There he would collect his horse and return to the palace. There he would shove all lingering thoughts of this woman in a deep dark hole to be forever forgotten.

# Chapter 9

Shane woke next to the fire as the sun streamed through the holes in the walls. An odd haze muddled his thoughts. Where was he? How had he arrived at this place, and why? He rolled onto his back. A woman kneaded dough. Lucsa.

She smiled at him. "In a few mites, these biscuits will be baked and we can leave."

Shane lumbered to a sitting position and stretched his uncooperative limbs. The crown prince did not sleep on the ground—even when travelling. But this was different. A tremor raged through him, loosening the hold on him, allowing him to move with greater ease. He rubbed at his face, trying to free his disarrayed thoughts. "We? Where might *we* be going?"

"To the castle, of course. Ya can nay fulfill yar destiny of becoming king from this small hut, my son."

"You aim to join me—in the palace?" He stood.

Her lower lip pooched out and she whimpered. Tears threatened. "Forgive me. I must be such an embarrassment to ya, my noble son. A poor, discarded woman. I only thought to aid ya, I did. Wished to know me boy, and encourage ya on to yar grand destiny. I imagine the king and queen would order ya to send me away nevertheless. And I know ya must bend to their desires—for now." She swiped at a tear and turned from him, sniffling. "I will remain behind. I would not want you to fall any further from favor with the king. It is enough to know ya live—and live well. I'll be fine here. I can survive another winter—if it be not too severe."

"I am sure I can find a place for you in the town below the castle, if not the castle itself." The words came from him without thought— and he regretted them in the very breath used to expel them.

She ran to him, threw herself into his arms, and held him tight. "Oh, thank ya, my son. I knew ya were an honorable man. Ya could not bear to see yar poor mother suffer. Ya're a good boy."

Pride unlike any he had ever known filled him. He embraced her. Felt the beating of her heart once more against him—a rhythm both familiar and comforting. An odd peace settled over him.

The outskirts of Lincolnshire lay on the horizon, and Shane's mind whirled. "Who am I to say you are, madam? I cannot very well say you are my mother."

"Nay, to admit such would lose ya the crown. I have heard of some who seek out a matchmaker in order to find a suitable bride. As son of the king, ya could desire such sound council, could ya not?"

"This is the role of a priest."

"One may be consulted once the choices have been significantly winnowed. As the crown prince, there will be many who desire to be the future queen. A simple priest could nay be expected to neglect his flock to properly scrutinize every candidate. I would be doin' all the most arduous labor in order to bring the best handful of potential brides to the priest for his final approval." Her peasant brogue eased the nearer they came to the town.

The idea could be plausible. Shane glanced at her once and

stopped walking.

Lucsa studied her well-worn garment. "I nay—do not appear, nor sound, a suitable applicant for the role in me present state, do I, Son?"

He shook his head.

"As a woman of some standing once, I can recall the proper mannerisms again. There be—are—several tailors in Lincolnshire. If ya—you have a few coins …"

"Everyone knows you here. How will we explain—?"

She measured her words and flipped out her skirt. "You could give me the payment, and we could part ways. I could request a new gown, much better than this—though nothing too regal or resplendent."

"How will you explain the sudden wealth?"

"If asked, I can say I've—I have—been hired to serve in the home of a noble family. It is true enough."

Shane glanced toward town again and calculated the costs of a commoner incurred of stabling one horse and the of purchasing another. The trek over the ridge was not easily traversed on foot, though he knew Queen Mariamne had done so when she fled the castle prior to his birth. He would not allow Lucsa to sharing his mount. He shuddered as he fingered his remaining coins through the pouch.

"How long will it take for the dress?"

"If they have something appropriate in the shop already, 'tis only a matter of a fitting—a few hours. Bronson usually has at least one finished sample of his work on display." She put out her hand. "I will also require a place to clean before I dress. I cannot very well put a new gown on me dirty body."

"I have not enough for all your needs, woman."

She stood akimbo, foot tapping. "Ya're the crown prince, surely the good citizens of Lincolnshire know ya're good for it."

"I did not announce my presence."

"Ah, ya did not wish to be dragged home and scolded?"

"Aye, something very near. I wished to be a man somewhere without the burden of my title—to get lost for a few hours. I never dreamed it would turn into this falderal."

Her eyes narrowed. "There be more than one in this town who'd take a lesser payment to have me keep their confidences a little longer." She put out her hand again. "Ten pounds should suffice."

"Ten pounds! Fie, woman."

"What can ya spare then? I'll make it work."

"I must purchase you a horse. I cannot offer you more than six and a few shillings."

Her hand lurched closer to him. "It'll have to serve."

They parted company with assurances to meet at the stable at midday. Shane drew up his hood and headed to speak with the marshal about a horse—a cheap one.

With Lucsa's absence came the nagging desire. *Run. Flee. Have nothing more to do with that woman.*

# Chapter 10

Lucsa had finally arrived in a deep-green satin gown. Her dark-brown hair, clean, lay in multiple braids scooped up in a net-thing he could not recall the name for. His mother still carried a handsome form—when it was cleaned and properly attired. She rode in silence behind Shane up the Kestron Ridge for the remainder of the afternoon. Now at midmorning, he glanced back at her in one of the turns.

"Is that it, my son?"

Shane raised his gaze to the castle-topped rock jutting up from the middle of the valley floor. "Aye. King Edgar's palace lies within the walls on the rocky perch." He turned to look fully upon her.

Hunger filled her countenance. She leaned forward in the saddle. Her tongue slid over her lips, and she muttered something he could not understand.

"Did you say something, Lucsa?"

Her gaze shifted to him, and again he saw the darkness swirl within. From this distance it did not threaten to pull him in, but before he could consider it further, she blinked—and it vanished. "No, my son. I marvel at your home. 'Tis majestic—a place fitting for your throne." Her words were smooth as polished gems.

He urged his mount forward. "You must stop calling me son."

"Who will hear?"

"You never know when a hunter or woodsman will pop out from behind a tree, or merchant come around the next bend. Furthermore, if you persist, you will be more liable to slip when we are in the company of others."

"As you wish, Your Highness—or do you prefer Master?"

He liked the sound of master, but it would not ring so pleasant in the king's ears. "Highness will suffice, Lucsa."

"As you wish."

Silence again accompanied the descent into the valley. When they could ride abreast, she drew alongside him until their mounts were even with one another. Fury bubbled in him. "If you are to play your part, woman, you cannot suppose to be my equal."

A wry smirk twisted her lips. "Of course, my lord. I should never presume to be more than a simple servant." She slowed her horse to ride at Shane's flank.

"You also take the honored role on my right," he muttered.

She dropped back and came to his left side. "Does this please you, Your Highness?"

He jerked a single nod as ire rubbed his insides raw.

"What might I expect within the palace, Your Highness?"

"I will find a place for you in the lower town. It will be safer there."

She huffed. "Do as you think best, my lord. I am here to serve."

Shane could not shake the darkness stirring within him. It twisted his belly and constricted his lungs. His heart thudded as though it would burst its bony cage. The heel of his hand rose to his aching temple. The horse beneath him blurred.

"Slade, my son." She drew even with him again. She pulled his mount to a halt, yanked a knitted glove from her hand, and placed it on his face. It lay as cool as a mountain stream against his searing flesh. "You are ill, my sweet." She slid from her mount. The crunching of her steps in the leaf litter thundered against his aching head forcing his eyes closed. The sound of her harsh footsteps returned a moment later, and a short reed was pressed into his hand. "Eat this, Slade."

"Don't call me thus, woman." He groaned at his continued discomfort.

"Oh, fie! Eat this, please, Your Highness."

"What is it?"

"Something to soothe, nothing more. Widow Ena has taught me a great many things of the healing herbs that grow in the forest."

Shane brought it to his lips with a trembling hand and chewed with slow purpose. The bitter skin broke, releasing sweet nectar from within the shaft. His vision cleared, his stomach calmed, the tremors stopped, and the heat dissipated. Glorious relief. He floated atop his horse with not a care in all the world. "Thank you."

A smile parted her lips in the most unpleasant fashion. "It is my desire to help, my lord. I only wish the best for you in all things." She mounted again. "I am ever grateful I was able to assist you in your time of need."

Mayhaps he should have her nearer to him. He shook off the thought. The malady had never plagued him before; surely it never would again. The safest course was to keep Lucsa far from the palace.

They camped at the foot of the ridge and rode throughout the long day at a gentle pace. Shane's mind churned with a wild flux of emotions. Fear gripped him as he wondered at the king and queen's reaction to the interloper he brought to their home. Desire twisted till he saw only the throne and the crown. Hope softened it in waves. He now had the opportunity to know the woman who gave him birth.

Gratitude stirred in finding her and the offer of aid she gave to him when he suffered.

The illness that continued to beset his body baffled him. Could this be a result of the widow's elixir? He'd ingested it over four days ago, and thus did not think it a viable culprit. What had happened three nights previous in Lucsa's hovel? Shane glanced back at her as she rode with her eyes fixed on the castle as it grew with their approach. He didn't remember anything after a few bites of her meal and a cup full of sour ale. He had woken feeling muddled. Had she done something to him?

Shane straightened, shaking off the irrational storm swirling his thoughts. The edge of the lower town could be seen on the horizon. He would be home in familiar surroundings before supper. There he could put this nonsense behind him and work for the crown he longed for more than all else.

They broke from the heavy trees, and the wind brushed Shane's sweat-covered face. His hands trembled again, and his stomach clenched in growing pain. He glanced back to Lucsa, who remained transfixed on the castle walls looming high above—her neck cranned to see it now.

"I will secure a room for you."

"Your malady has returned, my lord." She drew beside him and offered another reed. "I collected more of the fennel for such occasions. I am sure the king's healer will know best how to treat you." Her words came as a challenge, but she slowed to her respectful distance without further threat.

Chewing on the stalk, Shane considered her words. Carrington would know what to do. Had he not found a way to save those infested with the black poison of the horde at the time of the last war? Or had the cure come from Queen Mariamne? How did Lucsa know what would help him unless she'd caused it? Hate gorged up until he choked on it, but as the fennel took hold, his sanity returned. The fury abated, and all returned to right once more—more than right as the world danced before him in radiant waves of colors, smells, and sounds. Shane turned aside, entering the town.

Lucsa followed, chirping at the shops and their many wares with the eagerness of a child. "Your Highness, now that I am in your employ, I will need a regular stipend." She called out for all on the street to hear. "I will need a great many things—"

Shane whirled his mount, waiting until she came alongside him. "Fie, woman, what do you mean to do to me? The gossipmongers will be running wild with all manner of tales."

Her eyes widened, and her hand came to her chest. "My lord, I know naught of what you mean. I am here to serve as you have requested." Again her words carried, stopping several onlookers in their tracks. Under her breath she muttered, "You do not expect a royal hire to the crown prince to go about in the same gown every day or sleep in a small room in some tawdry inn. What would the gossipmonger say then?"

She sat straight, glancing at the buildings about. "Have you found a home suitable for interviewing potential candidates for your bride, Your Highness? It must be large enough for entertaining, so I might acquire a proper picture of each woman as a future queen."

A hum of excited voices bombarded Shane's ears. The wind stirred with the townsfolk's chatter. Shane seized the reigns of her horse and spun it around, leading her out of the town. "You will be the ruin of me," he muttered.

"I thought we agreed upon my role before we left Lincolnshire, Highness. What have I done to upset you so?"

"I thought you meant to use it only as an excuse if questioned. I never dreamed you would charge into town and announce it from the ramparts. Fie, woman, word will spread like a spark in a ripe wheat field. Every noblewoman in the kingdom—and some fair amount from neighboring kingdoms, no doubt—will be banging down my door in a matter of weeks. I have no compulsion to marry by winter's end. What have you done?"

She cocked her head, blinking at him like an innocent doe unaware of the bow in the hunter's hand. "It will take much time to sift through so many worthy candidates, my lord, then the priest, as well as the king and queen, will have to give their approval of a final choice. The wedding feast will need to be planned and prepared. The nobility of the kingdom summoned. It could take years before such a day arrives. You will have a great many days to indulge in your own dalliances, Your Highness." She shrugged her shoulders. "As king, you can summon any wench to your bed you choose. Who could speak against you?"

"The priest! God!"

Lucsa snickered derisively. "Then be wise in how you summon your companions, Highness. You need not announce them. And as for God, what do you really think He will do to you? Did not the kings of the Holy Book have many women? How would you be any different? God does not interfere in the lives of people, my lord."

Shane almost fell from his saddle. "Never dare speak so recklessly about the God of Veronia—the God I serve."

One brow rose high, "Truly, you serve this God?" she chuckled. "I thought you only served your own desires."

"I should never have brought you here."

"Mayhaps, but the town knows your matchmaker has arrived. What will they say if you send me away before I even start?"

Shane raked both hands through his hair. What options remained?

# Chapter 11

Shane rode through the castle gate, Lucsa directly behind. He knew it would only add to his problems, but he needed her where he could keep an eye on her. Some place he hoped to have more control over her.

"Your Highness, God be praised. The king and queen have worried over your absence," the guard said with a deep bow. Shane nodded and rode on. Passing through the inner gate, he dropped from his mount outside of the stable and threw the reigns to a squire. He helped Lucsa down.

"My son!" Shane turned to see Queen Mariamne running to him. She threw herself into his arms and held him tight to her chest. Releasing him, she took his face in both hands and scrutinized him. "You are hale?"

"Aye, mother, a bit of wanderlust—nothing more. I but desired a break from the pressing demands of my coming knighthood and official crowning as heir apparent. I never meant to cause you worry. Please forgive me." Shane meant each word he spoke. Guilt overwhelmed and threatened to crush the life from him.

Lucsa cleared her throat behind him, overshadowing the added guilt with ire. "Your Majesty." She stepped forward, curtsied to the ground. "It is an honor to be invited to your home."

Mariamne released Shane, considered the woman bent low in observance, and looked back to him.

"This is Lucsa, mother."

Lucsa rose, reached for the queen's hand—though it was not offered—and kissed Mariamne's ring. "The prince has hired me to serve as matchmaker for him. What a joy it is to bring the love of my prince's heart to him."

"Shane?" Mariamne's wise gaze washed over both of them. "Mayhaps we should move into the king's study to speak on this further." Mariamne turned and led the way across the ward and through the hall to the wooden door. "My King," she called after a small knock.

When entry was granted, Mariamne led them inside. "Your Majesty, your son has returned whole."

"Shane!" Edgar burst from his chair with a ruckus scrape of wood on stone and a wide grin. He took Shane's offered hand and pulled him into an embrace with a sound thump to his back. "I praise God for your safe return, my boy."

Edgar's smile faded when he glanced at his wife. "Your Majesty," Mariamne waved her hand to Lucsa. "Shane has brought a guest."

Edgar returned to his chair. Mariamne took the far seat as Lucsa gave a deep observance and only sat once Edgar waved her to the other chair.

Shane leaned against the wall for support. He wanted to run and hide as he'd done when he was a child from the punishment soon to come. There were no places within the castle that still remained a viable hiding place. He had exhausted them all during his mischievous youth. He straightened. He was soon to receive his spurs; he must take the consequences of his actions like a knight and show Edgar he was a man.

"Your Majesty, this is Lucsa. She has come under the guise of being the prince's matchmaker."

The queen's matter-of-fact announcement startled Shane. His stomach churned. He should have known the queen could not be fooled. She was gifted with keen insight from the Lord Almighty. *You are an imbecile.*

"A guise, beloved?"

"Look close, my king, and you will see clear the resemblance between them. Our Shane has gone off and found his blood mother."

Edgar rocked back. His gaze shifted from one to the other and back again. His jaw locked and his nostrils flared.

"It is true this is the woman who gave me birth, but I did not go seeking her, Majesty."

"You merely stumbled upon her?" Edgar said.

"An odd conversation led me to an old widow, who in turn directed me to Lucsa. Upon meeting, we determined the bound to be true."

"The Lord works in mysterious ways, Your Majesties," Lucsa said in sweet tones. "I believed my son long dead. To learn he was not only alive and hale, but the son of the king—well you can imagine my overwhelming joy. When Shane insisted I return with him, I did not think it wise, but I could not refuse him." She turned and dared lay her hand over Mariamne's. "You know well the beat of a mother's heart, Majesty. Could you have refused such a request?"

Shane stood unable to speak or even capture air. She lied with such ease. *What have I done! What have I done! Ruin. Ruin awaits the fool.* Another Scripture added to his own condemnation. *My son, fear the Lord, and the king, and meddle not with them that are seditious.*

Shane tried to swallow the fear choking him. He could not breathe and he tugged on the collar of his tunic.

"What do you mean to do with her here?"

The king's question was directed at him, but he could not find breath to answer. The room spun. His knees gave way. Darkness claimed him.

Shane woke. The lamps burned bright, the sun long since set.

Mariamne sat beside him, stroking his face with a damp cloth. She smiled. "There is my beloved."

He shook his head and pushed her hand away. "There is nothing in me to love, Majesty. I am an ungrateful cur. I bring you nothing but pain on top of pain." He squeezed his eyes closed against the threatening tears. When was the last time he had cried—truly cried?

She brushed his cheek with the back of her hand as Lucsa had done—but the feeling the queen's touch elicited was so unlike that of Lucsa's. Mariamne's tender spirit, the one that had comforted him all his days, made him want to curl in her lap and be cradled as a small boy. The other sent shivers of repulsion down his spine.

"Forgive me," he stammered. Unwanted tears wet his face.

"Of course, beloved. You need not even ask."

"But I must. I have taken your kindness and thrown it back in your face by bringing *that woman* here. I understand naught what comes over me."

"Turn your heart fully to God, Shane, and He will give you the strength to act as the righteous man I know you to be. Trust Him."

Shane sighed, sinking deep into the comfort of his bed.

"Lucsa says you have been ill."

"I know naught of the cause. It comes and goes with no apparent reason or source."

"Carrington has made a tea. He believes it will soothe and restore.

Rest now, my dear boy. It has been a trying time. To learn the truth, spoken in such harshness, and to find the mother of your birth, it is much to contend with."

"Where is she now?"

"The king has made arrangements for her to lodge on the second floor of the north tower. If she is to continue to pose as an adviser, it is the proper place for her. Few options remain open to us, for I do not believe she would be a woman quietly put off."

Rage from a source Shane did not recognize flared within him and spewed out of his mouth. "You are jealous of her. You hate her. She is my mother and not you."

"Shane?" Mariamne stood, retreating from his fury. "I do not hate her. I thank God for Lucsa. She gave me you. I will treasure such a precious gift all my days."

"You stole me from her. She wanted me—wanted to be a mother. You ruined everything for her." Shane knew the words were a lie—saw the pain they cause the one he truly loved—but he could not stop them or even control them. "I will give her what she has been denied. She will remain with me forever."

Mariamne closed her eyes, sadness marring her fine features. She gave him a small observance. "As you wish, Shane. She will remain as long as you desire."

"Slade! She named me Slade."

"You will always be my gift from God, Shane." She turned and slipped from his chamber.

Pain seized his chest. Regret drowned him. Tremors overwhelmed his limbs. He cried out in pain.

Alden shuffled in offering him the tea. Shane gulped it. His body relaxed, and sleep rescued him from his tears.

# Chapter 12

Mariamne curled into her husband's arms as he sat reading a parchment in bed.

"How is he?" Edgar put the document aside and kissed her forehead.

"Troubled." She pulled the quilt over her legs and snuggled closer. "I have feared over the pull evil has in his life for so long, my love. I have bloodied my knees in prayer against its hold on him. But now …"

"Has it claimed him?"

"Nay, but this woman who now dwells under our roof can be his undoing. She holds some power over him. He is hurt and confused, and she feeds his doubt and selfishness. The evil one controls her, Edgar, and I am sore afraid."

"If you speak true, she could be revealed by the light of God and dealt with quickly."

Mariamne shook her head, sitting up to look directly at him. "No. My spirit believes any actions against her would send Shane into the arms of darkness. We would lose him forever and Veronia would follow. No, Edgar, he must learn the truth of his own, and he has to be the one to deal with her. We must treat her with kindness—for his sake. And does not the Holy Word say, 'If he that hateth thee be hungry, give him bread to eat, and if he be thirsty, give him water to drink: For thou shalt lay coals upon his head, and the Lord shall recompense thee.' The truth of her will make itself known. But we cannot cease to pray for him in this struggle."

"When has there been a time when we have stopped praying for any of our children?" Edgar said with a roguish grin.

She curled back into his arms, and he kissed her again. "I know well the struggle between the dark and light that wars in him. If only I could save him this pain. But God must be the one to reveal Himself to Shane. God alone can fight the darkness seeking to claim our son. But Shane has to choose to allow his Savior to work on his behalf."

"Our God is faithful. He will not desert us—or Shane. We will trust and pray. Remember what the Scriptures say, 'Teach a child in the trade of his way, and when he is old, he shall not depart from it.' We have trained him well. Trust now that God will not allow him to depart from it."

She nodded against his chest. After an hour in prayer, they slid under the covers and slept well, surrounded by God's perfect peace.

Shane suffered several days of intermittent severe pain that came with sheet-drenching sweats, crippling stomach cramps, and tremors and cramping in his limbs. Each attack was answered with a tea that provided relief for a time.

At last, he emerged from his chambers on the third day and ventured down the stairs. His legs shook with weakness from his prolonged mystery illness, and his face was covered in sweat by the time he entered the hall. A subdued hum welcomed him.

Lucsa, sitting off to the side in the women's area, was the first to spot him. She rose with urgency and hurried to him as he made his way through the wide aisle between the men and women. She curtsied, took his hand and kissed it. Did something prick his wrist? If so, it was soon forgotten.

"Oh, how pleased I am to see you, my lord. I have worried so." Her eyes searched his face as he again questioned what possessed him to bring her into the king's home.

"I am well. Your worry is unnecessary. I thought you would have tired of the mundane nature of life in King Edgar's courts and decided to return home." He wanted her to go, noting her new gown of blue.

Lucsa's lower lip protruded in an unpleasant pout. "I could not leave without knowing you were well. The queen would not speak to me and refused to allow me to visit."

"It would be most inappropriate for a single woman—matchmaker or no—to visit the prince alone in his chambers. I am quite sure your presence has stirred enough gossip."

"I think it is because the queen hates me." She pronounced the words too loud for his liking.

Shane had spoken such himself, but with his head clearing of its dark humor, the thought was laughable. "Do not be a foolish woman. Queen Mariamne does not hate another living soul." He tossed his head as a light-headed giddiness washed over him. Others around the room were now taking note of him and acknowledged his presence with nods, smiles, and some nervous shivers. "Woman, you can return to your hovel at once if you feel unwelcome."

"I have not completed my charge, Your Highness."

"As you will." He waved a dismissive hand at her as he strolled away. He slipped into his seat beside the king, grateful to be off his trembling legs. A lightness, a pleasure he did not expect washed over him in warm waves. "Your Majesty." He greeted Edgar with a smile.

"Glad I am to see you out of bed, Shane, but be mindful of your time with Lucsa. There is much talk swirling already."

Anger flashed through him like a bolt of lightning. Not one full breath out of the man's mouth and he was already giving orders. Shane tossed his head again and growled low. "I will see her as I see fit."

Edgar sighed with a weariness that made the wrinkles on his face look more pronounced. *Could it be his hair is grayer than last I saw him?* Compassion for the man who raised him washed away the ire.

"I only wish to protect you, my son."

"My day of knighting is fast approaching, Majesty. I no longer require you to watch over me as you do Milana and Jak. I shall be fine."

"I pray you are right. It would cause me much pain if ill were to befall you."

"Lucsa is only a lonely woman. What can she do to me here under your roof, my king?"

"Nothing, most likely," Edgar said with a weak smile. "I merely wish for you to take care."

"Fine, I will take care around her."

Edgar nodded and returned to his meal.

As Shane looked around the room at the familiar faces, he found he walked in a new world. One which shifted from dark to light, joy to wrath, celebration to depression with the shifting of the wind. Two worlds now occupied the single space within him—but to neither of them did he wholly belong.

At the moment, he did not care. The food he ate tasted finer than any before, the laughter danced more joyfully, and the smiles were more radiant. He would bask in the moment as his senses celebrated his return.

# Chapter 13

Shane's unexplainable illness continued to plague him each day. He attempted to return to training. His stomach ached, doubling him over as he sparred with the sword. He waved his hand and stepped to the corral railing, wishing the malady would pass.

"Highness." Lucsa sauntered up with a too-familiar ease. Today saw her in a yellow frock. How many gowns would she possess by the time he rid himself of her. "I seek approve of this missive before 'tis sent."

"Not now," Shane moaned.

"Highness? You are ill again." She snatched his hand, and pressed something from her pouch into it.

He found two fennel reeds. Sighing he chewed one with eagerness. In moments he was himself once more. He nodded to her and resumed training.

"The missive, Your Highness?"

Shane stuck out his hand and took the vellum from her. It contained the announcement of the search for his bride and the requirements the prince sought. He thought each more ridiculous than the last. "Why do I care how tall she will be? Or if she can play the flute or crumhorn?"

"Highness, how would it look if you wed a woman you were

required to look up to, or one who only came to your navel?" She chuckled with a derisive smirk. "Wishing a lady to play a flute, or other reed instrument serves two purposes. She can entertain in your hall—"

"We have minstrels and murmurs for such times."

Lucsa scowled at him. "And if no entertainers have been hired for the evening, what do you do then?"

"Talk, or mayhaps play a few games."

"But if your bride were skilled at a gentle instrument, she could provide an extra measure of enjoyment to your hall. Learning such a skill also proves she can be instructed, she can learn, and she is patient and diligent in her studies."

"You stated there were two purposes?"

A mischievous grin swept across her face, and she leaned a little closer. "Playing these types of instruments strengthens the lips for you to enjoy all the more in your private moments, Highness."

As Griff called him back, Shane tossed the missive back. "It is not for me to say yea or nay. You must discuss it with Queen Mariamne at least, if not King Edgar. They will be the ones to send the sandesmen to the entire realm."

Lucsa stomped her foot at being dismissed with such ease. She whirled from Slade, her skirt twirling with her sudden motion. "Speak with the queen. Yes, yes, I will speak with her, but I do not need her permission," she muttered to herself as she stamped across the yard.

The image again assailed her of the queen embracing her child. The boy she had birthed but could not raise. Slade was hers to hold. But the way he looked at the queen. It could be nothing other than the love for a mother. Not so with her. Slade was her boy. He ought to look on her with such love. Lucsa stumbled. Why did no one ever look on her with such emotion?

"Where is the queen?" she said to the first maid she crossed.

"In her sitting room, my lady."

Lucsa brushed past her up the stairs to the third floor. Another maid stepped from the double-doored chamber on the left with a tray and disappeared down the back steps. Lucsa walked into the chamber without knocking.

"Lucsa?" The queen looked up from where she reclined reading with a raised brow.

"Prince Shane insisted I come speak with you at once."

Mariamne considered her for a moment, dismissed the woman standing nearby, and motioned for her to sit.

"Of what does Shane wish us to speak?"

"He has agreed to this missive being sent out announcing his search for a bride and instructed me to secure scribes to copy it and sandesmen to deliver it."

"May I see it?"

"As it does not concern you, madam, there is no need. As I said, my son has approved it."

Mariamne continued to consider her. Her voice never rose. Her posture never changed. Her haughty gaze never fell. "I will speak to the king, but he may wish to see what is going out in his name before it is released."

"You and your damnable king wish to control his every breath. He is a man, and you call him a boy. A day not far off is coming when he will sit on the throne, and he will no longer care to listen to you."

The overconfident queen remained the picture of calm and eloquence, making Lucsa's insides twist with fire. "It is the way of children to grow past the need for guidance of their elders. It is the wise who seek out their council anyway."

"Then it is a pity there are no wise ones here to advise him." Lucsa stood without being dismissed.

"Have a blessed day, Lucsa," Mariamne called as she closed the door with a thump. She stomped down the stairs, across the ward to the empty south tower tucked behind the stables, and down into the dark recesses beneath.

"I see why you hate her, master. She is an infernal hindrance to your cause, but I have your plan. It will not take long, master. Shane will be your faithful servant, and this wretched kingdom will fall and bow a knee to you. You will see, master. I will not fail you. Not again."

Lucsa continued to talk to the darkness as she shoved a door open deep under the tower. She took the stump of candle that remained lit and brought several others to life, illuminating the room she'd claimed for her own. Over the days she suffered in separation from her charge, she'd discovered this place and moved a few things into it.

A long table now sat against the back wall. She had taken some charcoal from her fire and drawn a multi-headed horned creature on the wall. In its mouth hung an upside down cross. To the right of the wall with her master's likeness sat a desk with several sheets of vellum. Some were stained with ink, others she had already scratched clean for use. A small chair sat in the corner.

Lucsa knelt in front of the table and gazed up at the drawing. "Oh, my master, I'm here to serve. What are yar wishes?"

A moment later she rose, snatching pouches and jars from one end of the table. "Yes, master. I understand. Yes, yes, I have everythin' we be needin'. Thin's from home and those stolen from the good healer. Have it all." She worked with the mortar and pestle crushing herbs. "Aye, master. Not too strong. Better the king suffers a prolonged illness and turn the throne over to your pet. Would be suspicious should he die too quickly."

She sat her potion aside, and pulled a jar from the pouch she always wore. "Now for Slade's medicine." She laughed. "Stupid boy has no idea what's happenin', master. 'Twill make yar work much the easier." She slid her ring off and opened the compartment. She added a few drops and returned it to her finger.

Next she pulled two fresh fennel reeds from another liquid-filled jar, letting them dry a moment. She placed them in her pouch along with the jar of Shane's medicine and the scrap of parchment containing the ingredients for the king. "A sprinkle in his cup, master, and the king will begin to suffer. The poison will attach to the metal goblet. Every drink will add to his discomfort. I know how 'twill please ya to see him in pain."

Lucsa was sure her charcoal god smiled and laughed with her before she snuffed out all but one of the candles and crept out.

# *Chapter 14*

Lucsa sat at her place, watching the women serve. She would not lower herself to serve in a rich man's home ever again—and she did not care what everyone thought of her sitting, waiting for her food while the queen served her. Training her eyes on the front table, she watched as the pompous king filled his fancy goblet with wine. Her heart raced, and her mouth went dry with the excitement bubbling like an underground spring.

She sighed with frustration as a maid interrupted him before he could drink.

"Your tray, Majesty." The petite woman stood on her toes to hand the tray up to the high table. Lucsa's insides turned as she watched Edgar smile at the woman, taking the tray.

"Thank you, Olivia."

As the worthless maid bowed her head and returned to her heels, her arm caught on the prized chalice, knocking it from the table. It tumbled—much of the clank muffled by the reed-covered stones. Before the girl could retrieve it, a commoner walking among the tables stepped on it, crushing the soft metal.

Lucsa blinked in disbelief at the turn of fortunes. In less than a heartbeat, her poison vanished into the reed-covered floor and the sand between the stones, and her weapon lay smashed beyond use. The vile woman and her unwitting accomplice bowed repeatedly, making their apologies to the forgiving king. *A real leader would strike them both down for being such clumsy fools.*

The woman hurried to the kitchen to fetch a new tankard, wooden and not as fine, the king thanked her again, and the meal continued without notice of Lucsa as she fumed. Oh she could always prepare it again. The fates could not be so against her that she would not succeed next time. She had promised the master. *I* will *make him suffer.*

Mariamne noted the royal physician, Carrington's, entrance late to supper and the slim nod when their eyes met. She exhaled trapped air as she turned to place the tray on the last of the tables. "Blessings be upon you this evening, Lucsa. May this food bring you renewed strength." The words were familiar as she said them often serving in the king's hall. This eve they caused an uncomfortable bite on her tongue. *Therefore, if thine enemy hunger, feed him: if he thirst, give him drink: for in so doing, thou shalt heap coals of fire on his head.* She recited the sacred words in her heart, and peace washed over Mariamne.

"I will try my best to stomach your swill." Lucsa snorted—though not loud enough for anyone to overhear. A smile plastered to her face gave no indication to those looking on of the venom on her lips.

Mariamne inclined her head and moved to the table where her daughter, Princess Milana and the knight's wives dined. "Is all well, Your Majesty?" Cy's wife, Annabel, said. Annabel had been her dearest friend from almost the moment Mariamne arrived in the palace so many years ago. They shared many secrets, and though she was the only woman in the palace to know of Shane's true origins, Annabel was not yet privy to the matchmaker's true identity.

"It is for now, my friend. Please pray it remains so."

Annabel eyed her but did not press for explanation with all the ladies chatting amiably around the table. She nodded her head, squeezed Mariamne's hand, and joined the lively conversation.

Mariamne's gaze returned to Lucsa, where she sat slump-shouldered two tables away. Her attention lay on the high table, where Edgar ate and laughed unaware of the threat thwarted this eve. Mariamne prayed yet again. *Deliver us, O Lord, from the evil man: preserve me from the cruel man: Which imagine evil things in their heart, and make war continually.*

"All has been done as you requested, Majesty. She will not suspect anyone has found her secret lair, and the herbs she has now can do no harm."

"Thank you, Carrington. You are a blessing to me." Mariamne stepped from the shadows, slipped into the kitchen, and up the back stairs to her chambers. Edgar sat in a chair in his nightshirt. His hands were clasped, his forearms on his thighs. Furrowed brows, and a deep scowl screamed his concern.

"Quite the eventful meal, would you not say, beloved?"

She did her best to smile. "Olivia and Marlow are not usually so careless."

He leaned back in the chair, his gaze searching. "Olivia and Marlow do not usually serve the high table."

Mariamne retrieved her nightrail.

"Beloved, is there something I need to know?"

"Edgar, do you trust me?"

He stood, spun her around, and cradled her face in both hands. "Do you need ask? I trust you with my life, my love."

She rested one hand over his. "Then I beg you not to make me speak of it. God is watching over us. He will see us safe. Please trust."

Edgar embraced her, kissing her forehead. "I will leave it in your hands and think no more on it."

Mariamne rose early the next morning and went to Cy and Annabel's home in the bailey. "Forgive me for drawing you from bed so early, my friends."

"Think nothing of it. I know something worries you." Annabel pulled her into a hug. "Come sit and tell us how we might assist."

Mariamne sat beside Annabel at their table, and glanced about. "Is Ethan still here?"

Cy sat opposite her. "No, he stays in the barracks with the others training for knighthood. Speak what is on your heart, sister."

Mariamne bit her lip, before whispering. "The woman Shane brought back with him …"

"She is his mother, is she not?"

Mariamne stared, then smiled. "You are ever the observant one, brother."

"His mother?" Annabel asked. "How did he ever—I did not dream such a feat were possible."

"I fear the evil one has had a hand in this. From his youth, Shane has struggled with the darkness. I believe he wants to do right, but he has not fully surrendered his heart to Christ. The Black Knight could not bring us down from without—"

"So now evil tries again from within."

"Aye, this is my thinking, brother." Mariamne reached across the table to the man she thought of as her own blood. "I need your help to keep the king safe."

His brows rose. "You know I will do anything."

Mariamne shook her head. "If I tell Edgar she tried to poison him, he will have her executed on the spot."

"Poisoned! But how … the cup." Annabel put her hand on Mariamne's arm. "The poison was in the cup Olivia spilled last night. I wondered why she and Marlow served in the hall. My sister said nothing to me."

"They came to me—red-faced to admit they were sneaking around together for a tryst."

"Olivia's husband died years ago, leaving her no children. Why did she feel she could not tell me of her interest in this man?"

Cy looked to his wife. "You are the queen's confidant. I the king's thane. We arranged a match with her from a minor noble family. Marlow is but a tanner."

"She did not think we would approve?" Cy nodded at Annabel's conclusion. "I will speak to her."

"I ask you not do so until the matter with Lucsa has been settled," Mariamne cautioned her. "Because of their innocent indiscretion— which they both have repented of—they found a room deep below the south tower Lucsa has conscripted for nefarious use. She has converted it into an unholy altar to the worship of the dark one."

Annabel gasped.

Cy narrowed his eyes. "Sister, the king must be informed."

"Please, brother, I am convinced if any action is taken against this woman, we will lose Shane to the darkness. He must uncover her wickedness. He must choose between the difficult truth and the pleasure of the lie on his own."

Cy sat back, folded his arms, and fixed her with a hard stare. "I like this not at all, sister. We play with fire most deadly."

"The fate of my son's soul lies in the balance."

"Your son's soul lies in the hand of God Almighty."

Mariamne laced her fingers and bowed her head. "God most high —Creator of the heavens and the earth. We beseech You today. We ask for Your wisdom and Your guidance. Show us how to deal with this evil within our walls, Lord. Evil is never to be tolerated. But, Lord, what of Shane? He teeters on a great precipice. I fear over him, my Father. You know well the beating of a parent's heart, Father. Please, tell me what we are to do."

"Our great Shield, protect us," Annabel's voice continued the prayer. "Send Your angels and guard us from the ploys of the evil one. We are Yours, and we seek protection under Your wing, Father."

Cy spoke next. "Give us eyes to see, ears to hear, and a mind to understand the tricks of this wicked woman. Let no harm come to Your children, my God. Reach out Your hand and protect us. Open Shane's eyes, Lord. Reveal the truth to him. Make Yourself known to him, this very hour, Lord."

"Amen and amen." Mariamne raised her head to look at Cy.

"We will watch—for now, sister. But I cannot promise I will tolerate her evil in my king's home until Shane comes to his senses. If the threat of her grows—"

"I expect you to save my husband—your king and friend, Cy."

He nodded.

Mariamne hugged them both and returned to the hall for the breaking of the fast, her spirit filled.

# Chapter 15

"I thought it sacrilegious to break the long night's fast so early each day." Lucsa fell into step beside Shane as he walked across the ward. "Most priests say it is a sign of gluttony to eat more than two meals in one day."

"King Edgar has always been in the habit of eating a small meal of cheese and meat left over from the previous night. It serves to use up what remains before it spoils. The time allows him to pray over the members of his home before they start their day. And the small sustenance helps them complete their tasks. Father Paul has blessed it as well." Shane rubbed his temple.

"I did not see you eat over much."

"Food sits foul in my belly of late, madam."

She spun the ring on her finger and took his hand, putting the back of her other hand to his forehead to distract him from the needle prick.

He jerked away, his eyes scanning about frantically to see who might have observed her unwanted intimacy. "Do not be so familiar with me, madam." A near growl punctuated his words.

She huffed, sliding the needle back into the ring before spinning it around again. "You sound like the queen, Highness."

Shane stopped. "What are you blathering about?"

"I tell you, the good queen—for all her high morals—does not wish me here. Any time she has opportunity, she threatens me."

"I have seen no such confrontation."

"Of course not. You do not think her so brazen as to accost me in your presence—knowing how you feel about me. You would never permit it, and she would lose your remaining affection. But I assure you, she wishes me gone."

"At the moment, I wish you gone as well, woman. I have training to attend. King Edgar speaks of his wishes to knight me and Cy's son, Ethan, at the beginning of the council of the lords." Shane rolled his neck, and a slim smile turned the corners of his taut lips.

She knew the effects of the opiate that coursed through his body brought him a wave of pleasure.

"A full two months prior to the remembrance of my day of birth." He hummed as his body swayed. "He honors me before the nobility so they will recognize me as heir apparent."

Lucsa grimaced. "But you must share your honor with a mere thane's son."

"Cy is near a brother to the queen and serves Edgar faithfully. Ethan has earned his spurs—far more than I." Shane started walking again. His shoulders relaxed, and his stride more a swagger. He no longer rubbed at his head.

Lucsa followed. "You nay earn what has been gifted you by birthright."

"But it is not my birthright, now is it? 'Tis Jak's."

"'Tis yours only, my prince. One day you will see there is no other option." They parted, her mind spun with new possibilities. She twisted the ring around her finger and walked back toward the ward.

She spotted Jak laughing as he led his horse from the stables. The boy resembled her son. Tall and lean with dark hair, but his face was round, not oval. His nose was stubby, like his fathers, and his eyes were too wide apart for her liking. He could prove to be a good servant for the master, but when he turned her direction, she saw the light within his eyes. He already served another.

Lucsa shrugged. Everyone could serve the master in one fashion or another. His death would force Edgar to crown Slade come what may. She walked toward the boy as he mounted. "What a fine horse, young prince."

"Thank you," Jak said, warning flashing in his eyes. "Can I be of some assistance, my lady?"

She ran her hand over the horse's neck, the ring turned and ready. "I thought since I was collecting names of potential brides for the crown prince, you may wish me to keep an eye out for a mate for you as well."

"I am still shy of fifteen, my lady. Marriage considerations will be long in coming for me, I hope."

"True, but if I knew your preferences, I would put those names aside for your consideration at some far-off future time."

"I thank you, but nay. I am not interested. I am off to hunt now. If you would excuse me."

Lucsa curtsied, patted the horse hard on the neck, driving the small needle into a pulsing vein. She used the last of her drug on the beast, but she could make more. "Good luck, young prince. Be safe."

Cy raced around the battlements shouting down to Jak's guard from over the gate. "Knox! Hold!" He raced down the tower stairs and burst out the door, startling the horses, but none more than Jak's.

"Sir, is there a problem? The prince wished to hunt."

Cy smiled, taking Jak's mount by the reins, noting its wide pupils and quick breaths. "Aye, looks to be a fine day for a hunt. I thought I saw Lord Jak's mount favoring his hindquarters. I would never forgive myself if the king's son were injured." Cy ran his hand over the animal. Its heart pounded and its skin twitched.

"I saw nothing amiss, sir," a guard said.

"I saw it from above, Robert. It was more of an oddity where the backend did not follow the front."

"That could be a sign of a back injury. Few horses recover from such," Knox groaned.

The horse pranced with restless angst.

"He *is* behaving oddly, Sir Cy," Jak said.

"Highness, why not take my mount for now? I would be loath for you to miss such a fine day. Rapier has not had a good run and could use the exercise. I will have the marshal look your mount over. I am sure he will be fine by the time you return."

Jak dismounted and re-entered the stables. "Thank you, Sir Cy."

Cy waved and turned the abandoned mount back to the stables. A child laughed; the horse snorted and sidestepped away. Barking dogs made him whinny and toss his head. His ears flicked in constant motion, and his gate fell in uneven, stumbling strides. As Cy led him past the armory through the inner gate, the smithy's clanging hammer caused the beset horse to rear up. His reins jerked from Cy's hand. The wild horse ran free through the ward.

"Take heed!" Cy cried to the maids at the well.

They screamed, dropping the earthenware containers, shattering them on the ground. The shrieks and crashing caused the horse to buck, kicking out his back legs wildly. He neighed loudly, bucking and rearing about the ward in frantic movements.

"Close the gates!" Cy shouted to the guards standing gawking in the open entrance.

As they scrambled to comply, the horse spotted the opening

between the ward and the outer bailey, lowered his head, and charged for freedom. Cy waved his arms to scare him off. The guards struggled with the ten-foot-high heavy-beamed doors. The horse kicked out its back legs and tossed its head with a frantic whinny and flared its nostrils. Cy stood his ground. "Hurry! He cannot get loose in the crowds in the bailey."

The crazed horse was only a stride away. Still Cy remained. A flash of flame waved in front of him. Scott, the royal marshal, held two torches between Cy and the beast. He yelled and shouted. The horse veered off. The gate banged closed.

Scott handed one torch to Cy. "Help me corner him behind the stables before he hurts someone or himself."

The two men, with the help of several squires, worked for an hour before the horse stood confined to the walled-in area. While several stood guard at the narrow entrance, others moved barrels and crates across the opening to prevent the beast from escaping.

"What malady has beset Chaucer?" Scott said, standing beside Cy. The two men watched the horse pace, paw the ground, and toss his head about in erratic swings.

"It came on most sudden, but the worst of it seems to be wearing off," Cy said.

"You sound as if he fed on some aberrant weed."

"I have no proof of such."

The marshal considered Cy. "But you have suspicions, sir."

Cy put his hand on Scott's shoulder. "Let him calm for another few hours before you tend to his needs. He cannot hurt anyone there. Let us pray it was a one-time malady. He is a fine horse, and it would upset the prince to put him down." Cy strolled away, working at the knot forming at the base of his skull.

# Chapter 16

Shane staggered down the stairs—his head pounding and his limbs trembling. He stopped several times, to steady himself against the wall. Every morning for almost a month he suffered with growing weakness and tremors. He closed his eyes, leaning back against the stairwell. Two more steps and he would be at the bottom. He stood, fighting nausea. He wiped his sweat-covered face with his sleeve.

"Slade," the familiar whisper forced him to open his eyes. Lucsa greeted him with her ever-present grin. He opened his hand. Using both hands, she placed the fennel in it.

"How long will I be like this, Lucsa? Your treatment makes me no better. I should speak with Carrington. I cannot continue this way."

She rested her hand on his forearm; the darkness swirled in her eyes, dragging him into their depths. "Oh, my son, you cannot. If you show weakness the king may withdraw his support in favor of the sniveling Jak. You must remain strong. Stay the course, Slade. Only a fortnight more and you will wear the crown and take your rightful place."

Shane's breaths eased. His head cleared and danced with euphoric delight to be free of the pain. "I am not being made king, Lucsa. It is but a mere formality to assure the line of succession. The king is still hale and sure to live for years to come."

"You know naught of the future, my boy. Things may happen quicker than you think."

She slipped away, leaving the notion to tumble in his head. *Am I ready to be king?* He smiled. He had spent his entire life preparing for the time when he would rule. Nothing could stop him—not this illness, not Lucsa and her whispers, not the king or the queen. Not even God Himself could keep him off the throne. *It is my right.*

Something within him flickered—fluttered. A light? A nugget of something remembered but only as the vague recollection of a long forgotten dream. He quaked again, but this was different. It came from deep in his soul, and it ran down his spine in icy steps of fear. As he walked out of the shadows into the hall—now long after the first meal —he tried to put it out of his mind. He hoped it would remain so confined.

Lucsa found the queen as she oversaw the education of the squires. The youths were leaving their morning lessons. Lucsa waited until the queen stood alone in the large open room at the bottom of the tower nearest to the inner gate. "So this is the labor which occupies the queen's days—wiping the noses of worthless vermin."

Mariamne's head rose. "Good day to you, Lucsa." There was no cheer in her words, but neither was there malice. The words came off her lips with ease but grated on Lucsa's nerves as if a razor were scraped across her bare flesh.

"When I am queen mother, I will not stoop to such menial tasks. I will never be found waiting the tables like a common wench or teaching the squires to read. Slaves need not know how to read. It only puts distracting thoughts in their heads."

Mariamne held her gaze. Something flickered there—for only a moment. Whatever passed through her never touched her lips or tainted her words. "If such should come to pass, Veronia will be the poorer for it. I pray Shane does not fall so far from the truth."

"Your prayers fall on deaf ears. Give up. There is no hope to cling to."

"It is better to trust in the Lord, than to have confidence in princes."

Lucsa felt the bit of the holy words as if multitudes of bees stung her. She turned, fleeing from the room, which felt devoid of air.

Next she found Milana, the true royal firstborn. Her beauty was the mirror of her mother's. Sleek black hair cascaded from her sweet oval face. Her green eyes shown with intelligence and vitality—and the light. Staring at the maddening girl, Lucsa's hands fisted. Tension filled her limbs until she quaked. Her chest heaved and she could hear her own ragged breath. She was loath to even set eyes on the girl.

*So beautiful and womanly, yet she refused to use her many assets to manipulate the men around her*. Milana remained the pure and virtuous woman Lucsa never managed to be herself. Why, by the time she was Milana's age, Slade was at least a year old. *If I fell to temptation than all women should*, Lucsa reasoned.

"Good day to you, Milana," Lucsa said, forcing a smile to her lips.

The young woman was not as good as her mother at concealing her true emotions, however. "Lucsa." Her greeting was dry, and her arms were held close to her as if she expected a blow.

"I have just left your dear mother and could not help but see your stunning resemblance to our beautiful queen. I am quite surprised some noble son has not laid claims to your heart as yet."

"My suitors do not concern you, madam."

"But I am the royal matchmaker," Lucsa smiled.

"You are Shane's problem, but do not claim honor not bestowed. King Edgar and Queen Mariamne did not contract your services."

Lucsa curled her lip and snarled. "I could find you a most desirable match. Such beauty could get you a king of a faraway land. You could be queen."

"I could be queen here, if the Lord wills it. Or my child could one day wear the crown."

Words leapt forth unbidden. "Neither you, nor your spawn, will ever sit on the throne of Veronia. If you pose a threat to Shane, I can arrange a great many calamities to befall you."

Milana threw back her shoulders, narrowed her gaze and spoke through clenched teeth. "And if I tell my dear brother, who loves me, of your threat—what would become of you then, witch?"

Lucsa drew back to slap the girl.

"Princess Milana, there you are?"

Lucsa's hand dropped to her side.

"Sir Cynric? Do you require me?"

"Aye, Highness, I wished to ask your advice on a matter of some import." He turned to Lucsa with a hard glare, causing her to draw back a step. "You do not mind, do you, madam?"

She shook her head and scurried away.


Lucsa fled the ward and disappeared into her dark chapel. "Master, I work for yar gain, but all me labors come to naught. *He* protects them. What must I do?"

She muttered as she ground and mixed new potions, smiling. "Yes, master. I will do as ya wish." After pulling the vile of Slade's treatments from the pouch ,she refilled her ring yet again. She scurried out of the chamber and dumped her latest concoction down the well. A puff of air escaped from her. Her shoulders relaxed as she strolled to watch Slade train. She took her perch high above and settled herself for the long afternoon.

Shane sparred with Ethan. Their blades clanged together with a glorious ring. Thrust, counter, block, parry, they fell into a rhythm, knowing the movements of the other as his own. Shane noted the well-defined bulk of muscle now outlined by Ethan's ill-fitting tunic. He felt the strength of Ethan's blows as they reverberated through his arm. Shane stumbled back from the ferocity of Ethan's attack.

Griff barked orders, "Anticipate, Highness. You are a heartbeat behind everything Ethan does." The captain walked around them. "Plant your feet. Dig in your heels. Give no ground." Another circuit. "Guard up. You open your ribs to be run through."

Ethan took the hint and rapped Shane's ribs with the flat of his blade. The cold steel reverberated through him, sending tremors to the ends of his fingers and out his toes.

Rage seared the spot of impact, erupted in his soul, and spewed out his mouth. "You cur!" Shane broke form and charged. Shane balled his fist and slammed it into Ethan's jaw. "You think you are better than I. I am crown prince. The only honor you have is due to the favor my father shows your lowly sire. Favor can be taken away, Eth. When I am king—"

"The Lord save us from such a time." Ethan stood his ground. His only reaction to swipe at his bloody lip with the back of his hand.

Shane swung again but missed. "I will see you licking my boots."

"Even if you could get an army to follow you, the sum total of them could not force me to grovel before such an unworthy wretch."

Shane lunged at him, caught him around the middle, and drove him to the ground. He drew back to pommel Ethan but found himself on his back before he could let his fist fly. Ethan straddled him, pinning Shane's arms down with his knees—his left hand wrapped around Shane's throat, and Ethan's right hand rose high and slow.

Griff caught the arm before it could be loosed. "You cannot, Ethan. Regardless of your feelings, God seems set on placing him in authority over us. You must honor such. 'Let every soul be subject unto the higher powers: for there is no power but of God: and the powers that be, are ordained of God.'"

Writhing, consumed by heat, Shane remained pinned to the ground—helpless, and humiliated. "Do you hear, Ethan? Appointed by God. A divine right to rule. You have no choice but to serve."

"Or swear my allegiance to another—more worthy than you." Ethan rose, kicking dirt in Shane's face.

Shane arched his back, popped to his feet, and hurled himself at Ethan. Griff caught him around the middle preventing Shane from killing him. Shane jerked free and raised his sword to the captain's throat. "How dare you presume to put your hands on my person. I am your prince." Shane pressed the tip of his blade into the man's flesh until a drop of scarlet appeared. "Kneel before me and prove you give me allegiance above all others."

Griff stood as though stone. His gazed narrowed and hardened. His breaths persisted even and steady as he ground out, "I bend a knee to no man, save King Edgar himself. To him I have sworn my fidelity. There may come a day, young prince, when I bow a knee to you and give my oath—but 'tis *not this day*."

Shane howled with fury. It consumed him until no other thought could remain—save murder. He shifted the weight to run the good-for-nothing knave through. The heel of Griff's left hand smacked into the blade, knocking it away. The captain's right hand snaked under Shane's sword arm, gripping onto his wrist with deadly strength. The sword fell to the dusty ground with a hollow clang. Shane's wrist twisted and contorted until it rested between his shoulder blades, sending hot bolts of pain through his arm and deep into his shoulder.

Griff stood behind him, pinning his arm in place while his left hand seized Shane's throat. "A bit of advice, *Highness.* Spend far more time at your training, then mayhaps one day you might chance upon a day when the good Lord smiles upon you and you best me." Griff put his foot in front of Shane's and shoved him forward. Shane landed on his stomach in the dust. "'Tis not such a day. Best you know for sure you can succeed, Shane, son of Edgar, when next you try. For if you fail, I will break your arm in the trying."

Shane rose to his feet. His limbs quaked, and his innards flooded with heat that burned upon his skin. The pounding in his ears drowned out all but the vengeance he would seek.

Every eye within and without the training corrals lay upon him. His very breath seared his lungs. His arm throbbed like the smithy's white-hot irons were jabbed inside it.

Griff stood, feet apart, arms crossed, daring Shane to try again.

"Your time will come soon, Ol' Griff. This I swear."

"Remember the lessons of your youth well, boy. Recall the words of Job, 'the Lord hath given, and the Lord hath taken it.' God can remove the honor bestowed on you and give it to another."

Shane stormed out of the training corral. Lucsa fell into step beside them. "Do you see now, my lord? They are all jealous of you. They want your power."

"How do I stop them?" Shane fisted his hands. "I will do whatever you say, Lucsa."

Her head tipped back. A smile lit on her face. "Come, I will give you wise council, my lord."

# Chapter 17

Shane hauled his head off the pillow after another fitful night's sleep. His knighting would occur on the morrow. Malevolent rage churned within him. How would he survive a day and a night in fasting and prayer, when he did not possess the strength to get out of bed?

"Highness, your father waits without to escort you." Alden shuffled about collecting the simple attire allowed him on this holy day.

"I know the way to the chapel, you fool. Tell him to be gone."

"Highness? 'Tis a father's honor …" Alden stood bent under the brunt of much of Shane's wrath in the last few weeks. But the man's loyalty and kindness never wavered. It pricked at Shane's consciousness, stirring the spiteful voice within to goad once more.

*Tell this imbecile the truth of your so-called father.*

"That man has no honor. He does not see fit to speak with me unless he is ordering me about. I must bend and cater to his every whim. The foolhardy, utterly useless things he forces upon me. It is my right to be crowned his successor. Why, therefore, must I suffer without food for an entire day?"

Alden pulled his nightshirt over his head. "'Tis time for prayer, Your Highness. To seek God's will—"

"Is it not clear? His will is to see me on the throne."

"Yes, Highness." Alden spoke no more as he dressed Shane. After only a moment, the door of the inner chamber cracked open.

Through the crack came a quiet, melancholy voice. "I will be in prayer for you, Shane. May God reveal Himself to you. May you find the fullness of His love, and may He grant you the deepest desires of your true heart." The door closed, and the king left. Shane heard the soft click of the latch to the outer door secure.

A flash of guilt churned in his belly like rotten eggs.

*He still seeks to control you. He wants to bend you to the narrow path of his God. There is more freedom for you, my son. More pleasure, more power. Stay the course—soon. Soon it will all be yours.*

A thought fluttered in his brain like a tiny butterfly. *But is not Edgar's God and mine, one in the same?*

Shane felt a prick on his toe. "You fool," he yelled. "You stepped on my foot." Shane pulled back to strike the old man.

Alden stared, shock and pain making his eyes grow wide. "Highness, I did nay harm you. I swear it." His gaze flickered to the raised hand. He straightened, squared his shoulders—as much as his weathered frame would allow—and raised his chin. "If you think me capable of injuring the man I have tended with love since the day you moved out of the nursery … If you believe me agile and spry enough to step on a toe when I stand on the far side of your injury … If you think me so spiteful … Then let loose your hand, Highness, and punish your old servant. When you are complete—if I still draw breath —I will seek another more to your liking to serve you."

How could the man speak so to him? The audacity, the calm, the love with which the old man spoke. The growing darkness within trembled at the reverberation of the truth spoken in unconditional love.

Shane's hand dropped, as air wheezed through his lungs. He

snatched his boots away from Alden, who reminded Shane of the manner of man he wanted to be. "I will see you on the morrow, Alden. Have my best suit laid out. The blue one."

"As you wish, Highness." Shuffled steps receded from the room. Shane stood alone—more alone than he had ever felt in his entire life.

Edgar moved beside his wife, lacing his fingers with hers. The worry—now ever present on her face—formed permanent creases in her beauty. Her sad green eyes searched his face. Edgar kissed her cheek. "I fear we have lost him to the darkness, my love."

She gripped his hand with greater force. "As long as he draws breath, there is yet hope." Her bold confidence lifted his heavy spirit. "There must be hope, right husband?" She faltered. His beloved had never doubted Shane would choose the Lord—until this moment.

Edgar drew Mariamne near. "God alone knows what the coming days will bring. In Him there is always hope."

She laid her head on his shoulder. "I will hope in the Lord my God, henceforth and forever."

Shane appeared in the archway at the base of the stairs. In front of him stood the nobility of his realm—the people he would one day rule —*Lord willing*. He shook off the last thought with a shiver of unease. No, he would be king.

*You have but to submit to it, my son.*

He brushed off the pestering darkness as though swatting at a summer infestation of flies. His focus returned to those before him as they formed two rows lining his path. Shane drew to his full height, threw out his chest, and raised his chin. His steps were slow, and deliberate. Even in the reed-covered hall, they barely sounded in the silence as he passed. He looked neither to the right nor the left, but marched out the hall and out of their sight.

Edgar did not follow him through the knights and men-at-arms who lined the ward or the townsfolk who continued outlining his path in the bailey. He knew Griff stood at the entrance to the chapel with Father Bartholomew. Shane would enter the chapel alone, and the doors would be sealed.

Yapping drew his attention as he passed toward his long-awaited imprisonment. Scruff, the pup he'd rescued months ago, leapt about on the leash of a squire, his tail moving with such speed it appeared to be wagging his entire body. Shane bent and stroked the mutt's head. Scruff leapt, placing his paws on Shane's knee and licked at his face. Though not a dignified thing for a future king to do, Shane cared not. Scruff stood as the last of his friends—the only living thing to welcome his company of late.

"See you on the morrow, boy," Shane said with a final pat and stood to complete his trek to his chapel dungeon.

Shane knelt before the high altar. Not even the blustering winter wind could be heard through the sturdy stonewalls. The tremors grew in his limbs. He did not recall seeing Lucsa as he marched to his destination. How would he survive without her ministrations for a full day and night? His heart thudded, rattling his chest—and his nerves— and pulsed in his ears.

Distraction was what he required. How did Ethan fair? They had not spoken since the day Ethan humiliated him in the training area. Ethan would also be locked within holy walls, but he chose to be down in the town. Shane missed him.

*Think naught of the lesser urchin. He, two years your junior, knighted on the same day as the heir. It is an affront to you. He has not earned the right to be knighted so young.*

Shane ignored the voice as a smile crept across his lips, remembering the mischief the two would throw themselves into with great abandon. Hiding in the well and scaring the maids, moving the horses from the royal stables to the nave of the chapel, stacking all the blades from the armory in the death holes. Shane laughed out loud recalling the delicate balance required in placing the many blades alternating the tips face out with the hilt facing out until they filled the narrow slit cramming in the last one to wedge them in place. Ethan and he had hid in a dark doorway to watch what would happen. They gave themselves away in fits of laughter as a guard pulled one weapon free, allowing the rest to tumble like logs in a waterfall out of the death hole.

Shane settled back on his rump, his knees aching and cold. What had happened to the affable friend of his youth?

*He grows jealous of your crown.*

Shane shrank back from the malicious voice, pain twisting his limbs. His head throbbed. "I come seeking the truth—" His words broke off as his stomach seized. He bent over, laying his forehead on cold stones. The coolness soothed his sweat-drenched face. He closed his eyes and writhed in the growing torment.

As the wave of agony receded like a constant tide, he glanced back under the pews before his eyes clenched closed against the hot tears drawn by the next surge of pain. He lay there a moment—hoping to die. His eyes shot open again; this time he looked.

There, under the second bench, lay a small pouch. Shane sucked air in his lungs and dragged himself to it. The small bit of leather looked familiar, but his addled brain would not recall it clear. He looked up. He lay near where Lucsa sat on the few occasions she ventured into the holy building. Lucsa—this pouch belonged to her. It never left her side. He opened it to find a single broken reed of fennel and one other broad green leaf. The surface of it shown like glass in the flickering candlelight.

*Eat and forget.*

"What will it do?" Shane asked the voice without thought.

*'Twill ease the pain, my son. Allow you to sleep—to forget your misspent youth with that boy.*

"But I should pray—not sleep." Shane tried to protest.

*Who will know if you do not bend your will to the king's wishes?*

"I will know." Shane groaned as another wave of pain—more bitter than the first—washed over his body. Every part of him trembled. His stomach heaved—bitterness covered his tongue.

*Eat—forget.*

Each muscle in his body coiled. He lay in a heap on the stones between the pews, tears drenching his face. The pain grew until he retched what little remained in his belly. Drenched in sweat, his body prepared to vomit again. In despair and agony, he took the larger leaf and chewed.

The sour leaf threatened to come back up before it had gone all the way down. His muscles convulsed and went limp—useless. He lay sprawled on the floor as his mind danced in a rainbow of colors and euphoria. As though released from his body, he floated and flew. He soared to the roof beams, circled over Mariamne's prayer gallery perched high above the women's pews, glided back down through the nave, swooped over the altar, and swished past the stained glass window—Edgar's prized personal donation in the construction of the humble house of worship.

Nothing could contain his spirit loosed by Lucsa's magic.

# *Chapter 18*

Swords clashed. Warriors roared. Horses' hooves beat the ground. A battle raged.

Shane lay on the battlefield, drenched in morning dew—or was it blood? His blood? He couldn't move. Not a toe wiggled. Not a finger twitched. Not even an eyelid fluttered.

The ground reverberated with the battle raging about him.

Shane's heart beat in an erratic wild rhythm until if felt like it would burst.

Sword against shield, blade against blade. Mail rattled. Armor clanged. Hate-filled oaths clogged the air.

Shane roused once more. Still his body would not respond. Not a single digit could he control. He choked on the fear consuming him and gagged to clear his airway.

Footsteps crushed the ground near his head. "He is mine!"

"You may have enticed him to listen to you. But you have yet to win his heart."

Swords clanged, echoing in his ears. Wind whirled around him in great pulsating rushes. Sinister cackles and holy shouts filled the air until a great cacophony of noise drowned out all thought.

The battle raged, pulling him again from the dark abyss. Thunder rolled. The earth rumbled. Unspent screams filled his body. His lungs would not accept air. His heart refused to beat. Whether from the battle, or his own frail body, Shane knew he would not live to see the rising of the sun.

Anger burst from him—hot and searing. *I will not even see my knighting, let alone sit upon Veronia's throne. Why does God hate me? Have I done such evil, God would kill me before I have a chance to live?*

*I will be with thee; I will not fail thee, neither forsake thee; fear not therefore, nor be discomforted.*

A violent tremor shook Shane to the depths of his soul. It broke cracks in the black callous surrounding his heart. Light broke through —a radiance brighter than the sun.

Guilt, shame, and a brokenness he could not imagine overwhelmed him. *Lord—help me.*

The battle evaporated in a puff of smoke. A depth of silence crushed him and filled him at the same time.

The bell, marking Lauds, reverberated from the steeple down the tower, across the chancel, over the altar, shaking the stones beneath him until his teeth rattled. Remembering the fierce battle, Shane bolted upright. He still sat within the chapel. No pews were upset, no bodies littered the floor, and no blood stained the stones. What had happened during the night? A vision? A dream? A pain-induced hallucination? He could not make his mind understand it. The tremors started again, and the aches returned. He reached for the pouch at his side and ate the fennel.

When the pain evaporated away, he stood, and moved back to the altar. He stared at the gold cross perched there, and a longing pulled at his heart. It drew him to follow. The dark whisper—but a vapor now—held no sway over him. In this new longing lay the light he remembered from the night. It contained the truth.

The weight of Shane's true character crushed him to the ground. He held his head in his hands. Tears pooled in his palms. "Father, what have I done? I allowed evil to woo me away from You—my Savior. Lord, forgive me. Rescue me from my sinful desires." His sobs echoed in the empty space. "I am an unworthy wretch, but I choose to follow You—if You will still have use of a fool such as me."

*Behold My servant whom I have chosen, My beloved in whom My soul delights; I will put My Spirit on him.*

An ocean wave of peace flooded him, rocking him back. The last of the darkness vanished in the all-consuming light filling him. The evil voice howled in fury, but the Spirit within Shane left no room for any other.

"I am Your servant, my Lord and my God. Teach me Your ways. Direct my steps."

Shane slipped from the chapel as the sun warmed the eastern horizon with oranges, golds, and glorious yellows. He climbed the back stairs, entering his chamber unseen. Alden stirred as he passed. "Sleep, my friend. All is well."

"Highness?" Alden rose, lumbering in after him. "It is still my duty to assist you?" The question shot guilt-tipped arrows into Shane's heart.

Shane lay his hand on the man's trembling arm. "You have always been the most faithful of all to me, Alden. No matter how I treated you, you have—" Tears choked off his words.

"I have loved you, Highness."

Shane could but nod. "I have been most cruel. I understand not how you bore it, but I ask your forgiveness, my friend, for I sore regret every evil thing I have inflected on you and said unto you."

Alden smiled. His stooped frame looked as though it lost twenty years of worry and age. "Dwell not a moment more on the past, Highness." He moved to the bed where his suit lay. "Shall we prepare you for this fine day, and your future?"

An odd nervousness shuddered Shane's insides. The future—what did God wish of Him?

Shane lounged in a hot bath until the water grew cold and at last rose to be dressed in his blue tunic, gold doublet, and black hosen. Midday found him sitting on his divan, tapping his foot in erratic spurts, waiting for the ceremony to begin.

Alden brought in a tray of breads and cheeses. "The nobles gather in the chapel now, Highness." He offered Shane a mug of weak ale, considering him with a raised brow. "We wait for Sir Ethan to return from town."

Shane nodded. "Ethan has earned this honor with his faithful training, depth of learning, his bravery, and his loyal, upright heart. 'Tis right we should wait for him."

Alden released the breath he held, and a smile dimpled his crinkled face. "Glad I am to hear you say such, Highness. Your time in prayer last eve has served you well. I praise the Lord God almighty for His answer to our many prayers."

The heat of his shame warmed his cheeks. "Ethan should have been Edgar's son—not I."

"Oh, Highness, do not say such things. It is the will of God you are born of the parents you have."

Shane could not look at him any longer. His stomach revolted at the little he had eaten. "Alden, would you do me a kindness?"

"You have but ask."

"Would you fetch the soothing tea which Carrington provided when I returned a month ago? It calmed by nervous stomach, and I fear I will have need of it before the day is spent." Alden bowed and turned to leave. "Ask him for a few doses, please." With a quick nod, the dear man shuffled out of the room as fast as his old legs would allow.

# Chapter 19

Shane stood, his chin low to his chest, beside and yet a step behind Ethan in the narthex. He could not meet Ethan's gaze. Tears threatened and his throat constricted. "I wish you well, brother," Shane whispered.

Ethan stole a glance over his shoulder, suspicion twisting his face.

Heat tingled on Shane's cheeks. He should run from this place. Nothing in all his days made him worthy to accept the coming honor and stand beside men the likes of Ethan. A fowl taste eased over his tongue at the thoughts of his own loathsome behavior. His fists balled as memory upon memory of his treachery and evil bombarded his brain.

"Ethan, son of Cynric, come forward," King Edgar called from the altar. Ethan held his head high as he walked with steady even steps. "Take a knee before your king, Ethan." He knelt with ease. "For your faithful service to me—your king, to your queen, and to the good people of Veronia, I do bestow upon you the title of Knight of Veronia."

Cy stepped forward and placed a red woolen cloak bearing the king's insignia over his son's shoulders as Edgar said, "This cloak is placed upon you so that you may find the strength to stand alone. May your acts of chivalry be the warmth for others colder than yourself."

Next, gold spurs were lashed to Ethan's boots.

"The spurs represent the right of a knight to ride unhindered throughout the land, dispensing justice tempered with mercy, protecting the weak, defending the defenseless, and helping the needy. By wearing the precious spurs near his feet, the knight shows his disdain for earthly treasures in favor of spiritual treasures."

Cy secured a belt around Ethan's waist.

"This belt is placed around you as a symbol of your chosen path. May it always remind you of the importance of this choice. The belt represents the unity of Chivalry. The color reminds the knight to be ever faithful in his duties, to be pure of heart, and to be respectful in his actions."

Cy then handed his son a shield bearing Ethan's coat of arms dominated by a tall, powerful lion.

"This shield stands for the honor and renown of you as Knight of Veronia. Use it and remember to guard yourself well."

Lastly, Edgar placed in Ethan's hands a finely crafted sword. "I give this sword to you as a symbol of your own actions. The sword represents the knight's right to dispense justice. The double edge of the blade ever reminds him to temper justice with mercy. As the steel must be tempered by fire and water, so must the soul of the knight be tempered by adversity and compassion. Never draw this in anger, and use it only for the service of God.

"Do you, Ethan, son of Cynric of Balmore, swear an oath as a Knight of Veronia in the faithful service of King Edgar?"

"Upon these gifts, and before God, my king, and those assembled, I do so swear to be a good and true knight, to uphold chivalry, its honor, rights, and privileges, to uphold the laws of Veronia, and to remain faithful to my sworn word, to hate evil and love good, to temper justice with mercy, to defend the weak. This I swear upon my honor, Ethan, Knight of Veronia." Ethan's oath rang out proud and sure.

Edgar drew his own sword, tapping it on Ethan's shoulders in turn. "This we do hear, and shall never forget, nor fail to reward that which is given: fealty with love, service with honor, and oath-breaking with vengeance. Arise, Sir Ethan, Knight of Veronia, and accept your king's honor."

Ethan stood to a great proud height. Edgar turned him to face those gathered, as they cheered with quiet respect within the confines of the holy building. Edgar motioned for him to moved to the side, and his gaze rose to the back of the chapel.

Shane trembled.

"Shane, son of Edgar, King of Veronia and Mariamne, Queen of Veronia, come forward."

Air sucked into every lung and stuck, leaving Shane fighting for breath. His legs quaked. *You do not belong here. Run.* His gaze found Mariamne sitting on the left in the front row. Her smile radiated confidence and pride. He dared turn and look at the king. Edgar stood tall, shoulders thrown back, chest out, chin high. A smile toyed with his serious features.

Shane found himself at the foot of the altar before the man who had raised him as his own.

"Shane, take a knee before your king."

Shane crumpled to the floor, his head hanging low, an unseen burden bearing down upon him. The weight of the heavy cloak added to his affliction, and he did not believe he would be able to stand, for he had no acts of chivalry to warm others.

Likewise, the gold spurs only served to remind him of the injustice, which lacked all mercy, others had suffered at his hands. Never did he protect the weak, defend the defenseless, nor help the needy. The gold spurs screamed to all where his true treasure lay.

A belt tightened around his waist. Had he chosen? Is this what had happened in the pre-dawn morning? *I pray it is so, Lord. For I do choose You.*

Cy then handed Shane a shield bearing a surprising heraldic symbol on it. The black on gold fur was emblazoned with a white standing buck. Shane knew well the symbolism this image spoke. The white meant peace and sincerity, while the buck represented one who will not fight unless provoked. Shane dared steal a glance at the king, who rewarded him with a quick flash of a smile.

The sword weighed heavy in his upturned palms. Shane thought to grip the well-honed double-edged blade, and cut open his hands for all the injustices he had caused others to suffered. *Lord, I beg of You, I want to temper justice with mercy.*

"Do you Shane, son of Edgar, King of Veronia, take the oath as a Knight of Veronia in the faithful service of King Edgar and your people?"

Shane struggled to swallow as fear and doubt threatened to choke the life out of him. "Upon these gifts, and before God, my king, and those assembled, I swear to be a *good* and *true* knight, to uphold chivalry, its honor, rights, and privileges, to uphold the laws of Veronia, and to remain faithful to my sworn word, to *hate* evil and *love* good, to temper justice with mercy, to defend the weak. This I swear upon my honor, Shane, Knight of Veronia." Shane's oath hissed with a fervor he felt in the depth of his aching spirit. He wished it to be true, hoped he would never fail to live up to the standard he claimed this day. He prayed he would never forget the unworthiness he felt at this moment.

Edgar drew his sword again. "This we do hear, and shall never forget, nor fail to reward that which is given: fealty with love, service with honor, and oath-breaking with vengeance. I dub thee Sir Shane, Knight of Veronia. Accept your king's honor."

Shane remained on his knee, as he knew more ceremony awaited.

Edgar turned, lifting the simple crown from the cushion Father Bartholomew held. It rested suspended over Shane's head. "Shane, son of King Edgar and Queen Mariamne, will you solemnly promise and swear to govern with King Edgar until his death, the people of Veronia and all our surrounding territories, according to our laws and customs?"

"I solemnly do so promise."

"Will you use your power to cause law and justice, in mercy, to be executed in all your judgments?"

"I do so swear." With each question and response, Shane's words grew more steady and confident. He took the oaths into his heart and swore he would never break them.

"Will you, to the utmost of your power, maintain the Laws of God and the true profession of the Gospel? Will you maintain and preserve unbreakable the settlement of the leadership of Christ, and the doctrine, worship, discipline, and government of His design, now established by law in the land?"

"All this I do so promise and swear. These things, which I have here so promised, I will perform and keep. So help me God."

Edgar placed the crown on his head, took his hand, and raised Shane to his feet. Edgar took one step to the right, leaving Shane center before the altar as he faced his people. People he now saw as friends—and not slaves. Friends he loved with a deep and abiding love.

Those gathered stood. The men took a knee, while the women curtsied low. With every head bowed, they spoke as one voice, "Long live Prince Shane. May God light his path and may his rule know mercy."

The words were subdued, but Shane could not blame them. There was much repair he needed to do to his reputation. He would begin this very hour. He bowed before them in humility.

Ethan stepped beside Shane at the king's silent urging. "My people, I give you Sir Ethan and Prince Shane, knights of Veronia. Welcome them and give them honor." Edgar paused for a moment as the crowd clapped. "Sirs, will you do us the kindness of leading us to the feast?"

Shane and Ethan stepped in unison down the aisle to the door. At the top of the steps they stood alone for a heartbeat. Ethan turned to him. "You are very good, Shane. I almost believed you meant those vows." He tossed his head and descended the stairs, not waiting for Shane or any other.

Shane watched him with regret. *Aye, Lord, there is much work to be done.*

# Chapter 20

Minstrels filled the king's overflowing hall with cheerful tunes. Troubadours entertained with epic tales of valor, love, and great feats of bravery. Gleemen tossed everything from fruit to weapons, stools to clubs, high in the air only to catch them again in great rings of movement. And a small troop of jesters, preformed in the time between the other performances until most of those gathered suffered from aching sides.

The frivolity and continuous movement blurred as Shane stared. He sat to Edgar's right at the high table. Those gathered laughed, and a few bold knights and men-at-arms tempted maidens from the women's table to dance in the small open space near the doors. He observed but he could not join them. King Edgar and Cy and Ethan, who also sat at the high table, clapped with the music. They cheered on the performers. Yet Shane only sat and watched, as an ill child sits at his window and watches his friends play without him. The jovial spirit never touched him.

He looked at each face, and almost to a man, he recalled some evil he had done them. A crude comment here, a cruel joke there, innocence plucked from a maid, and another damsel made to feel unlovely and unworthy. The list went on without end. Guilt and shame overwhelmed his spirit until none of the celebration could be heard or felt.

*You are an unworthy, useless wretch. You think you can be king?*

Shane struggled to breathe as the accuser brought to mind every evil deed. The same voice that tempted him to take the throne by any means only hours ago now condemned him.

"I am proud of you, son," Edgar drew him from the misery.

"You have not one reason in all my life to be so, Majesty. I have been unruly and unrepentant from my birth."

Edgar considered him. "You sound most contrite now, son."

"But how long will it last? How long before I fall back into my wicked ways and cause you pain once more?"

"With the Lord's help, I pray never."

The minstrel came forward for another round of lively music, and as those gathered sang along, any hope at conversation was drowned out. Shane sank back into his wallowing.

When at last the festivities faded, Shane came to himself. He looked around at the near-empty hall. He sighed and stood to leave. His limbs trembled and ached. His head pounded and stomach churned. He had only glimpsed Lucsa from afar and, therefore, she never forced upon him a twig of fennel for this day—yet while his heart reveled at not having contact with her, his body ached for the things she offered.

He shook off the desire to accept another thing from the woman. Alden would have the tea prepared. He needed *her* ministration not at all.

He trudged up the back stairs and caught Milana slipping out of Jak's room. "Milana," he whispered.

She stopped in mid stride, pausing as if considering her next movement. She turned, chin held high, and faced him in challenge. "Shane."

He walked toward her with heavy steps. "Forgive me, Milana."

"Why? What unkindness have you done me *this* day?"

He shook his head, shoulders slumped.

*She will never forgive you. How could she after all you have done?*

"A great number of evils have I committed against you. I have pushed you. I broke several fingers in your hand—"

"The injury happened a great many years back." She held up her hand and wiggled the once injured appendages. "Why bring such a long-ago event up now?"

"For I sore regret them. I lament lying to mother and father in order to lay the blame on you. But above all, Milana, I sore regret telling your beloved, lies about your virtue until he withdrew his offer for your hand."

She crossed her arms, but a tear slid down her cheek. "I knew you had done something to drive him away. What did you say to him? Did you tell him I was a fallen woman?"

"Worse. I convinced him you were a wanton woman who had indulged in all the men of the palace guard."

*Smack!* Her hand flew like a striking viper, and the sting left behind, poisoned his soul. "Why, by all that is holy, would you do such a thing?"

His head hung as it shook. "I am evil at my core, Milana. I resented your purity and your upright walk, for it showed me the cur. I, like Cain, did not wish to change my ways but to destroy you instead."

"This explains much, *brother*. Richard's leaving without comment, and his refusal to ever speak with me again, and that horrid woman you have brought into our home. You are as evil as she.

"Do you know she threatened to marry me off to some distant lord to get me away from the throne you so crave? And if that did not come to pass, she said a calamity would befall me."

She stomped her foot, sending a hollow echo along the length of the hall. "The Scriptures have warned you, brother, 'He that troubleth his own house, shall inherit the wind, and the fool *shall be* servant to the wise in heart.' You reap what you sow, Shane. I pray you can live with yourself."

Shane still could not meet her gaze as the weight of her wrath pressed on him from every side. He deserved all she flung at him and so much more. He had done her great injury by his malicious heart. How he wished he could take it all back and be a better man.

He thought on her words of Lucsa, but he could not reconcile them in his own mind. Lucsa only ever spoke of her mistreatment from the royal family. He saw her with them at times, but in those moments she was all smiles and gentility. A slim part of him yet doubted her capable of such conspiracy.

"I know the good Lord says we must forgive our enemies, Shane, I will seek His help to do so. But know this, I will never forget the pain you have caused me." She spun on the ball of her foot and flew through her door, slamming it.

Shane did not think he possessed the strength to make it the few steps to his own chambers. Alden appeared as he opened the door— tea in hand. Shane drained the cup and fell into bed before removing his clothes.

Morning light flooded his room. Tea sat steaming on his bedside table. He threw his lead-filled legs over the side of the bed and sat.

"Good morn to you, Sir Shane," Alden smiled.

Shane glanced down at his nightshirt. He marveled at the frail old man's ability to undress him in his stupor. "Thank you, Alden."

He nodded. "This day will see your first to meet with the council of lords. What do you desire to wear for such an auspicious occasion?"

Shane shrugged. He cared not, nor did he wish to sit beside Edgar in the place of honor to preside over the council. He would not, however, disgrace Edgar by refusing to show up. "Whatever you think best, Alden. I trust your judgment."

Alden considered him for a moment, his head tilted. Moments later, Shane stood in dark linen trousers, a fine green tunic, and a leather jerkin. Alden assured to place the belt and sword around his waist, and the spurs on his tall boots. Before he left the room, Alden covered his shoulders in the cloak and laid the crown on his head.

"Alden, I am not going off to war or some grand ceremony. I merely go to sit at council."

"But, Highness, you are a knight of the realm now and the heir apparent. You must be attired according to your station."

Shane sighed and allowed the garments to be arrayed upon him. Leaving his chambers, he again moved to the back stairs, but he climbed, instead of descending to the council meeting. He wished to speak to Queen Mariamne—like he'd done with his sister, he planned to beg her forgiveness and tell her of his deeds against Princess Milana. If anyone could set things to right, it would be the queen.

A tense, threatening voice drew him to the queen's door. He walked on the balls of his feet to avoid the clank of his golden spurs on the tiles. He inched to the crack in the doors of the queen's chambers.

# *Chapter 21*

"Now Slade wears the crown. You cannot stop me, Mariamne," the first voice threatened. Shane peeked through the crack. Lucsa looming over Mariamne where she reclined on a divan in the queen's sitting room.

"I have never tried to stop you, Lucsa. Such is a task for the Lord Almighty. The Holy Scriptures have promised me: 'Thou shalt be hid from the scourge of the tongue, and thou shalt not be afraid of destruction when it cometh.' There is nothing you can do to me which is not first filtered through the hand of my God."

"Your God cannot protect you. I will rule at Slade's side, and you will no longer be able to sway his choices. I will put an end to you and all your tiresome prayers."

"Lucsa you cannot stop me from praying, for 'I will offer to Thee a sacrifice of praise, and will call upon the name of the Lord.'"

"Stop!" Lucsa yelled, placing her hands over her ears.

"Do the pure words of truth offend you?"

Lucsa wagged her finger in Mariamne's face. "Slade will become king in the coming days. Then I will live here—pampered in *my* private chambers—and you, you will cower at my feet."

"When God ordains the far off day He chooses to place Shane upon Edgar's throne, I will follow the new king's wishes—no matter what they may be—for he will be my liege lord. But he will also forever be my son."

Lucsa made to lay hands on the queen but something prevented her. "He is *my* son, you cow! He will always be my son. I will have him send you far away so you never see him again. And the day will come before you know it. Edgar's moments are numbered. "

"If God wills it, then it will be, but it will not be at your hand, Lucsa. And if Shane wishes to send me far away, I will go anywhere he directs."

Mariamne's calm lay in stark contrast to Lucsa's furious agitation. As a clear noon day and deepest night hold nothing in common, neither did these two women.

Shane shuddered, frozen in place. One woman the mother of his birth, the other the mother of his days. He owed each an unpayable debt. A choice again lay before him, one he never wished to have thrust upon him—one he was quite sure he did not possess the strength to make.


Shane slipped back into the shadows as Lucsa stormed from the room. He waited until her stomping footsteps faded from hearing before he knocked on the queen's door.

"Enter," came her sweet call. She stood when she saw him. "Oh, Shane. I did not think to see you for most of the day. Is not the council about to convene?" She took his hands as he nodded.

"I wished to speak with you but a moment aforehand, Majesty."

She waved him to the chair beside her couch. "A pure joy to sit and talk with you, my son."

"Are you well, Majesty?"

Her brows crinkled. "Why of course. Why do you ask?"

"I know having Lucsa here has been a strain on you. I ask your forgiveness for bringing her under your roof—and for a great many other evils I have done you, my queen."

She leaned forward and laid her hand over his, where it rested on his knee. "Think no more on the matter. Lucsa is a trifling thing."

"You still do not hate her?"

She smiled and caressed his cheek. "I told you, I would be ever grateful to her for giving me you—the son of my heart."

"I know she has caused you pain—"

"But it cannot outshine the joy of you."

Tears welled in his eyes. No matter how he prodded, she would not speak against Lucsa. Mariamne held her tongue in grace and mercy for him. Shame and gratefulness overwhelmed him. He dropped to the floor before her.

"I deserve naught of your kindness, Majesty. I have been a reprobate from my birth, and I have blamed you for my evil behavior. Your name may indeed mean 'Rebel,' but your heart is ever true, loyal, and loving above all others. I alone carry the twisted, rebellious heart within my foul chest. Forgive me, please." Sobs tore through him.

She pulled him up on his knees and cradled him to her chest as she had when he was young. No regret or revulsion lay in her touch—only love. "Oh, my son, I know well the regret of a life ill-spent, but you have sought absolution. The battle for your soul was long and hard fought. Move forward from this day in the power of the Spirit, who will guide you and direct you. He will be faithful to create in you a new heart, one you can be proud to carry."

The tears would not stop. Her unconditional love broke away every hard edge and shattered every doubt. She believed in him, and so he found hope that change might be possible.

When his tears were spent, he sat once more in the chair across from her and told of his deed against Milana and Richard. Mariamne said she would speak to Edgar and they would go together to Richard's father, who now sat in the hall below as part of the council of lords.

"I will pray, Shane. God is faithful. If Milana and Richard's union is His will, this will not prevent it. Trust in Him to set things aright."

He stood to leave. Something she said triggered a memory. "Did you say a battle had been fought for my soul?"

"Aye."

"How do you know?"

"What do you mean, son?"

"While in the chapel I remember waking to the sound of clashing swords. It sounded as though a great battle raged around me, but I saw no one."

"I was driven to my knees all night wrestling in prayer. The Spirit reminded me, 'We wrestle not against flesh and blood, but against principalities, against powers, and against worldly governors, the princes of this dark world.' The Scriptures record battles between the heavenly angels and Satan and his demons, my son. This is no doubt what you heard."

That God would fight for one such as him staggered Shane's steps and addled his thoughts even more than whatever illness beset his body. He leaned against the cool stones outside the queen's chamber, fighting to make it all understandable.

On the second floor landing, Lucsa stepped from the shadows. Her eyes red from tears, her left cheek red and swollen. "My son. Oh Slade, you must protect me."

"What has happened? Who has dared do this to you?"

"I do not wish to say, Slade."

He gripped her arm. "Speak of it, and I will punish such a one."

"I could not ask you—it would bring you great pain." Her gaze rose to his. The darkness swirled in her eyes, but the pull of it no longer dragged at his spirit. He saw it for the evil it was, and he shrank from it. "If you refuse to speak, then I cannot help you, woman." He released her and descended two stairs before she called after him.

"It was the queen, my son."

He whirled, climbed the stairs, and gripped her arms above each elbow. His fingers dug deep into her skin.

"Son, you are hurting me," she whimpered.

He shook her. "Tell me true—if you can—what happened."

"I was summoned to the queen's chambers this morning. She yelled and screamed at me, saying you were her son. She threatened to have me thrown in the dungeon and worse. When I told her you would protect me, she slapped me."

"She struck you?"

"Yes, Slade."

"This very morning in her outer chamber?"

"Yes, I tell you true, she hates me and wants me dead."

Shane released one arm and started down the stairs, dragging her behind.

"What are you doing?"

"I have heard enough!" Shane stormed into the hall, marched to the center of the room, in the middle of all the gathered lords, and threw her down before the king, sitting upon the dais.

# *Chapter 22*

Lucsa knelt, hunched forward with the hands in the rushes. "What are you doing?" She did not look up at Shane as the words barely escaped her tight lips.

The lords murmured among themselves.

Edgar stood from his carved wooden throne. He glanced at the empty chair—a smaller version of his—and stepped from the raised platform. He held Shane's gaze unwavering. His voice remained low and calm. "Are you sure of this, my son?"

"It must be done."

"I understand, but is there no other way? Having set your course on this path, there will be no turning from it in the future."

"I have made my choice."

"Then I stand beside you, my son."

"You fool," Lucsa cursed, swiping at Shane. He jerked away, noticing the sliver of blood through the gash she sliced in his hose.

"Shut your mouth, and keep your hands off me, you foul creature!" The lords gasped at his outburst. Shane turned a complete circle to look each man in the face. "High lords of Veronia, I come before you as an imposter. I am not the true son of King Edgar and Queen Mariamne."

Loud chatter broke out. Shouts of anger, directed at both Shane and Edgar, filled the room.

"Sirs, I beg you. Hear my words for only a few moments and then hear no more from me ever again."

They quieted. Arms crossed or fists clenched. Shane's head whirled with a giddy power. Every gaze rested on him, and his heart pounded out its pleasure. "As Queen Mariamne returned from hiding so many winters ago, she believed the Lord Himself led her to where *this* woman had tossed me out. Little better than waste from a chamber pot, she left me in the depths of the woods to die. King Edgar at the time remained convinced he could not sire children and saw me as an answer to prayer.

"They returned to the castle with the intention of telling everyone the truth of my origins, but the good Lord prevented the telling for His own purposes. Everyone in the castle rejoiced so at Queen Mariamne's return after they feared her dead for months. They told the story of her hiding away to protect her unborn child. No other story would be accepted."

Shane turned and knelt before Edgar, his thoughts floating high above. A part of him wondered at being able to speak at all, for his lips and tongue did not feel like his own. "Your Majesty, you have loved me with a long-suffering, unbreakable love. While I, in turn, have spit on your name. I have brought shame to your throne. I have invoked the curses of your people against you. And yet you love me still. No greater example is there of God's love for a sinner than your love for me. I now, before these witnesses, renounce my former ways and do repent of them. I beg your forgiveness—though I in no measure deserve it."

"I forgive you, my son. Never have I been prouder of you than I am on this day."

Shane shook his head, fighting back the tears. "I am unworthy of the boon and the title, Sire. I am the illegitimate son of this horrid woman, and I return to you what can never be mine." Shane placed the upturned shield on the floor at Edgar's feet. In it he laid the folded cloak, the gold spurs, the belt and the sword. "I have not earned the right to be a righteous and just knight in your land, Sire, though I hope one day it will be said of me that I am such a man. I also now, before these witnesses, renounce your honor upon me of being your heir. This honor falls to your true son, Jak—The Just. May he rule after you in love and mercy as you have done." He set the crown on top of the other items.

Shane remained on his knees but turned his face to those gathered. They now sat in a palpable silence. "Noble men of Veronia, I beg of you not to blame King Edgar and Queen Mariamne for their generous and loving hearts. They took in a stray dog with great hopes of making him an honorable man. It is not their fault such a miracle lay beyond their reach. I have stepped aside. You will never be subjected to the horror I would inflict if allowed to wear the crown and sit upon the throne. I pray your rejoicing with such a fact will wash away any malice my presence may have brought to your king and queen. Please do not hold my ills against them."

The men gathered murmured and conversed for several moments. Some agreed not to censor the king, others called for justice.

Shane rose to his feet, cheeks wet with tears. "If you must have justice, then let it fall upon me and this woman. She bore me. She abandoned me for the queen to find. And just this hour she accused the queen of threatening her life and slapping her. Both are lies—but she knows no other way as the daughter of the father of lies. She begged me to take action against the queen on her behalf. Lucsa is the woman behind this evil, and I am her spawn. We deserve your wrath, not King Edgar nor Queen Mariamne."

"These are not the only evils she has committed." All heads turned to see the queen as she moved to stand beside Edgar. "I know it not proper to address the council, but there is a matter I have hidden from King Edgar to protect him and the soul of my son. For though he is not blood of my blood, Shane is now and forever will be, my son.

"This Lucsa, who cowers before you, has tried to kill the king."

Angry grumbles encircled them.

"She mixed an evil poison with her dark arts in the black chapel she created to worship the evil one. It lies in the depths of the south tower."

The grumbling rose to a clamor filling the hall.

"How could you not tell the king?"

"It is a sin to harbor evil."

"My family is in the upper rooms of the south tower!"

"Mine are as well. You have brought a curse upon us."

Edgar threw up his hand. "Silence! This kingdom is blessed by God. And no curse will stand against what God has already blessed, what He continues to bless." The ruckus died away. "Allow your queen to finish her revelation, and then we will allow you to judge our actions."

Mariamne took Edgar's hand. "My lords, the chamber was discovered within a day of her setting it up. Father Bartholomew was told, as well as Sir Carrington. The healer replaced all her herbs with harmless look-alikes."

Lucsa screeched a ferocious cry, but remained on her hands and knees. Though she writhed, she could not move.

"And Father Bartholomew prayed God's protection over us. In fact, between the good Father, Sir Cynric, Lady Annabel, and myself, there has not been a single minute since our discovery in which this kingdom and our home has not been covered by unending prayer. The

Father and Lady Annabel are praying as we speak. God has not left us nor forsaken us. He has protected us. Edgar is yet hale and draws breath."

"Jak lives as well." Cy stepped from the shadows. "The witch poisoned the young prince's horse so it would go mad and throw him. Jak never rode that beast out of the gates, for we have watched and acted."

"She also threatened Princess Milana," Shane stood, pointing at Lucsa where she cowered, as he recalled what he knew of the events. "This is the evil in our midst. This deserves your wrath, and I too as the instrument she chose to wield against you."

Shane took a knee before both the king and queen and waited for what they would pronounce over him. It also served to aid him in the growing weakness in his legs, which made standing near impossible.

Edgar's mighty voice rang out, rattling the tankards on the boards. "Noble men of Veronia. Men of virtue, righteousness, and mercy. Men of law and justice. You have heard the charges against all who stand before you. What say you men? What is to be the punishment for us?"

"Stone her!" came a thunderous shout as every finger pointed to Lucsa.

The oldest of the nobles, Lord Gwain continued, "Get rid of the evil in our midst. Burn her belongings and anything she touched. Wash the accursed chamber with holy water and have the priest bless it."

"And what of the rest of us?" Edgar asked.

The voices were not so loud now, they mumbled and talked. After a time, Lord Matthew stood. "I say we accept Shane's relinquishment and leave him to King Edgar and Queen Mariamne. He is no longer a threat to us. King Edgar is a good and godly ruler. His choice in bringing this boy into his home brought trouble on his own home but has had little lasting effect on any of us. I will not sanction any action against my king or queen. I again swear my fidelity to them."

"Aye," another lord added. Several more gave voice of their agreement too. No one voiced dissension aloud.

"You have not won. Master, help me kill them all," Lucsa said from her knees.

# *Chapter 23*

Shane swayed on his feet, his head whirled with light and color.

The nobles stilled, their hands hidden beneath the boards.

Edgar drew to his full height. The sweep of his hand brushed Mariamne behind him.

The air crackled with energy. The hairs on Shane's limbs stood on end. His heart beat in an uneven cadence.

"I am not the only sinner in this hall." The words ground between Lucsa's teeth like a gnarled bone.

No one breathed.

"The sire of the lad sits at your boards. He eats at your table, oh great king. He worships beside you in your sacred hall. You count him friend, when he abandoned the bed of his lawful wife to trifle with me. He left his seed in me so many times a child was inevitable." Her lips curled in a smug snarl as she glanced around the room, holding each man's gaze. "But his vows of love fell silent the day he learned of the bairn. Refused to see me when I fell in need. Withdrew his support and left us to die. He would not accept the child of his own flesh— accusing me of lying with another." Her voice rose, and with the strength of them she lifted to her feet. She no longer cowered on her hands and knees, but the effort of rising did not come easily. As in the queen's chamber, Lucsa struggled under some unseen hand restraining her.

"The woman spews lies. Why are we listening to her?" Sir Bede asked.

"I lie? What of the man who lies to all of you here today? Why blame me, but not the man?" she fairly screeched now.

The noise rattled in Shane's skull like a shrill mockingbird.

"I demand justice. If I am condemned for adultery and birthing a child out of the bounds of holy union …" She straightened to her full height, her finger sweeping before each man present. "then I demand the same punishment to the one who placed the bairn inside me."

"You are charged with treason against the king and the queen, and worse still, witchcraft," Edgar said.

She whirled and faced the king. The motion made Shane dizzy. "I demand justice!" The words ground through her teeth to be punctuated by a fearsome growl. "If this man never spoiled me with his promises of love, only to abandon me, I would not have been forced to make a way for myself in this cruel world."

"You could have sought sanctuary in the church," Sir Maitland said.

"The church? You fool. Who do you think condemned me? According to your own holy book, I sinned in the eyes of your God. According to the priest, it be an unforgivable sin."

"Only renouncing the name of Christ is unforgivable," Sir Bede spoke again.

"Oh, aye, when the church turned its back on me, I turned my back on their precious Lord. I allowed the dark one to claim me, for he alone promised never to leave me or condemn me. He promised me power." She turned back on Edgar, hatred swirling around her like a twisting wind in the valley floor. The rushes stirred, hair fluttered, wall tapestries waved. And Shane swayed.

A growl started deep in her belly. It grew until a roar burst from her lips. Lucsa lunged at Edgar, the razor sharp nails of one hand extended while the gleaming blade of a dagger flashed in the other as she lashed out. She aimed at the king's throat.

Edgar's sword flew between them. The flat of his blade lay before her eyes and reflected her evil back at her. The weapon filled with holy light and glowed as though it burned in the forge's fire.

Shane squinted against the light.

She shrieked. Her hands flew before her face in protection. She turned away only to face a room full of lords standing and pointing their blazing swords at her.

Mariamne's calm voice rang out above the din of angry men and the screeching woman. "Submit yourselves therefore to God: resist the devil, and he will flee from you. Neither give yourselves to the devil."

Lucsa's shrill squeal dropped Shane to his knees. The pain shooting through his skull felt like a battle-ax had been planted in it.

With her head down to avoid the holy light reaching every corner of the room, Lucsa covered her ears against the holy words and writhed in pain. Her body twisted and contorted. She screamed. It shriveled until her gown hung from her emaciated black flesh. Her hair turned to ash and fell away.

Shane sat on his rump and crawled away from her until he crashed into a long board. What was left of the woman who birthed him no longer looked human. Under four feet tall, all the flesh black as night, only the whites of her eyes remained. She sprang over him. Her gown left where she had stood, she sailed over Shane's head, landing on the boards before Lord Averill.

The aging lord fell back, knocking over his chair. His sword skidded away over the stones, and he lay sprawled across the rushes, looking up at the creature where it crouched on the table. "He is not my son. He cannot be. Tye is my son—the heir to my title."

The vile creature bellowed. Averill covered his face with his arms. Shane watched as in a single heartbeat, four lit swords pierced its body from every direction. One final howl burst from its lips as it threw back its head and writhed—and it was gone. In a puff of ash and smoke, the form vanished, leaving no trace.

The hall lay cloaked in silence. Shane felt the weight of it pressing on his soul. He thought he would die from lack of air. His heart thundered in his ears, beating out its relentless cadence, driving out all thought.

"'Tis finished," Edgar muttered. He reached out a hand to Shane.

He refused the aid, pushed to his feet, his stomach whipped with nausea and a sour taste flooded his mouth. Tears welled in his eyes. "Forgive me, Majesty." Shane fled from the room back up the stairs to his chamber.

Inside, he fell back on the closed door and glanced around the room. The ornately decorated room of a prince with all its luxuries. This did not belong to him—the unwanted son of a dishonored lord and spawn of Satan. He did not belong here. Sobs overwhelmed him.

# Chapter 24

Dressed in servant breeches, simple linen tunic, his oldest worn boots, and an old cloak, Shane crept to the gate. A whimper from the hounds' shed drew his attention. Scruff, wagged his tail at his master's approach. He squirmed wildly to the end of the length of rope holding him fast.

Shane glanced toward the outer gate. He needed to slip away undetected. An excited yelp held him in place. The pup's whole body shook with sheer joy. Shane drew near and knelt. Scruff planted his front paws on Shane's chest and licked him soundly with more small barks.

"Hush, you infernal mutt," Shane grumbled. "You will wake the squires and the whole castle." His hands sank into the coarse fur, and the dog nuzzled into him. "I cannot take you with me, Scruff."

The dog looked up, his head tipped and ears high.

"I am no one, with nothing to my name. I would sore welcome your companionship, but it would be better for you here. Jak and the squires will assure you get enough to eat." Shane ruffled the dog's head. "Learn your manners and you can sit in the hall and have all the bones you can eat, boy." Shane glanced off to the gate once more. His next words caught in his throat. "Do not be like me, boy. Learn your lessons well." His eyes moved back to the brown orbs full of love and eagerness. "You stay here and be a good dog. I have to go and learn to be a good man—and not even you can help me with that. I'm not sure anyone can."

Shane stood, and Scruff dropped back to his haunches. "One day —if I work at it hard enough—mayhaps I shall come back and show you the man I have become."

Shane turned and walked away, unable to breathe past the lump in his throat.

Scruff barked.

Shane whirled, pointing his finger. Scruff's head went down, his ears fell back, and his tail stilled. "You be quiet, mutt. You are staying." He turned and moved toward the gate. "You deserve better than me, Scruff. You are too good a dog to ever be with a man such as I." A tear slid down his cheek as the pup whimpered behind him.

One guard stood posted at the gate on the cold night. A light snow dusted his shoulders.

Shane hid under the cowl, pulling the cloak more tightly about him to ward off the chill. "Let me pass."

"You are more like the queen than you are willing to admit, Highness."

Shane's head snapped up. The cowl fell to his shoulders. The guard's head raised, slowly revealing Sir Cy. "Are you here to stop me?"

Cy shook his head, "No, Highness—"

"Stop calling me that! You know well the truth of my disgrace. I am no more a prince than a frog is a majestic warhorse."

"She would not want you to leave. She loves you—they both do."

"So you are here to prevent me from passing."

"I will not stop you, Shane. I learned long ago with Queen Mariamne, I cannot make another see the truth dangling before their own nose."

"Then allow me to pass. I have brought them enough grief and disgrace. I will not see more befall them on my account."

Cy stretched out both hands. On one palm sat a small leather bag that jingled with coins. The other hand held a sword. "If you are bent on running from your life, than take these with you. And remember, Shane, you cannot outrun God. Wherever you go, He will be there."

Tears threatened to fall once more as Shane shook his head. "I do not deserve …"

"None of us deserves mercy, son. Take these with you, so I might at least be able to assure our queen you went off with protection and a small sum to provide for yourself. It will ease her fears."

Shane inclined his head with reluctance. He strapped the sword around his waist and tied the pouch to it, tucking it under his tunic. "Thank you, sir."

Cy put his hand on Shane's shoulder as he turned toward the small inner door within the gate. Leaning against the door sat a bedroll. Cy slipped its strap over Shane's head so it lay diagonally across his back. "Always remember, you are welcome here, Shane. Anytime you want to return, the gates will be opened for you."

He nodded and stepped out into the bitter night wind. One foot in the bailey and one on the trail to the valley floor, Shane turned back for a moment. "Sir, would you do me one more boon? Will you tell Ethan I am sorry? He has always been the far better man, and King Edgar is blessed to have his services."

Cy nodded.

Shane stepped out. The door latched behind him with a finality that shattered his heart. He took one slow breath, raised his cowl again, and started down the steep path. He entertained no thought of where he headed, only that it be far from where anyone might know him.

*I will work until I draw my last breath to make matters right—to prove I am a man worthy of their love.*

Still long before first light, Shane walked through the town nestled below the castle. Movement caught his attention, and he noticed a traveling merchant loading his wears in a wagon. Shane thought to pass him by without acknowledgement, but stepped near, catching a teetering barrel before it fell.

"Thank ye, most kin'ly, laddie," the graying man with few teeth said.

Shane, soaked to the skin from the snow—now turned to rain—lingered a little longer. He continued to give the man aid until the wagon sat burdened with its load.

"Don't rightly know how to thank ye, laddie. Would've taken me near 'nother hour 'fore I finished."

"I assume this late in the season you will be heading south?"

"Oh. aye, right ye are. Headed home to Goxhill-near-the-Moor. 'Tis a lovely li'l hamlet near the coast."

Shane searched his addled thoughts, trying to recall ever hearing of the place before. "Does it still lie within Veronia?"

"Oh, aye, laddie, though truth be told ye go any farther south, ye be in King Vellcount's lands over the Great Maser Ridge, and any farther east, ye be in the sea." He smiled a toothless grin.

"Might I be able to travel with you, sir?"

The old man rubbed his gray, stubble-covered chin and tipped his head. "Well, don't rightly know any reason why not. Ye don't be one of them highwaymen, now do ye?"

"No, sir."

The man thrust out a gnarled hand, bent with age and a life of hard work. "I be no sir, laddie. Name's Wylie."

Shane shook his hand, still hiding under the cowl of his cloak. Wylie did not release him. "And ye? Have ye not a name, laddie?"

"Slade," he muttered.

"Well, Slade, my boy, ye best climb on up. I be leavin' now."

Shane settled onto the long board worn smooth in the center from years of a single rider. The old man lumbered up next and plopped beside him. Wylie clicked his tongue and waved the reigns over the backs of the two mules. "Come on, Arthur and Guinevere, let us be to home."

The wagon jostled through the quiet streets devoid of people so early in the morning. Wylie settled into a cheerful monologue that was only interrupted by an occasional song. Whether he aimed to entertain Shane or had forgot he sat beside him was unclear. Shane could not find the strength to care as he suffered from the trembling of his limbs, the churning of his stomach, and chills deeper than his wet clothes warranted—yet his face lay drenched in sweat. *You fool. You should have at least brought some of Carrington's tea.* Pain drowned out his own thoughts. By God's grace, perhaps he would die and his suffering in this life would end.

The fear that eternal torment awaited his wicked soul silenced all thought and made him tremble all the more.

Shane jolted awake as he landed on his shoulder on the hard ground. Flames danced before his eyes, distorting his view. Wylie's screams for mercy and the braying mules, added to the ache in his head. But the sound of the old man and his wagon clattering away evaporated into the growing mist. Shane must have been bounced off the wagon in the panic. He sat checking himself for injury. A dark sky loomed overhead. Was it still morning? He thought he remembered the sun beating on him. His clothes were dry. Night? Could a full day have passed without him knowing? Shane cradled his head in his hands.

"Look, men, he whimpers like a small girl." Sinister laughter brought him to his feet.

A bolt of fear brought him to full awareness like a lightning sparking a forest fire. His hand went to the sword at his hip. He surveyed the three men dressed in dark clothes before him. He took a step back toward the brush at the side of the rutted road. Sure his flank was protected, he narrowed his gaze on the men before him. "Let me pass. I have nothing you want."

Another stepped out from the deepening shadows at his right. The tip of his blade poked at Shane's waist. "I be wanting the gold that jingles so pretty there."

Shane drew his sword and laid it on the other man's tip. His opponent gave a quick flick of his wrist and the advantage was lost. Shane raised his hilt high as the next slice slid off his blade.

His challenger stepped back with an appreciative grin. "Well, lookie there, would you? The whelp has some training."

The other three drew their blades, and each tip leveled at him. "Let me pass. The roads of Veronia are assured safe by King Edgar and his men." Shane's legs shuddered under him. He lost focus on the assailants spinning before him. Sweat drenched his body. The weight of the sword in his hand became too much to hold. Its tip slipped toward the ground.

The four laughed. "Oh aye," the shortest man with wild red hair said. "As if any venture all the way here to Little Kinglet Hill."

"Our liege lord lives well over two hard days' journey. You have no hope of rescue in this forgotten hole," the one to his right said with a snort.

Had he traveled so far and not been aware of the passage of time? His stomach roared assuring him much time had passed. "I can take care of myself," Shane vowed. He swung his sword, swirled the tip of the first out of the way, stepped in and grabbed him around the throat with his left arm. "Let me pass."

A blast of pain erupted in his head, and he slumped to his knees. Struck from behind by an assailant he never saw, Shane fought to remain conscious.

A foot kicked his sword from his hand. One fist flew into his cheek while another foot kicked him low in the back. As he fell to his side, he thought he saw flickering lights in windows before fists and feet surrounded him. They pounded on him like a smithy fashioning hot steel. Blow after blow made contact. Bones broke. Blood filled his mouth. Gleeful laughter taunted. *Your days of avoiding training now come back to haunt you. You useless fool. Truly you are no knight.*

Pain—unlike any he had ever known—consumed him. *Please, Lord, let me die.*

# Chapter 25

Margg woke to the squeal of agitated swine. She groaned, and threw off her covering. The grunting and squealing intensified as she snatched a blanket, throwing it over her shoulders. Lighting a reed in the coals of her nearly dead fire, she brought a lantern to life and opened the door. "This better be good, you worthless vermin, or it's to the butcher with you all."

Rounding the corner of her small shack and held the lantern over the pigpen. A young male rutted at something sprawled in the middle of his enclosure, while the old sow grunted her growing disapproval at the intruder. Margg huffed her own agitation. Hanging the light from a nail, and removing the blanket, secured her hem scandalously high. "No point in doing extra laundry for a drunk fool," she muttered.

She opened the pen and stepped inside, the slop squishing between her bare toes. Snatching the light again, she squatted next to the prone body. The figure lay caked in mud from the pen but only wore his braies, and they were as filthy as the rest of him.

"Margg? That ya? What's the matter with the pigs?" The daughter of the old widow whose hut sat nearest Margg's poked her head through the railing.

"'Tis a drunk fool passed out in me pen. And what, are you doing out in the middle of the night, Car?"

"I was fetchin' Hannah. Momma's cough is real bad. Why's he in his under-things?"

"I assure you, I don't know, child." She stood and glanced around. "'Fore you run off, help me drag him to the well."

Car scurried over the pen with no other prodding. Margg hung the lantern again, turned the man over, and took hold of him under both arms while Car grabbed his feet. They slipped and stumbled until they dropped him by the well. The form groaned once but made no other complaint. Margg brought up water and dumped it over the body. Nothing happened.

"Most any ale-washed men stirs with a bucket of cold water," Margg said.

"Has he been bit by the barn weasel, Margg?"

"Where did you hear such a term, girl?"

Car shrugged, causing her messy brown curls to bounce on her shoulders. "Fellas leavin' yar tavern say it sometimes."

Margg pulled up another bucket full and dashed it over the fellow. "I suppose they do, Car, but your momma would have my hide to know you loiter at my tavern door listening to men talk about drunkenness."

"Ya aren't gonna tell her, are ya, Margg?"

"Don't ever let me catch you doing it, girl, or I'll paddle you myself."

"Yes'm."

Margg squatted again. "Grab the light, Car. There's something wrong with this fool." The girl returned moments later holding the light over him. "He's all beat up," the girl stammered. "Do ya think he's a bandit?"

Margg picked up one of the man's hand, holding it up to the light for a better look. "See here, Car. There's few calluses on his hands and little dirt under his nails." She ran her hand over his torso. "He has no old scars—though he'll have quite a few new ones. He's awful beat. Broken ribs and arm, I think." Her hand went down his legs, and Car followed with the light. "Knee's probably bad too." She picked up his foot next. "No sores, no big calluses here either. He's had good shoes."

"What's it mean, Margg?"

Margg stood, crossing her arms while trying not to get the mud from her hands on her clothes. "This man ain't no bandit or peasant."

Car's wide eyes glistened in the flickering light. "Then what is he?"

"I'm thinking he is a nobleman's son."

"Way out here? Noblemen don't come to Kinglet."

"No, which is probably how he fell to highwaymen. The outside thinks good King Edgar keeps us all safe, but his righteous rule doesn't touch our little corner."

"What'cha goin' to do with him?"

Margg smiled. She leaned over the man and rested her wrist on the girl's shoulder. "Well, I was thinkin', if I take real good care of him—nurse him back to hale and all—then it might just earn me a nicely sum of gold coins from some grateful lord."

"If I help, can I have one of them coins?"

Margg bumped Car's chin with her knuckles. "You go on and fetch Hannah. If we can bring him back, I'll share with you, little one."

Car leapt up with a squeal. "Thank ya, Margg. I'll be a big help. Ya'll see." The girl dashed off into the night.

Margg sighed. "It would've been helpful if you'd left the light, girl." She pulled up more water, rinsed off her feet, and proceeded to wash the rest of the filthy man. "You better be worth all this trouble and money, mister."

While she waited for Hannah to arrive, Margg dragged the unconscious man into the small room at the back of her tavern. She stripped off the last bit of his garments—now not only filthy but wet too—put him on the small raised pallet, and covered him with furs. She left the door open as she lit a candle and kindled a small fire. She knew Car would lead Hannah to the lit room and not to her home. Margg didn't allow men in her house. If they were too ale-washed to make it home, they slept it off here—for an extra coin, of course. Many took advantage of the safety in Margg's back room rather than chance the dark streets of their bandit-infested hamlet.

Though the room warmed, Margg slipped out across the yard, back to the pen, and retrieved her blanket. She pulled it tight about her, burying her numb fingers in its folds. When she entered the room again, she found the man writhing in pain. His forlorn moans assaulted her ears. His body convulsed in agony, causing the limb that worked to contract tight against his body.

"If these are your last breaths, mister, I won't get nearly as much coin for giving you a proper burial—not enough to warrant paying for one."

The form rolled to his side and heaved over in a nauseous vomit though little more than liquid and blood fell from his gaping mouth. His innards revolted again and again with great effort, but with little better effect. The space between the retching was filled with his tormented cries.

# Chapter 26

Margg stood enraptured by the man's torment, expecting him to die at any moment, and jumped to see the healing woman kneeling between them. Hannah had stepped into the room in the midst of the man's pain-filled throws like a whispering wind.

"Good evening to you, Margaret. Carling told me of the man you found. He is in much worse shape than I feared."

Hannah was the only woman in the village who insisted on calling her by her Christian name. It was one of the many things she despised about the woman. "He only started convulsing moments ago, Hannah. He made not a sound as I dragged him in here and placed him on the bed."

An indignant huff filled the air. "Hardly the proper care of a wounded man, Margaret. If he dies from your poor ministrations, you will have no one to blame but yourself for your lost reward."

Margg shot a glance at Car, who shrank back into the shadows. "Fear not, you will be paid for your services either way."

"Of course I will." The healer examined her patient's face with careful attention.

She might be quite skilled in the healing arts, but few harbored her good feelings. Hannah sauntered through the village as though she were the lady of a manor overseeing her underlings. A common kirtle or simple peasant dress were far beneath her, for she always wore the fashion favored by the gentry—though in linen and not satins or silks. Wherever she went, her proud chin sat hefted high so she might look down her nose at everyone she passed. She claimed to be the daughter of a dishonored lord—though none believed her.

"He suffers from the over use of the poppy." Hannah's nose crinkled as though she had eaten something most foul.

"He is an ill-liver?"

"There are occasions when physicians give their patients different derivatives of opiates. Many people favor the rapturous glory they experience with the poppy. They take more and more until they cannot live without it. It is a waste of a good life." Hannah tsk-ed with a haughty air. "I shall give him a little of the liquid to ease his pain."

"Is that the best treatment for one so lost in his harmful habit?"

Hannah looked up with a sneer. "When did you train in the use of herbs, Margaret? If you want him to live, it is best to stop his thrashing before he does further damage."

Hannah pulled a jar of clear liquid from her valise, and a slender tube of metal. She pulled the stopper out of the jar, dipped the tube in, and placed her finger over the top. She moved the slender strip of metal to the man's mouth and slid her finger so a few drops fell on his tongue. The man—in his pain-induced thrashing—hit Hannah's hand. The tube flew across the room.

Hannah sighed, "Carling, did you see where it went?"

Margg helped the girl look, and a few minutes later handed it back to the healer. As Hannah dipped the tube in the jar again, the man quieted. He lay still. The moaning stopped. He became as unmoving and unaware as when Margg brought him into the room.

"Well, that is rather unusual," Hannah sat back on her heels, the tube and jar resting on her lap.

"Isn't that what'cha wanted?" Car asked.

"But it should have taken a great deal more to quiet him. For his flesh to crave the poppy so earnestly, he should have been taking a great deal. But it would appear he took only enough each day to make his body need it. So little would afford him none of the rewards of frequent use but all the suffering."

She turned back to Margg, her brows pulling together. Hannah was never bewildered by anything. "Why would any man do such to himself?"

Margg crossed her arms. "Men seldom make sense, Hannah."

Hannah shrugged, put her tools back in her satchel, and returned to her examination. Her lean fingers moved over his sweat-drenched face. "Carling, be a dear and bring me a cloth and a bowl of water." Her hands moved down his neck, cradled his head, and manipulated it with gentle care. "Good, his neck appears uninjured." Next she pulled down the furs, and her hand ran over his broad, muscled chest. Hannah shook her head, "Broken ribs, internal injuries, he has so many wounds."

Carling returned with the items as Hannah lowered the blanket. Margg spun the girl away from the uncovered man. She snatched the water and cloth and pushed the girl toward the tavern. "Go sit inside, Carling. Hannah'll be finished soon and she'll go with you to aid your mother."

"But, Margg, I ain't allowed in the tavern."

Margg sighed. "Car, there are no men and no open drinks. I trust your mother would prefer you being in there than in here with a wounded man."

"Why? I seen him already?"

"Not like this, child," Margg muttered. "Go. It won't be much longer." Margg set the bowl and rag on the small table next to the prone man.

Hannah now worked at the man's feet. "Help me." She waved Margg to the man's head. "Sit behind him, clasp him around his chest, and pull against me." Margg moved into place, as Hannah gripped the man above his left knee. They pulled away from each other, and Hannah twisted until the resounding pop of his hip locking into place filled the room. The man groaned but made no other sound or movement.

Margg pushed him away to get up from the bed.

"Hold him yet, there is the knee as well." Hannah held down the man's leg below the right knee, and taking the heel of her right hand, she punched at the dislodged knee until it slid back in place.

Hannah allowed Margg to step away as she mixed ointments and elixirs. She treated and bandaged each wound until the man looked like he wore a death shroud. She covered him again with the furs and turned to Margg with the elixirs. Hannah held them suspended over Margg's hands but did not drop them or tell her what to do with them. Hannah looked down her nose and raised a brow.

Margg sighed, stepped outside and across the mud to her home. The fire lay cold. She sighed and dug three coins from their hiding place. Walking back she moaned at the growing light in the eastern sky. No hope for more sleep this night.

She dropped the coins in the waiting palm. Hannah inclined her head. "Put this on his wounds twice a day when you redress his wounds. Give him three drops every four hours. I will warn you it will be a miracle if he lives to see tomorrow."

"Redress his wounds? Every four hours? I've a tavern to run. I can't play nursemaid to this fool."

"I can do it." Both women turned to see Car standing in the inner doorway.

"How long have ya been standing there?" Margg snapped.

Car yawned. "Not long. I fell asleep."

Hannah turned. "It is an option if you want your reward, Margaret. If he does manage to survive your care," she sighed with annoyance, "I will return to monitor his progress. I hope you can afford to see him hale, Margaret. Your little watering hole is not the most lucrative. "

Margg stood akimbo, her glare narrowed on the hateful woman. "I do quite fine for myself, Hannah. And I am respected in this town. Can such be said of you?"

"I will concede our reputations among the common folk of Kinglet remains quite different. But I would not put much stock in the gossipmongering swirling about you, dear. Not all of it could possibly be true."

"Get out!"

Hannah shrugged and put out her hand. "Come, Carling, we have made your good mother wait long enough." At the door, she turned back to fling one last verbal dagger. "Be mindful of who knows of the man's presence. It may get more tongues to wagging. Furthermore, the ruffians who did this may return to silence him, or his family may find him and take him before there is much reason to reward you."

Margg curled her lip and snarled.

"I merely sought to help, dear. No reason to turn the wild beast."

Margg was left alone with the man. Only her fury-filled pounding heart and his labored breathing passed between them.

# Chapter 27

Pain. Torment. Light. Darkness. Muttered voices. Joyful shouts. Hunger. Muscle-constricting torture. Sweet watered-wine. Bitter potions. Agony. Nothing.

Shane floated and fell through each experience, not possessing enough strength to fight, and too much fear to let go. Clinging to life, and yet so near death. The tiny part of his soul to retain thought and sense knew he had to make a choice—but neither option held any sway over him. The nothingness between afforded him the claim to victory over death and the escape from eternal torment for his sins. The void between became his intimate companion, and he could not be parted from her.

"'Tis time to be wakein' up now."

The voice invaded his lost sanctuary with a sweetness of an angel. Why? Why must I leave my hallowed place and this dark comfort?

"'Cause ya can'ts gets better sleepin' abed all day, silly." Laughter danced like fairies frolicking through hidden glens.

A wet cloth brushed over his face, stirring his skin to life with its cool relief. The cloth left and returned to his neck and across his shoulders. When next it returned it slid with soothing passes across his chest.

Sparks fired in his brain, pulling him from the luxurious

nothingness. The water touched his bare skin. Where was his shirt? The warmth and weight of the covering over him slid down further to his stomach and panic flared. Shane reached to keep himself covered from the unwanted washing. His left arm would not respond. It lay heavy and unbending at his side. He swatted at the intrusive cloth with his other hand and grasped for the cover. He heard a yelp and a bump of something falling beside him. Warm fluff filled his hand, and he yanked the fur up to his chin. He tried to roll from whatever it was, but agony shot through him as if he dangled on a spit over the fire. He cried out.

"Now stop that," the small voice ordered. "Ya hurt yarself every time ya thrash about and Hannah says ya'll never get better if ya don't take more care. And I don't like being dumped on the floor neither."

"Car, best be heading home, child. Your momma will be needing you for supper." This voice meant business. Not angry nor threatening, but with authority that would not be challenged, the voice made the girl leave.

"He spoke today," the younger one said.

"And what did our sleeping brute say?" No humor, no concern— only a question as if this voice asked for the day's news.

"I told him 'twas time to wake up, and he asked 'why?'"

"Only a man would have to ask why he should wake after days upon days abed." Her tone changed. Anger kissed the words when next she spoke. "To eat so you might live, that's why, you fool."

Shane gave the shouts no acknowledgement, as he reconciled his thought of an angel speaking to him with the reality of a real girl bathing him. The thought made him shudder, and he fell back into his lover's dark and silent arms. Comfort and oblivion enveloped him.

Loud rumbling pulled him back to the world. Hollow wood clanked together, reminding Shane of the training corral. Shame washed over him like a frigid river as he considered his wasted days of arrogance, apathy, and avoidance. He took consolation in having returned the knight's accouterments, for he could claim no such honor. He remembered the beating and how easily the common knaves had taken him down. He never even landed a blow himself. He fought to return to darkness' embrace. Far better to be nowhere than to remember his humiliation.

The muttered voices grew in intensity and intelligibility, as if a wall were removed between him and a ruckus crowd.

"Margg, where's the blasted ale?" a thunderous voice demanded with a bang of something meaty on wood.

"Fie, George." The strong female voice yelled back from somewhere near Shane. "Your tankard sat full not a heartbeat ago. Give a woman a chance—less you want to come lug the barrel in there yourself."

Shane fought to open his eyes. Blurred unrecognizable shapes floated before him like a painting left in the rain. A brightly colored ill-shaped form stood before him and appeared to turn when he tried to speak. Shane licked his cracked lips and tried again. "Where—"

"Hush!" the woman—Margg, the fellow had called her—whispered. "Don't rightly know who beat on you so, but they may be out there." The swirl of color moved. Shane assumed she pointed. "Don't want them knowing you're alive, do you?" She placed a solid object on his chest, which looked to be little more than a lump of clay. "Take it," she ordered.

Shane wrapped his right hand around it and found it to be a tankard.

"Margg, by all that is holy, what's taking ya so long, woman? A man could die of thirst out here."

"By the sword, George, if you don't quite your moaning, I will tell your good wife where you hide every morning."

Shane gritted his teeth against the pain and dropped his head back to the pillow. He did not even have the strength to lift the tankard to his mouth.

"Car should be back soon. She'll help."

Shane tried to protest the return of the child, but the shapeless form vanished and the sounds muffled. He let his muscles go limp, almost spilling the tankard. "Where am I?" he whispered in a raspy voice he did not recognize.

Cold from somewhere near his head ruffled his hair and startled him a short time later. Margg had left through what must have been a door somewhere on the other side of the room. Shane forced his eyes open once more. He could make out the hazy outline of a girl in a torn and dirty dress, which sat too big on her small frame. Her brown hair formed a halo around her head. Like an apparition stepping out of the mist, she became more defined the closer she came to him.

Shane's hand rose to stop her advance, but the tankard was still held in his grasp.

"Well 'ello," Car said with a cheerful chirp. "Are ya thirsty?"

Shane snatched back the cup, sloshing some of the contents.

"Hey, do ya want help or not?" She stood with her hands on her hips.

Unwanted images of Milana formed in front of him. She had been about eight or nine years old, and Shane had snuck into her chamber and snipped one of her pigtails to about half the length of the other. "Shane, you horrid beast! What is Olivia supposed to do with my hair like this? It is unseemly for women to have short hair, and there is the

Christ Mass feast coming in a week."

"You are nowhere near being a woman, Milana. You are little more than a child," he had taunted her.

Milana had stomped toward him, kicked him soundly in the shin, and run off in tears. He did not recall his punishment or how Milana wore her hair in the coming weeks. But he remembered the sting and mortification of being kicked by a girl three years his junior. There were days he still felt that pain.

To have this child, who must have been a couple of years younger, so remind him of Milana from so many years ago rattled him soundly, he could not prevent her from taking the cup and helping him drink.

"Are ya hungry?"

"No." He groaned and pressed his head back against the pain. His traitorous stomach revolted against him, rumbling in loud complaint.

Car giggled. "Well, yar stomach is. I'll fetch ya some stew, mister."

If he had possessed the strength, he would have jumped up and run from the room. To be coddled over by a child little more than six years of age, heaped so much humiliation on Shane, he feared he would never see the light of day again.

# Chapter 28

Car hovered near his bed much of the day. Her curly locks danced with a life of their own as she babbled on about the village where she lived. Shane drifted from oblivion to consciousness, hearing only bits and pieces of her tales as she talked on without thought to her captive audience's interest. There were times she reminded him of Princess Milana in the days before his cruel jokes made her withdraw from him. Regret stabbed at his heart afresh.

"Where am I, child?" Shane asked, with a moan.

"Yar in the backroom of the Hart and Spoon."

"The Hart and Spoon?"

The girl nodded making her curls bob with more vigor. "It's Margg's tavern."

"A woman owns a tavern?"

"Sure, her husband owned it, and Margg helped, doin' all the cookin' for the men who came in—she's a good cook. Now, Margg owns it."

"What happened to her husband?"

The girl only shrugged.

"My personal life is my own affair, stranger. Don't go poking your nose where it doesn't belong if you wish it to remain attached to your face." Margg waved a dagger in front of him. "Now that you're in a talking mood, why not tell us your name."

Shane frowned. His gaze passed the shimmering blade, up the arm, and to the face of a shapely woman. Her simple, coarse, blue garment was clean, and modest covering her well. Her oval face was framed with long rich brown hair woven into a simple braid.

"Well, out with it, man. Everyone has a name." Her hazel eyes flashed at him as her dagger wiggled.

"Call me Slade," he muttered.

Car crinkled her small nub of a nose at the name but held her tongue.

"Well, Slade, if you will kindly tell me to which noble house you belong, I shall send them word of your whereabouts, and you can be gone from my backroom. I lose coin with you here. A palled man pays two coppers to sleep it off without the misses knowing."

"I am no nobleman."

The dagger near dropped from her hand. "What?"

Shane did not think Margg could look more shocked if he had stood at that moment and slapped her.

"Alright, mister, I don't have time for your antics. I don't care what your daddy says 'bout responsibility, nor your desire to sow your wild oats. You will tell me where you belong. Someone is no doubt looking for you, and I will not have them find you here, thinking I took you for ransom. Tell me which lord to send word."

"There is no lord, Margg. I am an unwanted cast off who has no name and no claim to any title or wealth."

"If you don't tell me at once, I'll add to your number of broken bones," Margg shouted, clenching her other hand into a fist and waving it and the dagger before him.

"As God is my witness, Margg of the Hart and Spoon, I am nobody."

"Awww," she shrieked and stormed out the back door, banging it open and slamming it behind her hard enough to make the walls quiver.

"Why does it matter who I am?"

Car shrugged with an innocent smile. "She hoped someone would pay her a reward for helpin' ya."

Shane slouched back onto his bed and drew the covers tight to his bare chest. "I am truly sorry to disappoint her."

Not long after Margg stormed out, Shane woke as the furs were pulled from him. He snatched them back and clutched them tight.

A woman in a simple gown stood beside him, her hands at her hips. Her russet-colored hair lay captured in a net thing at the back of her head, like some of the noblewomen Shane remembered seeing at the castle during annual gatherings. It had a silly name he couldn't remember. The statuesque woman scowled at him. "Carling told me you had come to life again."

"Who are you and what do you want with me?"

Car giggled, peeking out from behind the woman's skirts. "She's our healer, Mister Slade. She saw to yar wounds after Margg found ya."

Shane's gaze darted from one face to the other as he clung to the furs. "Are there no men in this forsaken hamlet?"

"Of course there are men, you imbecile," the older woman rebuked. "There is no need to cling to your covers. I have seen all of you already." She reached for them again and Shane jerked away, holding them secure.

"Leave him be!" Margg ordered from the tavern door.

"Margaret, I should check his wounds to assure none has the rot."

"Hannah, you can check whatever you like, but you will receive no more payments from me. The man is a ne'er-do-well, and I will not waste any more of my hard-earned coin on him."

The woman huffed. "Then I will take my medicines—" Hannah reached for the jars sitting on the table near his head.

Margg seized her by the wrist. "Those have each been paid for in full. Leave them or lose your hand."

The healer stood with a spine made rigid with indignation. "Do not presume to lay hands on me. I am still of noble birth—"

"You have yet to prove those proud claims, healer. And I will presume to touch anyone who dares think they can steal from me—while in my own home no less. Now, get out. Your services are not needed here any longer." She narrowed her gaze on the other woman and lowered her voice to a hiss. "Unless you intended to provide the man other services?"

Hannah huffed again, spun on her heel, and thundered to the door. "Well, no one has ever confused my healing with your whoring pleasures, Margaret." She left the room, slamming the door behind her.

Margg roared and hurled the tankard of watered wine after her. "That sanctimonious witch!" She turned and wagged her finger in Shane's face. "She will never step foot in my place again, mister. If you have need, you'll go to her, and you'll pay for it yourself. I don't care if you die—never again. Do you understand me?"

"Aye, Margg, never again," Shane said, trying not to tremble under her fury. She stomped from the room, slamming the other door. Shane let out the breath trapped in his lungs and relaxed.

"What's whoring mean?"

Shane's head snapped around. Car's brows were pulled tight together. "'Tis a very unkind thing to say about a woman. I hope never to hear such a vulgar word on your lips again.”

“Oh, I got ’twas bad by Margg’s growlin’—she always throws somethin’ when she’s mad. We’re lucky she put her dagger away. But what does the word mean?”

“That is a question for your mother, child.”

“Momma’s sick. Hannah says there’s nothin’ she can do for her,” she sighed long and mournful. “I think it is ’cause momma can’t pay her no more. Margg doesn’t think momma will see sprin’.” The girl stated the fact as though saying a flower would no longer bloom.

“I am deeply sorry, Car. I would help if I could.”

She smiled at him and retrieved the tankard. “Ya’re nice, Mister Slade. I like ya.”

“You do not know me, child, or you would not say such things.” Shane cowered under his heavy covers, struggling to find a position that afforded him some relief from the constant pain. There was none.

# Chapter 29

A chill blast of air kissed his toes. A cold, heavy item clamped around his ankle. Shane raised his head with effort and pain. "Margg, what ever are you doing?"

"I am putting on a fetter."

Shane laughed and regretted it. He struggled for a steady breath. "Woman, I cannot bear my own weight to rise off this mat and sit without help of a whelp. Where do you imagine I might go that you cannot apprehend me with ease?"

Her gaze bore into him like a hot poker. "I know well the schemes of men. You will fain weakness as your strength grows and leave when I least expect it. You will repay me the money I have lost for your healing, Slade of the unknown origins. You will stay chained here until I receive every last shilling."

"I swear it."

Margg spun away into the outer room. "You have no other choice but to swear it, fool."

Shane tried to cover his freezing feet. Where was that girl when he really needed her?

"Car?" he called and sucked air through his teeth at the pain the act elicited. The child did not come. He lay shivering, near tears at the agony wracking his body.

"Where is Car?" Margg demanded as she passed through the room sometime later.

"I know naught, but you left my feet uncovered, woman. The cold is causing me pain."

"Ye know nothing of real pain," she muttered and opened the outer door. With both doors open, a brisk gust blew through the room, adding to his discomfort. He heard her call for the child repeatedly—then nothing.

A short time later, they both reentered the room. Margg stood behind Car, shoulders set as words ground between her teeth. "Mister, you have hurt Car's feelings with your ungrateful moniker for her. You'll apologize."

Shane's gaze fell to the child. Her head hung, but he could see wetness on her cheeks and the red puffiness of her eyes. "Car, I truly have no idea what I said to upset you, but I am sorry."

"You called her a whelp, you unappreciative clod!"

"When did I call her that?"

"When you said, 'I cannot bear my own weight to rise off this mat and sit without help of a *whelp*.' Do you recall it now?"

Shane threw back his head and stared at the dark, web-covered ceiling beams. He reached out his hand toward the child but did not look at her. He felt small fingers slide into his hand and hold it tight. Turning to her, he saw the pain clear in her face and it brought tears to his own eyes. "I told you, sweet child, you would not like me if you knew me. I am a cruel man who can wound even without the strength to stand. I have no control over my own tongue. I meant you no ill with my venting. Those words were said in my frustration of being trapped abed, not in response of the excellent care you provide me. Truly, child, I would not be alive if not for you, and Margg. Forgive me—if you can. It was honestly never my intention to hurt you. I am sorry."

Car released his hand, laid her arms across his shoulders, and rested her head on his chest as she slipped onto the bed beside him. "I forgive you," she whispered.

Shane fought to breathe as much from her pressing against his wounded flesh as from the overwhelming feeling of absolution she so freely gave. He could not find a place to lay his hand, and letting it hang off the bed added to his discomfort. He looked to Margg for help. She rolled her eyes at him and placed his hand high on Car's back, tapping it so he would in turn pat her.

Car wiggled closer and he whimpered. She lifted her head to look him in the face, shifting her weight again. He yelped, and Margg lifted her off.

"I'm sorry," Car said, worrying her lower lip.

He forced a smile. "'Tis nothing, child," he said, holding his breath.

"Go now and fetch Slade his dinner," Margg said. Car disappeared into the tavern.

Margg turned on him, wagging her finger in his face. "That poor child was abandoned by her father before she was a year old, lost her older brothers four years ago and is about to lose her mother. If you cause her one single moment of pain—so help me God—I will …"

"I am an imbecile, as you have already pointed out, Margg. I cannot swear to never cause her pain. But I will swear on the Lord God Almighty, I will do nothing consciously to hurt her. You have my word."

Margg spun away, muttering, "The word of a man. What good is that?"

Margg burst into the room early the next morning. "'Tis time you earn your keep, Slade."

"What would you like me to do flat on my back?"

"You are not an invalid. You can sit up, so you will sit and chop the ingredients for the meals." She plopped a stool down near the fire.

Shane clutched at the furs covering him as she moved toward him. "I swear I will do any manner of thing you request, dear lady, when I have clothing to cover myself. Not so much for my small dignity as for the innocence of the child who sits in my room so many hours a day."

She crossed her arms, glaring at him.

"I have endeavored to remain covered as she has attended me, but if I am to be out of this bed for more time than her helping me to sit up, I require clothing."

She leaned near his face and snatched one of his medicine jars from the table. "Then you have a choice to make. Is it to be clothes or your precious escape?"

"What are you talking about? What is that?"

"Poppy, of course. Don't play the innocent fool with me. Hannah told me how you have used so much of this your body craves it. If Car didn't give you a dose every morning and evening, your body would be suffering more from the lack of it."

"Poppy? I do not indulge in such harmful practices of the weak and feebleminded, woman. I have committed a great many sins, but drunkenness and abuse of such things as opiates are not among them. Your healer is mistaken."

Margg stood and scrutinized him, arms again crossed.

Shane found the effect distracting as it pulled the plunging scoop of her neckline dangerously low over the great gifts God had endowed her with. He shifted his gaze toward the door.

"You're telling me you never felt the lightness of head and the dreamlike joy in the simplest of things, only to later suffer tremors in your limbs and a gnawing ache in your belly."

"How would you know of such things?"

"Men have staggered into my tavern for much more than ale."

He turned toward her again with a raised brow.

"I do *not* provide it for them." Her fists sat perched on well-cut hips.

Shane looked away, his mind reeling. "I have experienced these things, madam, but it was not of my own choosing."

Margg snorted.

He snapped. "One who claim to be my friend, my ally—truth be told, she convinced me. She was someone from my past. This woman did this to me. She was a witch of the dark arts and used her ministrations to control me and keep me bound to her."

"And you knew nothing of her treachery?"

"Not until it was too late and I lost everything. I know not the contents in that vile jar, Margg, or what will happen if I do not take it. But never will I allow that poison to pass my lips again. Smash it against the wall or do whatever you like. I will not tolerate it in my presence."

"You sound most regal in your demands, *my lord*." She added to her mocking tone an irreverent curtsy. "As you wish. I shall sell it to cover your sorry hide. But remember your oath when the pain comes on you later."

Margg snorted at his determined silence before leaving out the back door.

Shane shook in rage at the long reach of Lucsa's evil.

Margg returned with a worn tunic and breeches, which she had to assist him into. Once dressed and re-shackled, she brought him a bushel of vegetables, a small bent knife, and a large kettle. Car came and knelt beside him, being careful of his splinted leg. He watched the child as she cleaned each vegetable and chopped it on a wood board on her lap. He did likewise, though with less skill.

"Your pieces are all so similar, Car. I hack at them in such a clumsy manner that mine are all manner of sizes."

"Momma says ya have to do a thin' many a time afore ya can do it well."

"Your mother is very wise. How is she? Does she not need your tender care more than I?"

Car looked up, her gaze steady and calm. "Momma ordered me out of the house. Told me ne'er to come see her again. Margg said it's 'cause Momma doesn't want me to see her die. I think it's 'cause she wants me to get over missin' her before she is ain't here no more."

"I am afraid you will always miss her, child."

"That's what Margg says too. I stay at her house now, on a pallet near the fire." She pointed out the open back door to the small wattle-daub building across the yard. "Margg's nice to me, and she goes to see Momma every day. She brings her broth and builds up her fire. Margg says she's a little weaker every day and doesn't know why she keeps fightin'."

Shane reached down and stroked Car's cheek with the back of his finger. "Perhaps she holds hope for healing so she can be your mother again."

Car smiled at him. The warmth of her sweet innocence and her acceptance and kindness wiggled its way into his heart—planting a seed of hope.

# Chapter 30

As Margg promised, Shane suffered in agony for several days as his body demanded it be fed more of the poison. Car never left his side as he dry-heaved relentlessly and cried out in pain at the effort. His muscles cramped and drew in his limbs—those not splinted—tight to his body.

"Please, Margg, can't I give him a little medicine?" Car begged.

"No!" Shane moaned in the throws. "I will not take it. I want to be free of its hold over me. No more," tears streamed down his face. "No more, please."

Margg handed the bowl of water to Car. "You heard him, child. He wouldn't take it, even if I still had it. Go fetch him some fresh water. The coolness will help."

As the girl left, Margg knelt by his side and rubbed a damp cloth over his face. "You're tougher than I thought, mister. I'll give you that." She brushed some of his hair away from his forehead to allow more of the cool cloth to touch his skin. "She must've been feeding it to you for some time, for lack of it to torment you so. But take heart. This cannot last forever. 'Twill end soon."

"If it does not, I beg you, kill me."

Car gasped at the doorway. Margg waved her in, kissing her temple. "He doesn't mean it, child. 'Tis the pain." She handed the girl the cloth and slipped from the room.

Margg had been right—the tremors and muscle cramps died away sometime in the middle of that same night. Shane, at last, slept.

When next he woke, his mind danced with awareness. The dark chamber where he lay felt more cheered. Car came in, and her smile was wider, her tiny lips deeper red, her beautiful blue eyes sparkled more. Sunlight from a high window lit her hair in every tone and hue of gold.

"Ya must be feeling better. Ya're smilin'."

He reached out and touched her face. "Who could help but smile around such a beautiful girl?"

Her cheeks pinked and one leg twisted on the ball of her foot as she shied away from him.

"Has no one ever told you how pretty you are, Car?"

She shook her head.

"Then I will make it my mission to tell you every day to make up for the lack of others who are blind to the truth."

She laid, on him hugging him tight. Though it still hurt, the edge had gone from his deepest pain, and he hugged her back.

"Alright, enough of that," Margg barked. The green of her dress reminded him of the grass of a meadow on a bright spring day. Her skin kissed with a warm glow and her figure well formed. Her long hair lay braided down her back, and when she moved it swung with a joy that bubbled up in his own chest.

"You look lovely this morn, Margaret."

"Don't call me that," she said, twisting her exquisite lips into a deep scowl.

"We are going to the Christ Mass," Car said with a small joyful leap. "Now that ya feel better, do ya want to come with us?"

Shane looked to Margg with hope, but the woman gave a sharp shake of her head. He glanced back to the girl with regret. "Oh that I could, Car. The Christ Mass is my favorite time all year. But with my leg in a splint, I am sore afraid I could not sit in the pews. And I definitely could not kneel for prayers."

Car sulked.

"Do not frown so. You are too pretty to wear such a sad face. You go and say a prayer for me. Heaven knows I need them."

She flung her arms around him in a second quick embrace. "We'll bring ya back a Christ Mass cake."

"That would be a nice treat."

Margg led the way to the door and let Car walk out before speaking. "There is no one out and about on this morn, and the tavern will be closed all day." She pointed to a bushel on the floor, "But tomorrow's coming and there will be hungry mouths to feed. Make yourself useful."

Shane finished the vegetables with a speed he never thought possible and spent some time moving about the room to explore. Margg had attached him to a long tether of solid steel links, but he noted the ring, which secured the chain to the floor, lay loose in its bolts. The planks holding it were dry. A firm kick—with a healed leg —or a good twist with a rod jammed through it would free him. He shook the notion from his head. He owed Margg. He would stay and do whatever she required of him. He would begin his penance and work to make a good name for himself. He might yet earn his forgiveness.

He continued to venture around the small space, seeing what else he might learn. He next spotted a needle and thread on the mantle, and an odd notion struck him. Setting himself on the stool once more, he took the corner of one of the thinner furs from his bed and cut off a piece. He shaped and stitched it together with uneven, ugly work Queen Mariamne would have scowled upon, but for a man who had never picked up a needle—other than to poke some unsuspecting prey—they would serve their purpose. He took a little of the unspun wool from the basket near the door and stuffed it inside a hole he left open. He sewed the monstrosity closed, and looked at it.

The snout was crooked, and all four legs hung at different lengths. He used a bit of red thread to sew a mouth—as lopsided as the rest of the face. And dark thread to sew in crosses to make eyes. It was ugly, and Shane could not even assure Car would know what animal he attempted, but he thrilled at the excitement of giving it to her. The thought staggered him to his bed. *Shane of the highborn fools. The man who never gave a kind thought for another soul. You, you like this child. Even more than that, you love her—or at least what your wicked heart understands of the foreign emotion. Those who know you best would never believe it.* He looked again at the sad excuse for a bear and shook his head. This might actually result in her disliking him.

He hid it under his pillow and lay back on his bed. Moments later, the door burst open. "Slade, we brought ya a cake!"

He struggled to sit and put out a hand to accept her treat.

She gasped. "Oh, yar hands are all bloody."

Shane had paid little attention to the numerous needle pricks and knife cuts as he labored on the toy.

"What have you been about?" Margg demanded, seizing his wrist to examine his hand. She glance down at the chain running out from under the furs to the ring bolted to the floor.

Shane stuck out his ankle to show her he remained her captive. "I was making a gift to give in honor of the Christ Child."

Car sucked in a breath and bounced up and down. "A gift? Who for?"

"Well, you brought me a gift of a cake, so I guess it must be for you."

Car's eyes grew to an enormous size, her mouth hung open, and she clenched her hands so tight to her chest they turned white. "For me? Really? I've ne'er gotten a gift before." She clapped her hands and spun around. "What is it?"

Shane smiled at her as Margg stepped back and considered him with a tilt of her head. "Put out your hands."

The girl's hands shot in front of him with the speed of a loosed arrow.

"Close your eyes."

She clamped them closed until her nose crinkled.

Shane pulled the bear out from its hiding place and held it over her hands. "Now I want you to remember. I did not have much time to work on this, and I am not very skilled."

"It's okay. I'll like it. I promise." She wiggled with an energy that would not allow her to stand still.

"It will be alright if you do not find it to your liking, Car. I will not be offended." He placed the fuzzy bundle in the palm of her hands and marveled to see her smile grow even bigger. "Alright, you may look."

She gasped and turned it this way and that, looking at it. "It's a bear," she said with joy—much to Shane's relief. "Oh, he's perfect. Thank ya." She threw herself around Shane's neck nearly driving him back into the wall beside his bed.

"I am pleased you could tell what he is, and I am overjoyed that you like him."

"I'm going to call him Slade."

"Please do not."

She looked up at him, mouth downturned. "Why not?"

"'Tis a poor name for a noble bear, and it would be confusing to have two named Slade under the same roof. What were your brothers' names?"

Car crinkled her brows and looked back at Margg, who answered. "Eric and Tanner."

"Well, those are both fine names," Shane nodded. "Or you could mix them both together. You could call him Eriner or Tanric."

Car giggled. It was by far the sweetest sound he'd ever heard. "Those are funny names."

"Well, he is a rather odd looking bear," Margg offered.

Shane nodded. "Quite odd. Such an unusual creature deserves a name befitting him."

Car held the toy, considering him as her head tipped back and forth. "I think I like Eranade best."

"That is quite a mouthful. Are you sure?"

"Maybe, Slaicner?"

Shane tussled her hair, "Call him whatever you like, child."

She hugged him again and Margg spoke. "Best be off, little one. I will be along after I check on your dear mother."

Car skipped from the room. Margg stood in the open door, looking over her shoulder. "You confound me, mister. You show no signs of having ever worked at any labor. You talk like the self-important nobility. Yet you make a toy for a child—by sewing, no less. Something a nobleman would never be caught doing. Needlework is relegated to the world of women."

He held up his hands. "'Tis obviously something I have never tried my hands at before."

"Well, that was clear by the hideous shape of the ill-formed creature. Was it truly intended to be a bear, or did you just accept whatever she called it?" Margg's sharp edge resurfaced.

"I aimed for a bear, but it was only a child's kindness to see such in my poor craftsmanship."

Margg nodded and stepped from the room. The door was almost closed when he thought he heard her say, "Thank you, Slade."

# *Chapter 31*

The festive holiday season turned to the cold months of deepest winter. Shane mended; the splint around his right knee and the one on his left forearm were removed. His strength grew and with it the chores Margg assigned to him. Earlier this day, he stacked wood in his room, both for him to use and for Margg to grab for the fire in the tavern. Now he sat outside his door on the stool from his room working to scour pots free of burnt dinner remnants. He found the water too hot, which served to make the lye bite at his broken, cracked skin all the more.

Car came to stand on his right, looking at him in a rare moment of silence. She slipped her hands around his neck as she laid her head on his shoulder.

"Do you require something, child?"

She shook her head without raising it. "Ya look sad."

Shane considered this for a moment. "I suppose I spend too much time thinking about what once consumed my days."

Car released him. Standing near his knee, her bear poking out of the pocket in her dress as always. She clasped her hands together and stared with earnest.

"You do not wish to hear my sad tale, Car. Then you will be sad too."

"But might make ya feel better."

He shook his head as thoughts tumbled about unbidden.

She placed her small hand on his arm, "Please?"

"Oh, I think you will be the undoing of me, Carling of Kinglet." His eyes scanned the high mountain peaks, which formed a near unbroken ring around the tiny valley. "Is every winter like this?"

"Wha'cha ya mean?"

"There are only occasional gentle rains here. I have not heard heavy winds or driving rains, and the snow stays high up the mountains."

Car glanced around as she considered his observations. "Momma told me once, she moved here 'cause the mountains stand guard 'round us and protect us from the worst weather. It that wha'cha ya mean?"

"I suppose it is."

"What is it like where ya grew up?"

"There were a great many winters where I could not go outside for days, for the rain fell too heavy and the wind howled through the cracks in the shutters. It was a rare winter to see snow fall, though, and if it did, not enough fell to play in and it did not last but a few hours." He looked at her and smiled as he exchanged the cleaned pot in his hands with another dirty one waiting at his feet. "Though the winter I was born, I am told, was the worst winter anyone could ever remember. Snow fell everywhere. It lay deep across the valley, and all travel stopped."

"Yar birthday is in the winter? Is it soon?"

Shane shook his head with bemused regret. "You have wiggled another tidbit from me, Car. You are ever so clever."

She stood a little taller as her grin filled her tiny face.

"Oh, I am eternally grateful you never knew me there."

Her face twisted in confusion, "Why?"

"You would not have liked me. I played mean tricks on people I cared about, and I said and did cruel things. I know I displeased God. He offered me so many wonderful blessings, and I treated them all with contempt. I have led a wasted life, Car, and I fear God may be sorry He ever created such a wretch as me."

Her hand again rested on his forearm—warm and tender. "Ya could always tell God ya're sorry. Momma says He wants to forgive everybody."

Shane closed his eyes with the sensation of having been slapped. *I sought forgiveness from King Edgar and Queen Mariamne. I apologized to Princess Milana and dear old Alden. I even wrote a letter to Prince Jak, and asked Cy to pass on my words of regret to Ethan. Why have I never thought to seek the absolution of God?*

Shane laid his forehead against Car's. She giggled and raised her chin until their noses touched—hers felt cold. "What'cha doin'?"

"I am hoping your wisdom will seep into my feeble head, dear one."

"Slade, yar silly," she said with great giggles.

Shane raised his head and scanned the buildings he could see from where he sat behind Margg's tavern. The road out of town stretched in front of the small way station, leading to the only pass out of the ring of peaks. Along the other direction, the road meandered into the center of the village. It lay lined with a few small shops, and the owners lived in private rooms, either above, or behind like Margg.

"Do ya see somethin'? Is someone comin'?"

"No, I was looking for the steeple of a church."

"Oh, Little Kinglet Hill don't have a proper church—not like the ones Momma told about from outside. There's a building with lots of benches in it that once was used for village meetin's, mass on the

Lord's Day, and a school too. But the old priest died, 'fore I was born —now a cranky monk comes once a month. But he don't come in the winter."

"Who said the Christ Mass for you then?"

"Nobody. A few of the old ones used to tell us what they remembered of the story, but now they are in heaven and no one 'members no more. We just go and pray and hope God 'members us."

"Does no one in Kinglet read?"

"Read?" The sharp retort came from Margg as she stood in the doorway behind him. "Of course we can't read. What would simple farmers, herders, and craftsmen need with reading?"

"You could read the Scriptures. Everyone carries such a need. And you, Margg, could enter into binding agreements with the merchants who come through town. They could never cheat you."

"Are you saying, then Slade, that you can read? Only nobility is taught to read," she raised a single brow and challenged him to deny his noble rearing again.

"There are many occasions where others than nobles are taught to read," he muttered, though none came to mind at the moment.

"I can't picture you as an acolyte, and you are definitely no monk." She leaned close to whisper in his ear. "I have seen the way you look at me."

He shook his head as much in denial as in an answer to her statements. Grabbing a long stick, he moved it across the damp earth. M-A-R-G-G.

"What's it say?" Car asked jumping up and down.

"That is Margg's name, and this is yours—Carling." He wrote out her full name.

She knelt in the mud and traced the letters with her finger. "Do another. Write yar name, Slade." He crinkled his nose and shook his head. "Write fire." He did, under her name. "House—write house." She stood again, bounding around him like an untrained pup, stirring memories of Scruff. He swallowed the heartache choking him afresh.

Car pulled him out of his recollections, pointing to everything she could see within the yard. When everything sat named in the mud, she moved to things she could not see, like *love, happy, laugh*. Shane wrote every word, filling the yard as far as he could reach from his chain tether, with her thoughts.

"Time to prepare supper, Car."

The child groaned, but Shane was drawn by the slim smile that played on Margg's lips. The words brought her some measure of joy, and that small flicker made Shane's heart soar.

Margg caught him looking at her. The smile vanished. "You have work to complete, Slade. I need my pots—if you want to eat."

He stacked the three clean pots together and handed them to her. "If I had a piece of slate and a bit of chalk, I could teach you both. It is not a difficult skill to learn, but it takes time to master."

"You do not have time for such trifles."

"Please, Margg? Please. I wanna learn to read. Momma says there are amazin' worlds to learn about in somethin' called books."

"Kinglet has no books, Car. There is no point."

"Merchants come through here all spring and summer—so you say. They can bring you anything you wish—books included."

"And who might be paying for these fine books, mister?"

Shane inclined his head, returned to his stool, and pulled the last pot into his lap.

"It is as I thought. Men—they are always promising grand things with no thought for the practicality of doing such. It leads to nothing but heartache and pain, child. Never fall for the daydreams of men. We have to live in a world of getting enough to eat and keeping a roof over our heads."

Margg disappeared through his room, but Car stepped close. Gripping his upper arm with both hands she whispered, "We always have mud and sticks. Will ya teach me with those?"

He could not contain his smile. He bopped the end of her nose with his fingertip. "It would be my pleasure to instruct such an eager and willing pupil."

Car danced and twirled, singing out her thanks, until Margg called to her from deep within the tavern. She ran off with bursts of joy, which eased the old pains still lingering in Shane's heart.

# Chapter 32

The snow line crawled up the peaks. Shane heard the rush of
water grow each day in a stream somewhere across the road from the
tavern. Margg fussed at the delay of the opening of the pass as her
supplies diminished.

"I will have to close the tavern soon if a merchant cart doesn't
arrive. I've lost customers already, for I have run out of ale and have
taken to serving bitter beer and watered wine," Margg said one
evening.

"I wish I could help, but I lack the divine power to melt the snows
any faster for you."

"Men, always wanting the impossible—divine powers, indeed."
She moved back into the tavern. The last customer had left hours ago,
but Shane knew she could not bear to sit about. She would find
something to do, whether it be sweeping the rushes, wiping spills,
stacking cleaned tankards, or some other chore. If Shane had learned
anything in his weeks with Margg, she would work off her agitation
and go to bed late.

Car pulled him to the door once Margg was out of sight so he
could evaluate her lesson scrawled across the mud near his room.
Shane looked at it closely, rubbing his bearded chin. The sensation
made him smile, for he had always hated beards—until he ran away

from his life and who he had been there.

"Did I do good?"

"You did quite well. Your name looks rather fine, and the words you copied are well formed." He leaned down to be close to her face, propping himself up with his hands braced on his knees. "But, my pretty girl, I think you forgot two letters from your alphabet."

Car turned, looking at the long line of single letters at her feet. She moved to the beginning and started reciting them as she passed each one. "A-B-C … G-H-I-K,"

Shane cleared his throat, and she tried faster. "F-G-H-I-J. It's J. I forgot J." She gave a triumphant bounce. Snatching up the stick, she drew the letter above the I and K.

A deep thud came from the tavern. Shane's head snapped around. Two heartbeats later—as he strained to hear—the sound of male laughter floated to him. Then came Margg's muffled growl.

"What's the other letter I missed? I can't find it."

Shane grabbed her by both shoulders nearly shaking her. "Car, you must listen to me. You must do exactly what I tell you."

Something else crashed in the tavern. "What's that?"

"Margg is in trouble—"

"We have ta help her!"

"I aim to, but you must do as I tell you—no argument."

Car nodded her head, eyes wide as tankard rims.

"Run to Margg's home and hide. Find a spot where no one will find you." Shane spun her around and pushed her. She stumbled forward two steps and turned back. "Go now!" The girl ran as if the hounds of hell themselves chased her. Shane was standing at the inner door before she was out of sight.

Cracking the door, he saw five men surrounding Margg. Several held her down, one worked to undo his breeches, and another tore at her clothes.

Shane seized the fire poker, rammed it through the ring in his chain anchoring him to his room, and jerked it with a mighty twist. Bolts of pain shot through his side. As he expected, the floor gave way, and he was free. He dropped the ruined poker and, picking up the chain, slipped into the room.

Shane approached the closest villain. Swinging the chain over his head and looping it around once more, he gripped both ends at the back of his neck in one hand and squeezed. The scoundrel released Margg's right arm and drew his sword to swing it over his head at his attacker. Shane clamped his hand over the man's swinging wrist with his free hand. As he held the sword hand, the man dropped unconscious. Shane released him, but kept hold of the sword and lashed out with a powerful swing and near took the head off the man turning to face him.

With her right leg now also free, Margg kicked out at the attacker standing between her legs, crushing his offensive weapon. The man bellowed and dropped.

Shane yanked the chain free with a snap of the fallen man's neck. As Margg still lay pinned to a narrow table, Shane used his heavy, metal binding like a whip, striking the two remaining brutes across the face. They leapt away, releasing Margg completely.

Shane bent to retrieve the lost sword, and a fist slammed into his tender ribs, re-breaking barely healed bones. He gritted his teeth against the pain and brought the blade up—running the man through.

As Shane struggled to capture air in his lungs, a warm back pressed against his. The shoulder bones rested below his, and the long rope of hair lay pinned against his spine. The crown of her head rested back against the base of his skull. Shane felt the heave of her erratic breathing in near-matched rhythm to his own.

The man Margg kicked regained his feet. One of the two remaining attackers came into view over Shane's right shoulder. Margg twisted, pressing more against his left shoulder than his right. "They are trying to draw us apart," Shane warned.

"Well, kill yours and I'll kill mine," Margg snapped.

They pushed off each other, lunging at the men before them. Shane felt the press of his opponent's blade on the tip of his sword. A flick of his wrist and Shane's blade was free to do the same. The two blades danced around one another without an advantage. The furniture and cramped space of the tavern limited them to smaller movements as each thrust and parried, banging their hands and arms together as often as their blades.

Shane remembered well playing a similar game with Ethan when they were confined inside on rainy days as children. He recalled the maneuver Ethan had used to take the advantage. Stumbling back as though knocked off balance, Shane created distance between them. When his attacker raised his arm to run him through, Shane crouched low. He sprang up a heartbeat later, knocked the other man's blade aside, and slammed his shoulder into the man's gut, lifting him off his feet. He threw the man down onto the edge of a table, causing it to flip and fall onto his opponent. Shane grabbed for his ribs. He kicked the table away and thrust his sword through the attacker's heart before he could stand again.

Shane whirled only to come tip to tip with the dagger Margg always carried at her back. She looked at him, blood drops sprayed over her face and chest. She panted for breath but lowered her weapon. Shane's gaze roamed the room and found all assailants dead. The sword fell from his hand, and he sagged against the tall bar beside him.

Margg stepped forward. "Are you wounded? I see no blood." Her hands ran over his middle until he gasped as she passed over his ribs. She took his wrist, draping the arm on his uninjured side over her shoulders. Her other arm encircled his waist, and she turned him to his room. "Best get you to bed before you collapse." She tossed back the furs and eased him down. "If you can sit there for a few moments, I'll bind the injury again."

He managed a nod as he squeezed his eyes closed against stinging tears. He heard her curse and opened his eyes to look at her. She held her right palm out, and he took it to see what distressed her. A long ragged gash snaked from the center of her palm down the side of her wrist dripping with blood. Shane pressed the strip of cloth, intended for him, on the wound and wrapped his large hand around, holding firm. "I am truly sorry you were injured."

"'Tis but a scratch." She tried to pull free.

"No 'tis deep and will require sewing. Even so, I fear it will leave a scar."

"It matters not. Who would care?"

Shane held her for several more moments before she wiggled free "Truly you fuss for no good reason." She gathered another cloth.

Once his chest was bound tight, she helped him lie back. She covered him and she spun around the room. "Car?"

"I ordered her to hide in your home." Shane hissed through teeth clenched against the pain.

Margg nodded her approval until her gaze fell on the loose ring of his chain sitting on the floor at her feet. She picked it up, scowling at him. "How long have you been free?"

"How long was I fighting?"

"How long have you *known*?"

"That the wood was so rotten it would easily release the chain?" She nodded.

"Christ Mass."

Her voice softened. "You knew you could be free any time in the last months and you remained? Why?"

"As you said, I owe a debt. It is one I will see paid."

Margg glanced over her shoulder at the tavern and shuddered. "Consider your debt canceled."

Shane shook his head. "I only wish any of their clothes that are still wearable and any boots that might fit. I still owe you much." He whimpered in pain. "And it would seem I still need you yet—if you be willing."

She inclined her head again without looking at him, but he saw the glint of tears on her cheek in the candlelight.

"I regret you had to take their lives. 'Tis a burden—"

She waved him off with a flick of her hand. "A burden I know well already, don't fret needlessly." She moved toward the outer room. "I will drag them off to the woods for the wild animals."

Shane struggled to move.

"Don't. I can manage." She paused. "Is there anything else you wish to salvage?"

"The sword with the round pommel that holds a green gem. It was a gift before I left. You may hold it until my debt is paid in full."

She turned, narrowing her gaze. "These are the men who attacked you before?"

"It would appear so."

Margg squared her shoulders and raised her chin as she turned back to deal with the bodies. "Then we have done the world a service this night. We have sent evil back to hell."

# Chapter 33

Margg removed the useless fetter from Slade's foot while he slept. She swallowed hard on her pride, and the next morning apologized for the raw welt the thing had left behind. She even sent for Hannah to provide him ointment and clean cloths to wrap it. But the re-injured ribs meant another couple of weeks passed before he could bear the pain to return to his chores.

The first of the merchant wagons arrived a week later, and her tavern returned to its lively hum. Margg's shoulders lost their hunch, and she found she could breathe with ease once more.

Slade stepped into the tavern and moved toward the kitchen. The cowl on the worn outer tunic he'd plundered from the bandits they killed covered his head as always. He preferred to remain hidden anytime he ventured out where others could see him. Margg could not determine if this was for his own protection or the saving of her honor. Either way, she appreciated his discretion.

"Margg, when'd yous get so rich yous could afford to buy you a servant?" Brett said, a glare bouncing off his bald head.

"The day I found him half-dead in my pigpen. Worthless fella had no other place to go, so he works here now for scraps and a pallet."

"Where'd he 'ome from?" Seth, another man, with missing teeth, asked.

"Don't know—don't care. Don't talk much, which is fine by me. Now are you boys here to drink or to report back to someone about my personal affairs?"

"He's an affair?" a dark figure hummed from the corner.

"Fie, but you are the worse tavern tattlers. You be as bad as a gaggle of gossiping women. Drink or be off with you."

Margg moved away from the men taunting her. She tossed her head, feeling the sweep of her braid against her back. Men—vile creatures one and all.

Slade caught her eye. He tried to remain in the shadows, slinking from chore to chore. She knew his ribs still pained him, for she saw him favor his side or attempt to pick things up only to drop them and try again from a different angle.

At this moment, Slade stacked wood near her hearth. He had yet to regain enough strength to heave an ax to split it, but he carried what he could wherever she had need. She also noted he lacked skill at whatever she asked him to do, but he did each task without complaint. Slade ducked out of the room again, on to the next activity.

*Strange fellow, that one. A fine-looking man, with sad eyes, but who is he really?* She huffed, turning back to filling tankards. *Fie, woman. What is the matter with you? Quit dreaming about things you know will never be and focus on what you can control.* She set her jaw, glaring out at the men drinking themselves into a stupor—*not a one of them better take out their poor choices here on the woman who shared their beds.* They would not be the first to pay for such cruelty.

Shane wheezed as he leaned against the doorframe away from prying eyes. Some days his bones pained him worse than others. Today was one of those days.

"Slade, come see." Car coaxed him from the outer door with an eager wave of her arm.

Shane sucked in a slow breath and hobbled forward. She seized his hand and pulled him outside. He ground his teeth.

There in the dirt, she had scrawled words and even a couple of simple sentences. He ran his hand over her head. "You are doing quite fine, Car. You will be reading in no time."

She jumped, wrapping her arms around his waist.

He yelped in pain.

"I'm sorry, I'm sorry."

Shane leaned back against the wall of the tavern, threw his head back, and waited for the worst of the spasms to fade. He could not pull breath into his lungs, so he knew there was no way to comfort the girl.

She began to cry.

"Car, there is no call for tears. Slade over did this day, and his ribs ached long before you touched him. A girl your size couldn't really do a man any harm."

Margg's cold retort cut him deeper than the searing pain in his side. She never afforded him a kind word, never looked with kindness on his efforts to repay his debt. The woman would feel more if she were made of stone.

Margg strolled through Car's hard work, brushing it aside without thought. "Come, Car, let the man whimper in peace. It will only last longer the more we coddle him."

"Margg!" Shane pushed away from the wall with a wince as he held his side. "Carling has worked hard studying her letters. She wrote every word you carelessly stomped through. You may not want to improve yourself, madam, but you have no right to trample on her dreams for a better life."

Margg whirled, her mouth agape but her eyes narrowed. "What do you know of little girls' dreams? Will these squiggles keep her safe from stronger, older boys who prey on innocence? Will understanding them help her support herself? No! She's a girl, and she'll always rely on some man to assure she's cared for. But trusting men with our welfare makes us the target of their hate, their fear, their angry outbursts …" Margg took one slow deliberate step toward Shane with each of her last words. She pushed him back against the wall and snarled in his face. "My dream for Car is for her to live a life that never depends on a man. Then she'll be safe." She kicked at the words left in the dirt. "This'll never get her such!"

Shane put his hand on her upper arm. Her lips sat so very near his. He was sure he could taste them already. A longing pulled deep. He stamped it down as fury swirled in her eyes. "Who hurt you, Margg?"

She swatted away his hand. "I'd never have the time to list them all."

"I am sorry—"

She shoved him, banging him against the wall again. Air hissed through his clenched teeth. "I don't want your apologies or your simpering pity. Never speak of it again or you'll have more than a few broken ribs to pain you.

"Come, Car, you don't have time for this folly. Your mother needs her dinner." Margg snatched up the girl's hand and dragged her away.

Shane watched her saunter off. The angry swing of her hips, the stiff hold of her proud shoulders, the sun's glint on her hair—only served to make his heart quicken its beat. *Why must you always be drawn to the ones who hate you?* His head dropped back with a hollow thud on the mud wall, and he groaned.

# Chapter 34

Shane met Margg in front of the tavern. She cocked one brow and scowled at him. "Might I be allowed to deliver the meal to Car's mother?"

"Why?"

"I wish to meet the woman who brought such a sweet child into the world."

She put one fist on her hip. "Why? Do you intend to persuade Nara of the merits of learning to read?"

Shane's head sagged as he gave it a slow, weary shake. "No, Margg, I would do naught to undermine your authority with the girl. I merely wished the woman to know she has a fine child."

"Do you think her addled? Everyone knows what a grand child Car is—what are you really about?"

Throwing up his hands in surrender, Shane turned to leave. "Put the thought from your mind. I sore regret I ever asked." His words dropped to a pitiful mutter. "It matters not. I would never be good at encouragement and spirit lifting. It would only serve to add to my inadequacy."

He took three steps before she stopped him. "Well, if you must— here." She held out the bowl for him. She pointed down the road out of town and Shane spotted the wisp of smoke from a leaning chimney.

The door lay useless against the chipping daub house. Shane knocked on the frame, breaking a few more pieces loose. "Excuse, madam? Please, be not alarmed. Margg has sent me with your bowl of broth."

A faint wheeze came from within, followed by a wet, hacking cough. "Come," a whisper of a voice called.

Shane stepped on the dirt floor no different than outside. A small dark table sat in the middle of the room. Beyond, lay a heap of rags near a hearth with a dying fire.

The rags moved. "Ye must be—the fine young man—who's come to stay—with Margg." Her breathy voice barely had strength to make the words heard, but the poor woman could only manage to string a few together before she wheezed for a new breath or stopped in a fit of coughing.

He stepped to the side of the table where he could see the face of the withered woman lying under the rags. Only a few wisps of hair remained on her head, gray as her face with its pallor of impending death. Her sunken eyes looked toward him with an eerie haze. Margg spoke truth in her wonder of how the woman still breathed. She looked to be nothing more than thin skin-covered bones. "I much doubt Margg ever said such things, but I am appreciative of your kindness, Lady Nara."

"'Tis truth I—speak. I think me Margg—fancies ye. She has said how ye care—for my Carling. How ye—teach her to read." The words were spoken with awe.

Shane could not control his skeptical snort. "Well, she has never given the least indication she cares for me or my teachings."

"Oh—my boy—don't judge poor Margg—by her rough manner.

She—hides behind it.—She oft speaks of how well Carling—is doing at her—lessons, and—how my girl teaches her—what she's learned. And Margg speaks of little else but ye—" She erupted in an awful fit of deep coughs.

Shane felt the effort of them in his own aching ribs.

"Please weary not yourself on my account," Shane stammered. "I promise to reserve my opinions of the tavern owner. Truly, I knew naught of how she felt."

"Never tell her I—breathed a word. She would—have my head." A weak chuckle was followed by more coughing.

"I swear, she shall never hear it from my lips." Shane paused debating, on how much more to pry into Margg's private affairs. "Might you know what happened to her husband?"

"He was—a beast. She came—here many times, bloody—broken. One day—the tavern remained closed—longer than usual. I went in the back—found poor Margg covered in—the blood of her—unborn child. We almost—lost her too. My Willham—raged at the man—for treating his woman so poorly. They—went off in the woods. Jarman never returned. Willham—feared someone would learn—of what he had done and—the next week, he left Kinglet."

Shane struggled with the emotions whirling in him over the argumentative Margg. He wanted to shake her for treating him like an enemy when she favored him. But more, he wanted to run back to the tavern and scoop her up into his arms and hold her. He wanted to promise her no one would ever hurt her again.

His blood flared at the thought of her wicked husband, and the vision of him impaled on a pike and torn apart by wild animals gave Shane solace. *Oh, but to lose a babe before it has even taken breath. Lord, I cannot fault her, her hatred of men. Such pain no mother should ever bear.*

The old woman coughed again, bringing Shane back to the chilly room where she lay. He set the bowl on the table and knelt by the fire, "Let me add a log. You must be cold."

"It matters little—my boy. I cannot feel the war—warmth—or the cold anymore."

The log laid upon the coals, he collected the bowl and moved closer to Nara. When he stepped out of the deep shadows and knelt beside her, she gasped, triggering another long fit of coughing.

Her boney hand covered her gaping, toothless mouth. Nara's eyes bulged from her head. "'Tis ye," she stammered. "Oh, ye have finally come." She laid her hand on his.

Shane stifled a shudder at the cold, clammy thing. "Madam, you know not of me, for never have I been to Kinglet before."

She shook her head. "Long I have known of the trouble now upon us." Energy filled her body as she raised her head from her filthy pillow stirring a rank odor. Her voice came bold and unbroken. "God revealed it to me when I fell ill. The Lord Himself promised one would come who would raise my Carling to be a woman after God's own heart. This same one would turn back the evil once again seeking foothold in our land."

"Nay, my lady, I cannot be the one of which God spoke."

She raised her hand to cradle his face, stirring the air and filling it with the stench of decaying flesh. "Long have I dreamed of this face. Ye are he. I have no doubt." She smiled with a contentment that flooded the room and spilled out into the growing night. "The Father promised me I would not go to my reward until I saw ye with me own eyes. Oh, son of the second birth—boy of the double parents—the one lost but now found, how I have longed to meet ye."

Tears streamed from his eyes. "Nay, my lady, it cannot be me. I am no man God could use. I have made such a mess of the blessings

He showered on my ungrateful soul. I have lost any chance to be a warrior in His divine battle call."

Her smile grew, as did the earnestness of her plea. "Ye are precisely the man God *will* use—for what must be done can only be done in His strength. Ye must but be available to Him."

Her eyes closed, and a holiness like none other Shane had ever experienced blanketed the room. His heart calmed from its erratic pounding as peace flooded his spirit.

When next she spoke, Shane knew the words were not her own. "You have been chosen out of all others, for you have seen and felt firsthand the evil threatening your home. You, My child, have been raised up in the truth. 'My son, keep thy father's commandment, and forsake not the law of thy mother. Bind them continually upon thine heart, and tie them about thy neck. When thou goest, it shall lead thee; when thou sleepest, it shall keep thee; and when thou awakest, it shall talk with thee. For the Commandment is a lamp, and the Law is light: and reproofs of instruction are the way of life.' For 'as many as I love, I rebuke and chasten.' You are My beloved. And in you am I well pleased."

Shane couldn't breathe. He fell prostrate on the floor beside the holy woman. He buried his face in his hands. "I am unworthy."

She put her hand on the back of his head. Her own whispery voice returned as she spoke again. "But He—is worthy, and He—has seen in ye—what ye cannot. 'Have not I—commanded thee? Be strong—and of a good courage—be not afraid—neither be thou dismayed—for the Lord—thy God—is with thee—whither so ever—thou goest.'"

She took several slow deep breaths. "Oh thank Ye, Father." The hand slid from his head. The wheezing breaths ceased. Shane raised and looked on Nara, who now lay still. A small smile yet graced her lips. Her unseeing eyes turned toward the door.

# Chapter 35

Margg found Slade leaning against the pigpen at first light. He didn't seem to be in pain, but the color had drained from his face. Her heart skipped a beat. She told herself it was only because she fretted over Nara, and not that she thrilled at his return—not in the least. *He is a burden. One who eats my food and sleeps for free in the room I get good coin for. I would be better off if he went back from whence he came—this moment.* Even so, the sharp pain in her heart at the thought nearly made her stumble.

Slade turned to her as if noticing her for the first time. His eyes were red and bloated. *Crying? What would make him cry at Nara's?*

"Nara, is she—"

His head hung.

"Well, at least she no longer suffers. Have ye told Car?"

His head shook listlessly.

Margg sighed, irritation renewing her wish for him to leave. "I will see the thing is done. And the house burned."

"Burned? What of a proper burial?"

"Nara lingered with a wasting sickness for near a year, Slade. No one in town would dare enter her home to collect her diseased body. And I think even fewer would allow her to be buried in holy ground for the same reasons."

"She was a holy woman." Slade's words were bold and had the bite of anger behind them.

"She still breathed when you entered her home?"

He gave the slimmest of nods.

"She spoke to you?"

"Aye," he whispered, hiding his gaze.

Margg put her fists on her hips and tapped her foot. "And with what, might I ask, did dear Nara fill your head, Slade?"

He would not speak.

"Did she speak of me?" Her heart fell to her stomach. *What does he know?*

"She spoke most of Car and of her grateful heart that you care so for her daughter. But in her words to me, I felt … peace … comfort and truth unlike any I have ever known."

"You think she spoke for God?" Margg snorted as his gaze searched her face. "Some say our Ol' Nara was a prophetess of the Most High, others a witch of the black arts." She shrugged and stepped away. "You make up your own mind, but I never saw anything but an ordinary woman in her."

"I know well the touch of evil and how vastly it differs from the holy. Nara carried the Spirit of the risen Lord within her." He smashed his fist on to the opposite palm to punctuate his statement.

"As you say."

When Margg arrived at Nara's deteriorating hovel, she collided with Slade as he stepped from the doorway. He cradled a slender bundle in his arms, wrapped in a clean cloth. "Is that one of my sheets?" she asked, blocking his way.

"Add it to the many things I owe you."

Still she would not move from his path. "What do you aim to do?"

"I will see her buried in holy ground."

"There is no priest in Kinglet Hill to speak the rights over her."

"I know them well enough to see the thing is done proper."

"And what if the good folk of Kinglet stop you?"

A strange look washed over his face. "If this be a matter in line with the will of God Most High—to see Nara laid to rest in His sanctified ground—then I will face naught of opposition. If, as you say, the people stop me, I will know God does not wish it. Now, if you could be so kind—while Nara yet weighed but a little in the end, she is still a burden near past my feeble strength. Will you let me pass, Margg?"

"Don't come running to me when they threaten to burn you along with her," she snapped, stepping to the side.

"Mayhaps you would do me one further boon and direct me to the holy ground?"

She pointed toward the town. "Follow the road past the bakers, turn left, and walk to the end of the lane. The sacred dead are buried under the great oaks there."

"And where might a spade be found?"

Margg shrugged. "Ask John, the tanner who is adding to his home. Man has more children than seems fitting for one fella. His place is near the end of town, but you can't miss it. Follow the unending pounding."

She turned back to her tavern. "I'll wait for you to return before setting the house to flame. It shouldn't be long."

On the main road, they parted ways, Margg telling him again he was wasting his time.

"'Tis my time to waste."

"No, 'tis mine. There are things you need to be doing for me."

Nana was a fine woman and all, but Slade didn't need to dote over her —she was dead. There was the living to think about. Did he spare her no thought at all? What had Nara told him? *Does he know?* Margg searched his face for any signs of disgust or fear.

Shane laid Nara's body on a gentle rise under the shade of the massive oak. He took only a moment to catch his breath, shoved the nagging pain aside, and headed off to find a tanner named John. He came to the end of the road where a group of homes nestled at the foot of the mountains. He looked at each but saw no building underway. He groaned. No one was about to ask directions. The light morning breeze shifted and brought with it the sound of rhythmic tapping. He followed the sound to a sprawling home tucked under the trees in a narrow hollow between the steep slopes of two peaks.

The man pounding the cross bars of a frame together drew Shane up short. The man stood at least a head taller than him, and his shoulders near twice as wide. Shane wondered if Margg sent him here to be pummeled again. The man's arms had to be the same breadth and length as Shane's legs.

"Ya want somethin', mister?"

Shane pulled his gaze from the mountain of a man to see a miniature form of the father—though in truth the son was about Shane's same size.

"Well?" the youth asked again. His size made it hard to determine his age, but he might have been twelve or thirteen.

Shane cleared his throat of fear. "I am looking for a man named John."

"And what might you be needin' with this John?" The father turned from his work and walked toward him. Shane swore the ground trembled with each step as he closed the large gap between them in but a half dozen steps. The hammer he swung over his shoulder could pass for a battle club.

"I—" Shane's voice squeaked. He cleared his throat and tried again. "I was told I might borrow a spade from him."

He crossed his arms, and Shane marveled they would span it. "And who might be loaning out me tools?"

"Margg. The owner of the tavern."

"I know of Margg." John growled, making Shane's ribcage rattle. "Well, I assume yar the fella she keeps holed up in her back room. What manner of evil is she doing with ya in there?"

Shane's head shot up, revealing more of his face than he intended. "No manner of evil in the least, sir. She found me beat near to death, and cared for me until I was healed. Now I am working off my debt to her. There is nothing more to the matter." He ducked his head under his cowl once more.

"What be yar name, my good man?"

"Slade," he muttered. No point in telling this man any different— no matter how he hated the moniker.

"Well, Slade, what might Mistress Margg want with me spade?"

"She does not want it for anything."

"Then why are ya here?" The words were spoken, but they boomed from the man.

"I have need of it, sir."

"Again I ask—what do ya want if for?"

"I aim to dig a grave for Nara and provide her a proper burial."

John's arms fell to his sides. His voice came as a reverent whisper. "The poor dear has at last gone home." He stomped the last step toward Shane, pounded him on the shoulder, and continued on past him. "Why didn't ya just say so sooner? Let's be about this grim task."

He kept walking back toward the road as he yelled over his shoulder. "Matthew, tell yar momma I'm goin' out with the tavern boy."

Shane moaned at the man's rough touch, worked air back in his lungs, and hastened to catch up. Shane found he took two steps for each stride John made. "Are you not forgetting something?"

"Lent me spade to Rawlins, we can collect it on our way. Might see if Tate will loan us his as well. Two digging will make the labor pass faster."

By the time they made it back to where Nara's body waited, John had collected five other men of the town and six spades. As others, both men and women, gathered about them, they made quick work of digging the hole and lowered the body into it. As Shane stood, he startled to see Car stepping beside the grave.

She bent and scooped up a handful of earth. Releasing it into the pit onto her mother, she said, "This is my momma. She was good to me and taught me right from wrong. She loved me all my days. And I will love her all of mine." Car walked around the grave and wrapped her arms around Shane's leg. He pulled her close, resting his hand on her back, hearing her sniffle.

Margg stepped forward next to drop in her handful of earth. "Nara was my friend when I had none and a shelter in my time of need. I will miss her counsel and her friendship. May God welcome you with joy, Nara."

Shane had never heard Margg speak with such tenderness. As she walked to stand on his other side, she would not look at him, but something about her sparked the flicker in his heart to a full flame.

"Nara was a godly woman—regardless of what some may say in jealous slander. She never failed to pray for me and mine whenever we had need. Our small hamlet will be the worse without her," John dropped a heap of dirt on the body.

The others who came to pay their proper respect spoke their words over Nara, then the men filled in the rest of the hole. As they finished, another man came and placed a stone, carved with Nara's name on it, on the ground at the head.

"When I heard of Nara's prolonged illness, I set to work on it. She was good to my girls when they were growin'. 'Twas the least I could do."

Shane now spoke for the first time. "We gather to speak our farewells and gratitude to our sister in the Lord, Nara of Kinglet Hill. I knew her but moments. Even so I felt the presence of God Most High upon her. I trust in the words of the Holy Scriptures. 'We are confident, I say, and willing rather to be absent from the body, and to be present with the Lord.' Lord, welcome this faithful one into Your arms. And remember with kindness those left behind."

He dropped the handful of earth he still held in his hand and recited the words he had heard the priest say on more than one such solemn occasion. "Forasmuch as it hath pleased Almighty God of His great mercy to take unto Himself the soul of our dear sister here departed, we therefore commit her body to the ground; earth to earth, ashes to ashes, dust to dust; in sure and certain hope of the Resurrection to eternal life, through our Lord Jesus Christ; who shall change our vile body, that it may be like unto His glorious body, according to the mighty working, whereby He is able to subdue all things to Himself."

"Amen," each person said.

Those gathered turned and left without further word. Margg looked to Shane with a tenderness he did not expect. "Thank you."

Her lips again called to him. His need to pull her close and comfort her resurfaced, and he rocked to the balls of his feet to close the small distance between them.

Her gaze dropped from his, and she tossed her head in agitation. She huffed, turned, and walked away. "Well, supper won't cook itself."

Shane stared after her.

"She is gonna miss Momma," Car whispered, slipping her hand in his. They walked back to the tavern a half pace behind Margg, who remained aloof from their companionship.

# Chapter 36

The distance Margg kept between them on the way back to the tavern remained in the days that followed. Shane only spotted her on rare occasions. She did not tell him what she wanted him to do and never commented on any task he took on to complete of his own accord. She would leave his meal on a table, and he was expected to know when and where—otherwise he ate it cold.

"Do you know what vexes Margg?" Shane asked Car one afternoon as she worked on her writing.

"What does *vexes* mean?" the girl asked with a tip of her head.

"Why will she not speak to me? Have I done something to upset her?"

Car shrugged. "I didn't know she wasn't talkin'."

"There are a few floorboards loose in the tavern. Do you know who might sell nails in town?"

Car shook her head.

Shane grunted his irritation. "Well, I suppose it matters not, I have no money to purchase such anyway." He picked up the ax and moved toward the woodpile. If he chose the right logs and did not work at it over long, Shane found his ribs would tolerate the labor of wood splitting. Today he knew it would feel good to vent his frustration on the hapless bits of trees.

"You feelin' up to that, boy?"

Shane turned to the booming voice rattling his insides. "Well enough to split a few, John. What might I do for you this day?"

"I came to ask for yar help, if ya be willing. Can't pay ya much."

"Mayhaps you might spare a few supplies from your building. Such would suit as adequate payment."

"Supplies?" John crossed his arms, the hairs of his mighty beard jutting out as if standing in military formation. "What might ya be thinkin'?"

"There are several boards loose in the tavern floor. I thought you might spare me a handful of nails to anchor them down before someone suffers an injury. I would not want to see Margg bear the blame for such an accident."

John's massive hand shot out. "Nails I have a plenty. That I can do for ya. Will loan ya the hammer too."

Shane shook his hand, knowing he would never be able to manage the huge instrument John used as a hammer.

He spoke to Car as he followed the man out of the yard. "Finish your lesson, pretty girl. I will return to check on it later. You know where I have gone, should Margg ask after me."

Car waved and turned back to her stick and the letters she scribbled.

"Wouldn't mind you teaching a few of my youngin's their letters neither. Not much call for such here in Kinglet, but I'm a man hopin' for better things for my little ones."

"Margg's many tasks fill much of my days, but mayhaps after midday meal on the Lord's Day. Cannot imagine the good Lord would see such learning as real work, when it could serve to allow one to read His Holy Book."

John's hand slammed into his back, and Shane staggered forward.

"I think I may just like ya, Slade." John laughed, and the sound echoed off the mountaintops.

Margg continued to be distant, and so Shane spent his late afternoon hours for the rest of the week helping John raise the walls on the three new rooms of his home. With seven bairns and another on the way, the family had long since outgrown the three rooms of the original structure. Come the Lord's Day, Shane walked with Car to John's home. As this was yet another Sabbath without their visiting monk, many of the townsfolk milled about the center of the hamlet, talking with one another.

Slade skirted around the gathered people and down toward John's home.

"Slade, my friend." Shane braced himself for the blow that always followed the boisterous greeting. "Are ya ready to instruct me brood?"

Six of the seven tanner's children sat on a log outside John's home. "I thought it prudent to bring my first pupil. Car can instruct the little ones in their letters. I, on the other hand, will work with the older group, who I believe will be swifter to acquire the skill. We will proceed at greater speed."

"Fine, fine. We're ready for some learnin'." John sat on the end of the log and picked up a stick in front of him.

Shane nodded, instructed Car to take the three youngest children to a muddy patch near the path, and moved to work with the rest.

Shane straightened from where he knelt to inspect his pupils' work and rolled his aching shoulders. "This would be a fair amount easier with slate and chalk," he muttered. Turning his attention to the sky, he sighed.

"Forgive me, John, but I fear it is time to call an end to our instruction for this day. Margg will soon serve the evening meal. There are always many on the eve of the Lord's Day. Some whole families come. Margg will be in need of Car's help." He waved for the girl to join him as he turned to leave.

"The monk visits next Sabbath, but I expect to see ya back for another lesson following." Again, John slapped him on the back.

"You and your family are all fine students. I will be honored to return, though I expect you will soon outgrow need of me."

Shane turned, and Car slipped her hand in his as they walked toward the tavern. Soft and small, it fit inside his palm like the girl fit in his heart. She covered the roughness with her simple gentle kindness. Shane gave her hand a squeeze, and she looked up at him with a grin.

At the center of town, Car pulled him toward the crowd drawn by a bit of merry music. He loosed himself from her grasp at the edge of those gathered and raised his cowl with some haste.

"Car, Margg will be waiting," he called as she disappeared between the many legs surrounding the musicians in the center. Shane sighed and turned to leave.

An arm slipped through his and stopped his progress. "You are not darting off so quickly, are you now, Slade? Stay and enjoy a bit of merriment." The healing woman brushed against his side.

"Margg will have need of our help."

"Ol' Margaret survived quite fine before you arrived, good sir. And while you are most gallant, your efforts are wasted on her." She turned, steering him toward the others.

Shane tried to pull from her grasp.

She snuggled him tighter toward her. His arm now rested against her bosom. While one arm remained entwined around his, holding fast, her other hand reached up and brushed back his hood and caressed his cheek. "The woman is far beneath such a fine man as you."

Shane jerked his face from her unwelcome touch. "You know naught of Margg—nor me." He wiggled and pushed until he pulled himself free of her. He straightened his garments. "Truly, if you saw the certianity of the matter, madam, you would know Margg is far too good for the likes of me. Good day to you." He hurried away before she could seize hold of him again and near ran back to Margg's tavern.

He lifted the bucket at the well, plunged in his hands, and drank deeply before splashing his face. He ran his fingernails over his cheek, trying to rid himself of the sensation the healer had left there. Shaking himself to release the last of the water from his beard and wiping his hands on his breeches, he entered his room and headed toward the tavern to help Margg, however she might allow him this night.

*Smack*! Shane's cheek stung with a slap before he reached the inner door. He blinked past the stars as Margg's rage-filled face came into view. She had flown through the door in front of him and it slammed shut behind her in almost the same moment.

"By all that is holy, woman, what—"

She raised her hand to strike him again.

He snatched her wrist and held her offending hand away from his blistered face.

"You are welcome to leave," she snarled.

"Why? What have I done?"

"Go to your lover. I do not want the likes of such a man under my roof."

Shane huffed and raked his free hand through his hair—the action brought King Edgar to mind, and he nearly lost his grip on the whipping hand. "I assure you, I have not one notion as to what you are ranting about. I have no lover."

"You were seen entwined arm in arm with the vixen. Do you stand here and lie to my face and deny truth?"

Shane shook his head. "Do you speak of the healer woman?"

Margg struck out with her other hand and set his other cheek to burn as the first. "Go to Hannah and let me alone. Never again do I wish to see your vile face."

Shane took her other wrist and pinned them both above her as he backed her up and held her against the inner door. "I have no idea what manner of gossipmongering you have indulged in this fine afternoon, Margaret. But you will stop slapping me, for I have done naught to warrant your wrath. Hannah is the one who deserves your nasty ire. For it was she—and she alone—who seized ahold of me and held fast. I worked as quick as was possible by any a man—save John the tanner—to extract my limb from her fearsome grasp."

He leaned into her, hovering but a breath above her enticing lips. *Oh to claim them*—but he dared not take such liberty with her just now. "I have no interest in the healer woman. Truth be told, she does not stir me as some women have."

Margg's breath caught, and her luscious lips quaked.

He wet his, savoring the thought of stilling her lips with his.

Her breaths came in quick pants, and a cloud of fear darted through her eyes.

He straightened, releasing her and stepping back out of her reach. "However, if my presence has grown wearisome or a burden upon you, I will find somewhere else to lay my head. Though I will not go far, as I still owe you a debt, Margaret of the Hart and Spoon. Tell me your wishes that I might obey." He took a knee. "I am yours to command, my lady."

# Chapter 37

A ragged breath rattled in Margg's chest, and her heart thundered in her ears. *Would he kiss her?* He vehemently denied love for Hannah, spitting out her name with disgust. She grasped for the hope that he might have feelings for her—but he withdrew—asked to be commanded. What would he say if she ordered him to love her? But he didn't. He didn't kiss her—and he couldn't love her. She was soiled, by her place in the world, her work in a common tavern, her past. He could never love the likes of her.

A thud sounded on the other side of the door. "Margg? Are ye serving or not? The tankers are running dry."

She gripped the door latch. "I care not what you do. I have no need for you," she jerked open the door and slammed it closed.

"George, which do you demand first, food or drink?" she choked around unshed tears.

The man shrugged and moved back to his table.

Margg filled the tankards, then moved to the kitchen. Car had bowls full of the stew Margg had begun earlier in the day, ready to be carried to the tables. "There's only families in there now, Car. You may help me deliver these."

Car picked up two bowls and followed her. "What about Slade?"

Margg whirled on the girl, slopping hot stew over her thumb. She cursed and leaned into Car's face. "Never speak that name again. I will not bear it in my presence."

Car's eyes were wide. She held her breath and nodded. Margg turned to set the food before their patrons. The two worked side by side for the rest of the night. Margg tried to brush away all thoughts of the man she wished had never been thrown in her pigpen. She should have left him to his fate.

Her heart convulsed, and she swiped at a tear that would not be constrained.

Car yawned as they stacked the last of the clean tankards, ready now for the morrow's guests.

"Time for a good night's rest, little one. You did fine work this day." Margg did her best to smile. She put her arm around the girl's shoulder. As they walked toward the back room, Margg faltered. Mayhaps she should go out the front and around the tavern to avoid running into him again.

Car pushed open the door before she could change their course. The back room sat dark and cold. Slade was gone.

Shane shivered, moving closer to the fire he had built in Nara's hearth. Any closer, though, and his clothes would light. Did it really matter? Margg had thrown him out. Never would he be the man he hoped. He thought he could work for his redemption in Margg's tavern. But there was no hope for him.

His head dropped back against the wall, and another chunk of wad dropped off. It skittered over his shoulder and down his back, causing another shudder to rack his body. Margg's earlier warning came to mind. These deteriorating walls could still hold the wasting illness that had taken months to claim blessed Nara. He no longer cared. He snatched up Nara's fur and wrapped his trembling body in it.

As his body warmed and he tried to empty his mind of the woman who crushed his heart, Nara's words came back to him unbidden. 'This one will turn back the evil now finding a foothold in our land.'

The words cut him, and he cried out. "Lord, I am an unworthy wretch. How could I ever hope to turn back evil when I am evil itself and not even wanted by those in this hamlet? I have failed before ever I began." He buried his head and hoped the sickness that had killed Nara would make quick work of him.

"There ya are."

Shane raised his head to see Car standing with her hands on her hips. Could Margg have sent her to find him? His heart fluttered to life.

"What'cha you doin' in my old fallin' down house? Ya've been missin' for days, and John is getting' quite cross with ya."

John—yes he had use of another pair of strong hands. He had sent Car, not Margg—never Margg.

Car moved into the room and climbed into his lap. She wrapped her arms around his neck and tucked her head under his chin. She warmed his cold heart and body.

"I missed ya, Slade."

His arms slipped around her, pulling her closer. "You did fine without me, I am sure."

She shook her head against his neck. "My heart hurt, like when Momma died. I thought maybe I'd done somethin' wrong. I know ya and Margg are mad at each other," She raised her head to look in his eyes. "If ya don't like Margg no more, does that mean ya don't like me neither?"

Shane kissed her forehead. "I like Margg very much, and I love you, sweet girl, with all my failing heart."

More of Nara's words sprang to mind. 'The Lord Himself promised one would come who would raise my Carling to be a woman after God's own heart.' The prophetess of God believed he would raise Car as his own. Like Mariamne and Edgar, he could be the parent to raise her, to love her, to show her how to follow God. But was he the man for this awesome task? Did he know how to follow God well enough to lead the way for this girl?

He looked into her trusting eyes again. *Lord, I need to be that man for her.* He pulled her closer and kissed her cheek. With her still in his arms, he rose to his feet. *From this day forward, all I do is for her. I will be the man she needs me to be. God help me, I cannot fail her.*

He carried her out of the house and set her on the ground. He took her hand and stood in a shaft of a bright sunlight. A verse from long ago sprang to mind. *But I say unto you, Resist not evil: but whosoever shall smite thee on thy right cheek, turn to him the other also.* He smiled, remembering the sting of both his cheeks from Margg. *But I say unto you, Love your enemies: bless them that curse you: do good to them that hate you, and pray for them which hurt you, and persecute you.* That is what he would do. He would love Margg, regardless of how she felt about him. He would show Car how to love even when you were not loved in return.

# Chapter 38

Margg swiped at another enraging tear. She had told Slade to leave—wanted him out from under foot—out of her life entirely. He had obliged her. He had disappeared, and no one had seen him in four days. Yet his room sat unused as if waiting for his return—and she avoided walking through it whenever she could. She still saw him lying under the furs, racked with pain, heard his labored breathing, and smelled the heavy musk of his unwashed body.

Another tear slithered down her cheek. She was better without the distraction of him. She didn't need the gossip, which had come with housing a handsome man in her back room. And the man *was* majestically cut and formed.

Margg turned to ask Car to grab something in Slade's room. Where had that girl gotten off to now?

Slade had been good for Car, she conceded. Teaching her reading —though Margg still didn't know where she would ever use such a skill. Car needed a man—*that* man—to raise her up proper and teach her things Margg had never learned. Car needed Slade. *I need him.*

Margg stepped into the intolerable empty space and stopped at the laughter she heard tumbling through the open outer door. She moved to the doorway and peered out.

Car stood jabbering away to a shirtless man next to the well. The man threw back his head and sprayed water in an arc from his drenched hair. The bare back facing Margg, displayed a smattering of fresh scars. A bump along one rib showed where his injuries had not been set properly. Slade would suffer from it all his days, she lamented.

She watched as Slade took a small knife and trimmed some of his unruly hair. He pulled a tunic over his head and covered his finely honed body in rough fabric. After binding his hair in a warrior's knot, he turned to address Car, who bounced around him with uncontainable joy. His beard was now trimmed short and again revealed the line of his well-carved jaw. Margg sighed to see him.

He smiled at Car's antics—yet he could never spare her anything but his menacing scowl.

Margg swiped at another tear.

He gripped Car by the forearms and lifting her off her feet, spun her around and around. Only stopping when he needed to grab hold of the pigpen to steady his dizziness. And he laughed—oh how he laughed. Their merriment could be nothing less than angelic merriment.

She stood in the shadows, in the cold, far removed from their joy and the warmth they shared.

Slade, once again steady, reached down and scooped Car up. His arms wound tight around her waist, and hers snaked around his neck. She nuzzled under his chin, and he kissed her head.

Margg fell back against the doorframe, tears washing her face.

Margg dropped the rag on the counter and turned to the front door. She had sent Car to pallet long since and now decided she could not avoid her own cold, lonely bed any longer. She noted the high stack of chopped wood along the back wall, and her eye caught on the open door to Slade's room. A glance inside revealed he wasn't inside. She staggered off to her bed and stifled the threatening tears with her pillow.

She rose early the next morning and slipped passed Car sleeping near the hearth. The back room still remained empty, but a fire lay burning in the tavern. Wood stacked neatly next to it for the day. The pots sat scoured clean, ready for her to use. The stove was lit, and vegetables of all kinds were chopped on the cutboard. A shank of venison hung from the hook in the ceiling beam.

Margg ground her teeth as a tear again threatened. Slade was not gone, he just refused to be seen.

Shane slipped out the front door of the tavern and walked toward John's home as the sun began to light the sky. As his feet covered the ground, his mind raced over his past. *Lord, please, I no longer want to be the man I have been. I want to be a man You can be proud of. A man who Car would be proud to say raised her.* He cleared his throat of the pain strangling the life from him. *Lord, may I be a man Miss Margaret would like to know.*

With few words, Shane took to mixing the daub John, his sons Tristan, and Matthew, and he would use to cover the wattle they had placed within the frames. Today they hoped to add the daub to the two inner walls. It would take weeks yet to find, cut, and strip all the rightly sized spindly branches to fashion the remaining wattle for all the outer walls—and weeks after that to weave it all together before another nauseous concoction of mud, straw, water, and dung was caked to it. In the time it took to collect and prepare the outer walls,

John hoped the inner walls would dry completely.

"It is not some villain who needs a good thrashing, my friend."

Shane looked up at John hovering over him, then back at his fist sunk deep in the mixture. The odor of the dung and mud hit him fresh again. He pulled his hand free and shook the filth into the tub. Shane rose to his feet and reached for the handle of the wide basin he'd worked in.

John refused to take the other side—crossing his arms. "What evil torments ya, friend?"

Shane straightened and looked off to the house and the waiting walls. "My own evil."

"What evil have ya committed?" John asked with a laugh.

Shane shook his head and stooped to pick up the laden tub on his own.

John put his foot on the rim, pinning the already unbearably heavy container to the ground. "I asked ya a question, Slade."

Shane stood but refused to meet the man's gaze. "Every manner of evil your mind can think to conjure."

"Murder?"

"I have killed, though I believe it was in protection of another's life and my own."

"I hear no evil there." John looked over his shoulder toward the hills, his foot tapping a rhythm on the tub. "Ya know, I've seen myself many a man twisted in a state like ya are now. Never known it to be about past sins, though." His fingers rubbed through his beard. "These venomous vines tying ya up in knots can only be a woman's doing."

Shane looked at him. "Now, do not go blaming another for my own troubles. I tell you truly, John the tanner, there is no one to blame for my current difficulties but my own sorry hide."

One fat brow above John's narrowing eyes rose high. His hands dropped to his side, and he bent for the other side of the tub. "Never seen a man so hard on his own self as ya, Slade of the miserable wasting."

Shane snatched up his side and walked toward the waiting wattle. "That sums up my life most accurately—a miserable waste."

They finished the daub on the morrow. The next dawn saw the Lord's Day shining bright. Shane had been waiting for this moment near as long as he had been in Kinglet Hill. The monk would be present this day, the weather had turned enough for travel, and he was a last hale to attend. This day he would unburden his soul and see how he might earn God's forgiveness. The heavens testified he was making a mess of things on his own thus far.

# Chapter 39

A man in a brown robe, nearly as wide as he was tall, stood at the front of the meeting room. Shane followed the last few villagers inside as their grumbled mutterings wafted back to him.

"Another day to pay our due."

"Paying that fat brute is all we ever do."

Every villager knelt before the monk.

The man stood looking down his stub nose with his fingers laced together just above a rope that held a giant wooden cross around his waist. His thumbs drummed on the expanse.

Shane took his knees with the others. He remained far removed from the holy man against the back wall. The monk cleared his throat, but it did naught for the croak from his voice. Words tumbled from him in a single lifeless breath.

"If thou wilt diligently hearken unto the voice of the Lord thy God, and wilt do that which is right in His sight, and wilt give ear unto His commandments, and keep all His ordinances, then will He put none of these diseases upon thee, which He brought upon His enemies: for He is the Lord that healeth thee. God's blessings be upon you."

"God's blessings be also upon you, Brother Jonah," the congregation droned as one.

Shane heard only obligation behind the words and no true desire to have the Almighty shower blessings on this man.

"Give, and it shall be given unto you: a good measure, pressed down, shaken together and runneth over shall men giveth into Your bosom: for with what measure ye mete, with the same shall men mete to you again."

The moment his last command passed his lips, everyone stood.

Shane watched as each family walked forward and dropped their hard-earned and scant coin into Brother Jonah's bag. Shane did not follow the others forward but stepped out as John and his family walked by. "Is this a normal service for you?"

John shrugged as his bairns ran about chasing one another and the other village children. "Aye. The brother comes once a moon, reminds us to obey God, blesses us, and we present our offerings. Has happened this way as long as I can remember."

"How do you know what the Lord requires of you, if all he does is tell you to obey?"

John scratched his chin. "I figured if I paid for God's work as Brother Jonah instructed, that was what was required. Have ya been taught different?"

Shane's fists clenched tight at his sides. "Oh, aye, a great deal different." He stomped back into the meeting room before John could say more. He passed the last villager on his way out, and Shane watched the fat monk shake the bag bloated with coins.

The monk grumbled. "'Tis less each month."

"Mayhaps the good people of Kinglet Hill do not feel they are getting the full value of your services, monk. Or then again, mayhaps you have already bled them dry."

His round head shot up. "I am a servant of the Most High." His fists perched where Shane could only assume his hips should be located. "Now, my son, have you come to present your tithes to His most holy work?"

"Nay, monk, I come seeking confession."

"But the Lord says, 'All the tithe of the land *both* of the seed of the ground, *and* of the fruit of the trees is the Lord's: *it is* holy to the Lord.' You must present your tithe to the Lord, my son."

"The Good Book also says, 'As every man wisheth in his heart, so let him give, not grudgingly, or of necessity: for God loveth a cheerful giver.' I am a beggar in this hamlet, working for nothing more than my keep. I have no coin to give you. Now will you hear my confession or nay?"

Brother Jonah shook his head and waddled toward the door. "I do not hear confessions, my son. There is not the time. I have other villages to minister to—many, many more, which is why I come but once each month."

"What good do you do if you have no time to instruct these people, no time to pray over them properly, and no time to allow them to unburden their souls?"

The monk stopped beside him but remained within the shadows of the building. He craned his neck to look up at Shane, but his eyes narrowed. "I do as I am called by God, my son. What right do you have to say that God is in error in calling me?"

"I do not call God into error. God is never wanting in any manner of thing He chooses to do."

Brother Jonah stood a little taller and nodded with an upturned nose in agreement.

"I do, however, seriously doubt you were ever called by Him to do anything at all whatsoever. And certainly not this. What you do here in the name of God is the work of the devil himself."

A sausage-sized finger wagged in his face. "Mind your words, boy. I could call curses down upon you."

"Blessed be God, and the Father of our Lord Jesus Christ, which hath blessed us, with all spiritual blessing in heavenly things in Christ," Shane said as warmth bubbled up in him unlike anything before. "How shall you curse, where God hath not cursed? Or how shall you detest, where the Lord hath not detested?" Rage added heat to the holy warmth within Shane, yet he floated from the building like he walked with the Lord God Himself. *This will be the last time Brother Jonah comes burdening Your flock, Lord. I swear it!*

Shane blinked. He looked to the right and to the left. He stood in a thick grove of trees. "Where am I?" he muttered. He raked his fingers through his hair, loosening many strands from the knot he now favored. He turned around and caught a fleeting glance of the tallest structure in Kinglet—the mill on the river running through the village.

"Lord, I recall not how I came to be here, but ..." he faltered. He had yet to give his confession. God would not hear his plea. He still stood as God's enemy—a sinner of the blackest heart.

Leaves rustled, and a twig snapped beyond the nearest trees.

Before Shane could discover the source of the noise, Holy Scriptures learned long ago flooded his mind. *Then I acknowledged my sin unto Thee, neither hid I mine iniquity: for I thought, I will confess against myself my wickedness unto the Lord, and Thou forgavest the punishment of my sin.*

*If we acknowledge our sins, He is faithful and just, to forgiveth us our sins, and to cleanse us from all unrighteousness.*

*Thou hast forgiven the iniquity of thy people, and covered all their sins.*

Shane shook his head. He had no one to confess his iniquities to.

*I will confess against myself my wickedness unto the Lord.*

As if the ground shook beneath his feet, the words rattled in his soul until the meaning behind them became clear. He dropped to his knees. "Lord, I confess my great and many sins to You. I have spoken lies, for I follow the father of lies. I have broken Milana's engagement with my lies. I have hurt her and the man she loves. I have spoiled women …" tears choked his flow of words "so many maidens, Lord. Hold not my sins against them. Help them to find men who will love them true—despite what I have done to them."

The words, once begun, could not be stopped. For over an hour his soul bled his guilt, through tears running from a spirit that grieved each and every moment of disobedience, unkindness, and hatefulness.

He settled back onto his heels as he sat still and quiet, his head bowed. Shane scoured his memory as he did one of Margg's pots. He did not wish to leave a single sin unspoken to the Lord. When no more evils came to his mind, he raised his face to the heavens. "Lord, I sit here before You this day. If there be any iniquity I have left unconfessed and forgotten, I beg You to bring it to mind."

Shane waited. Nothing more was added to his unruly list of ills.

"This is my vow and my plea, Lord God Almighty. I swear to serve the good of Your people and not myself. I pledge to teach Carling of You and raise her as I was raised, surrounded by Your truth. I will work until the day in which I can earn Your forgiveness."

*He is faithful and just, to forgive us our sins.*

Shane leapt to his feet. "As my first act of penance, I will assure that worthless monk never more darkens Kinglet's door." He stomped toward the village. "Never again will that man steal from Your people."

A half an hour later, Shane plodded into John's yard. Car sat with her pupils working on the rough slates John had provided them.

"There ya are, Slade."

"John, I need a piece of parchment."

"Parchment? But we have slate?"

"Vellum would do as well, but I must prepare a missive at once."

"A missive? To who? And who will carry this message of yars? We have no sandesmen here, my friend."

"Let me see to all the details. But it must be done at once."

"As it is the Lord's Day, I will have it for ya when ya come on the morrow to help harvest the materials needed for the next portions of waddle."

Shane nodded and moved to the log to review the work of his students.

# Chapter 40

Over three Lord's Days had passed since Slade became a ghost, doing chores around Margg's tavern while she slept or toiled elsewhere. She hadn't caught a glimpse of him once. Car—to her credit—never said his name, but she beamed with such joy it didn't matter. The girl was smitten with the man. And why shouldn't she be, Margg groaned, even as her throat went dry and a twisting started in her middle that churned until she could no longer stand straight. The Lord had cut Slade a fine and handsome form, and he was good with the girl.

The rhythmic sound of chopping wood filtered to her, and she moved with caution to look out into the yard that lay between the tavern and her shack. Slade chopped log after log. His strength had obviously returned, as he split most every piece with one swing. He wore no shirt, and the sun glinted off his bronze skin beaded with droplets of sweat. It would not be long before laying a fire would be unnecessary in the warm summer months. But still he worked to prepare.

She returned to the tavern, filled a tankard with his favorite ale, and slipped out into the yard.

He did not look at her as he laid the ax to rest on the next waiting log. "My lady," he inclined his head, took the cup, and downed a deep draft. "I thank you for your kindness."

"So whose bed have you found to share?" The sharp retort leapt from her tongue, and she regretted it before her mouth closed.

His head slipped lower as he sat the tankard on a nearby stump and raised the ax once more. "I have lain with no one since I arrived."

"You don't sleep out of doors, do you?" She wanted to sound concerned but knew her words dripped with disgust.

He shook his head. "I have slept—what little I can—at Nara's old place."

Margg turned to look off in the direction of the meager hovel—though the tavern blocked her view. "Nara's? I …"

The ax banged into the wood with a *thwack*.

Margg turned back to Slade. He took an armload of the chopped pieces and added them to the stack outside the door of his room. His room—that's how she still thought of it. Slade belonged here with Car—with her.

He walked back toward her, his shoulders and head hanging low as though he'd lost his only friend.

"Is John and his family hale?" A compulsion forced her to keep the conversation going. She wanted … she needed for him … closing her eyes, she tried to breathe—tried to think. She looked at him again.

He paused in midstride, his head tipping to the side. "Aye, quite well. He has nearly completely enclosed two of the three rooms with waddle. We will be spending the next couple of evenings scouring the forest for the last of the materials." A small smiled turned the corner of his mouth. His head was still so low she almost missed it, but it made her heart flutter. "Though in truth, I fear the forests here 'bouts have already been stripped of any useful treasures for us."

"Surely John's additions have not stripped the forest? Kinglet has much useful timber surrounding it." She bit down on her lip to stop the critical flow of words.

His smile faded, and he inclined his head still without looking at her. He reached for the ax. "Of course, my lady. How foolish of me."

The words were not a retort or an insult but were breathed with defeat. He chopped a couple more logs as she stood there. "Is there something you require of me, my lady?" His head hung lower yet. Soon it would touch his chest. "Do you wish me to leave again?"

"No!"

He startled at her abrupt command. She huffed a deep sigh. "No," she tried again more softly. "Feel free to come and go as you please. You may again use the back room."

"I will burden you no longer, my lady. Nara's place serves me in good stead."

"Car would be pleased to have you around again."

"Dear Carling sees me enough. I would not wish to keep her from providing you aid."

Margg whirled and stomped toward the tavern. "As I said, do as you please. 'Tis clear you have no regard for my wishes." She stopped inside the door and dared look back at him. He sat on one knee, his hands clasped as though in prayer. After a moment he stood, drew up the ax, and sent it hurtling into the hapless log with such force the two halves reeled away. He sat another, and it too was cleaved in half with brute force. Log after log fell before him in rapid succession.

When nothing more remained of the pile before him, he sunk the ax blade deep into the chopping stump and stomped from the yard. The scattered pieces of his wrath littered about.

"Could you not stay for me?" A single tear slipped down her cheeks and she swiped at it angrily as she returned to the kitchen.

Car toddled alone on her way back to help Margg in the tavern. Her slate held in her left hand as she wrote bumpy words with the chip of chalk in the other hand.

"Oh!" She drew up short as a figure appeared in her path. Starting at the sandaled feet of the obstacle, she scanned up over the long black straight dress to the white-haired man smiling down at her.

"God's blessings be upon you, my child."

"I'm not yar daughter," Car said as a hand went to her hip. "And why are ya wearin' a dress?"

His kind smile grew. "'Tis not a dress, young miss. 'Tis the robes of my office. I am a priest."

She considered him. "Ya don't look nothin' like the monk who comes to the village once a month. And it isn't the Lord's Day yet."

"I am here on other business this day, but I hope to attend your Lord's Day when next your monk returns."

"That's on the day after the morrow," Car said with a shrug and sidestepped the man to continue on her way.

He turned and walked beside her. "Those are some mighty fine letters you are writing there, mistress …"

Car walked a little taller, holding out the slate for him to see better. "I've been practicin'."

A small chuckle fell from the priest's lips. "Do you have a name, young one?"

She nodded.

"May I know it?"

"Momma called me Carling, but everyone calls me Car now."

"Well, Mistress Carling, I was hoping you might help me with a great kindness."

She stopped and looked up at him.

"Can you point out the person who taught you to write such fine words?"

"Oh, aye." She waved for the man to follow her and skipped the last bit toward the tavern. Slade was stomping from the woodpile toward the road just as they walked up.

"Slade, this man is come lookin' for ya. He's not wearin' a dress. He's a priest."

Shane's head rose to look at the dark-robed man. His encounter with Margg but moments ago had left his insides churning like butter in her contraption. He stared but did not see.

"So this is where you have hidden yourself away, young Lord Shane."

Shane blinked as his heart startled, and recognition dawned. "Father Bartholomew …" he sputtered.

"His name is Slade, mister priest."

The father reached down and patted the child's shoulder. "I have no doubt it is the name he gave you, but it is not the name with which he was christened. I preformed the rite over his squalling form myself."

"Ya knew Slade—or Shane—when he were a baby? Yar very old, mister priest."

"Car, run along now and see to your chores in helping Margg."

"But—"

"Now, child. The good father and I have much to discuss."

"Father? I thought he was a priest, and holy men aren't suppose to have bairns."

Shane knelt and gripped her shoulders. "It is the title given to a priest, Car. I did not say he was *my* father—I know naught of the man. Now, go and give aid to Mistress Margg, please."

# Chapter 41

Shane pushed to his feet, though his legs threatened to buckle. Car disappeared into the tavern, and he turned his attention back to the holy man before him. He fought to calm his breathing, but his constricted lungs would not allow air to enter.

"You look hale, my son."

Shane moved to steady himself, leaning against the pigpen. "What are you doing here, Father?"

"I received the request you sent," Father Bartholomew pulled the rolled bit of parchment from the pouch hung over his shoulder.

"I sent that to the holy house in Winter Bend, and I put no signature to it." Shane searched his face.

"Aye, 'tis true. I had gone to Winter Bend to seek the Lord's favor. There is much troubling news in the land. When the missive was brought before the brotherhood for discussion, I heard a familiar voice in the lines. And seeing the scrawl of the pen, I confirmed the hand of my former pupil."

"I again ask—why have you come? Who serves the king and queen in your absences from the palace?"

"I had to find you, Lord Shane."

Shane stood straight and stepped toward the priest. "I am no lord, as well you know! I cannot go back. I have no place there."

"You must return, Shane, if not to ease the queen's heart, then for Princess Milana."

"Milana? She hates me. I have ruined her union to Lord Robert."

"Princess Milana is missing."

"Father," Shane threw out his hands to encompass all of Kinglet. "Do you think I hold her here—against her will?"

Father Bartholomew shook his head in the annoyed manner he always used when Shane interrupted him. "Nay, my son. But the princess left a note when she disappeared days before her wedding to Lord Robert. She stated she had gone to seek you out that you may stand by her side as she said her vows."

"She would never—"

*Smack!*

Shane reeled from the blistering of his cheek. Before he could recapture air in his lungs, fists pounded against his chest.

"Margg!" Car yelled. "Stop! Don't hurt him."

"My child, please," the father tried to intervene.

Margg jerked from the priest's grasp. "You're a wretch! You liar!"

Shane seized both her wrists and held them fast. "Aye, of that there is no doubt. But what manner of evil have I done you this time, woman, that you assault me so?"

"'I am no nobleman.' Did you not say these words to me?"

"I spoke truth when I said such."

Margg screeched and yanked against him to break his hold. Her foot flew and he struggled to dodge the kick. "You are none other than the missing heir, his Highness Lord Shane. How much more noble can you be?"

Shane's jaw clenched, and his teeth ground together as he spoke, "I am no blood of the king nor the queen. I was found thrown out in the forest, left to die, by the witch who birthed me. Queen Mariamne took pity on me, and as the king thought he could sire no children of his own, I was raised as the heir. It was an honor I scorned and was wholly unworthy of. I tell you true, I am little more than vermin, Mistress Margaret. I did not lie to you."

His gaze shifted to the priest, "Tell her, Father. I am a man with no name."

Margg quieted by a little as the priest spoke.

"My child, Shane speaks honestly when he says no royal blood courses within him. But he is much loved by King Edgar and Queen Mariamne. They have grieved the loss of him most bitterly."

Margg's eyes glared at Shane.

"If it is still the reward you seek, I will ask if they will pay you for the trouble I have caused."

Margg shrieked and yanked free from his grip. She slammed both fists into his chest, driving him back into the railing of the pen. "I want nothing from you. *You* are nothing but a foul wretch." She whirled from him and flew into the back of the tavern.

Shane led Father Bartholomew to the meetinghouse, where they sat together on a bench discussing the state of the kingdom. He rubbed his cheek, the sting of Margg's wrath still biting through his short beard. He hadn't lied, but he hadn't really told her the truth either. Her hatred of him only grew.

He scrubbed his face of the latest guilt and tried to focus on the matter at hand. "Father, if the entire kingdom is searching for Princess Milana, why did you come seeking me? I know naught of this matter. I have been here all the days of my absence from the castle. And I say yet again, Princess Milana would not come seeking me."

"Should we not talk about your young woman first?"

Shane shook his head vehemently. "Nay, Father. She is not my—anything. Milana is our concern, and I say once more, she would not look for me."

Father Bartholomew cocked his head and considered him for a long moment before his hand rested on his shoulder. "Aye, as everyone agreed. Most did not believe the note was even in the princess' own hand. But whoever left the missive sought to bring you into the odd affair. You are apart of it, regardless of your own thoughts on the matter."

"What is it you ask of me?" Shane's shoulders slumped.

"I know not, but will you pray with me? Mayhaps God will reveal His plan for you."

Shane nodded, and the father's words of entreaty flowed with power—though Shane heard few of them. His mind filled with images of Milana, their days growing up, and his constant torment of her. She would not seek him, he was most sure. But why include him? What could he do that thousands of the king's men could not? 'This one will turn back the evil now finding a foothold in our land.' Shane quaked as Nara's words reverberated in his skull.

Was this what the holy woman had spoken about? Again he asked, *Lord, what am I supposed to do that all the king's men could not?*

"I have to go and find her." Shane's words burst from his lips of their own. It wasn't until the priest raised his head that he realized the prayer had not concluded.

A knowing smile filled the old man's face. "Then let us commission your quest before the Lord." Again he bowed his head and continued to pray.

Shane stepped from the meetinghouse to see to the matters

needing to be completed before his departure. Father Bartholomew stood in the doorway. "I may yet earn my forgiveness," Shane called out as he waved.

"Have you remembered so little of your lessons, my son? You cannot earn forgiveness."

Shane choked and concentrated on not falling. It was true then, nothing could be done to put things to right again. He tossed his head; it did not matter. His soul be damned, but he would die trying to find Milana.

Shane staggered into John's yard.

"Slade, my friend, ya are early this day."

"I have need to speak with you. And truly I pray you still call me friend when my tale is complete."

John crossed his arms and fixed a hard stare on him.

"I am leaving Kinglet Hill."

John gave no reaction.

"It has come to my knowledge that Princess Milana is missing."

It was as if John had turned to stone, for he made no movement at all.

"I go to seek her."

A single brow arched high.

Shane shifted the weight between his feet and worked at the knot in his neck. He could not meet John's gaze and contemplated the tuft of grass at his feet for a moment. "John," he swallowed down the lump threatening to strangle him. "Most men do not know me by Slade. It was the name the mother of my birth gave me. Most know me as another." He gulped for air that would not be captured. "I was raised in the castle of King Edgar and Queen Mariamne—as their son.

They call me Shane."

No gasp sounded and no mighty fist flew against him. Shane dared look up.

John continued to stare.

Shane returned to shifting his weight between his feet. *What should he say next?*

"Do you think me a dolt?"

"Nay, John, I never—"

John gave a curt nod and seized Shane's hand. "From the first day ya stepped to my door, I knew ya were a man not accustomed to using yar hands." He pried Shane's hand open and looked at the palm. "Ya knew not a wit of how to handle a tool or what to do with it. Only now after months of labor have the blisters faded and calluses formed." He let Shane's hands drop. "These are the hands of a nobleman." John walked away a few steps as he continued to reveal the truth. "Add to the hands the proper king's tongue and the ability to read—any simpleton would know the manner of man ya be, sir. Or am I to address you as His Majesty now?"

Shane shook his head and finished his tale as John listened once more without moving.

"So why come and tell me of yar departure? Do you wish me to join ya?"

"Nay, my friend. I ask a small boon. Would you, or mayhaps Matthew, keep a watch out over Mistress Margaret?"

John's chin rose and his gaze narrowed. "Margg's always managed to see fine to her own affairs. I don't think she'll be favoring me or mine sticking our nose in."

"I am sure she will not, but I fear she has grown soft to the meager aide I have provided her in the last months. I would not want my absence to cause her as much trouble as my presence."

"It will be done." John considered him for a moment more. "Wait here," he ordered. He returned a few moments later with a waterskin, a bedroll, and a cloak of rough wool. He handed them to Shane. "These are not much and not of the quality a prince would be accustomed to, but I give them to you with my continued friendship."

To refuse would be to disrespect the man, Shane knew. He inclined his head and took the offered items. "I am more than grateful, for your friendship most of all."

John's chest puffed up, and his chin rose high. "It is not often a simple tanner can say he is friends with the king's son."

# Chapter 42

Margg swiped at tears as she stormed through the back room. Seeing Slade's bed … *No not Slade—Shane. Prince Shane.* She swayed, unable to remain still as her churning feelings whipped about, yet unable to move forward. Stuck in a torrent of emotions more fierce than any winter storm, Margg fought for an even breath. *Prince Shane, heir to the throne. He may not be the true son of the king, but surely he had more standing than she. Prince—*She couldn't get past the title. *It explains much. Why would a highborn prince find love with the likes of a lowly tavern maid such as I?*

The thought rocked her until she thought she might collapse on the bed—his bed. He could never love her—would never consider a woman like her worthy of his affections. Fresh tears washed her face. Her throat burned from her attempts to swallow them. "Rid your thoughts of him, Margg," she scolded herself. "He leaves to find the princess and rejoin life at the castle. You shall never see him after today." Sobs surged up through her and tumbled out, shaking her body with their force. *He could never love me.*

"Please do not cry, Carling." Shane knelt on one knee before the child and wiped a tear from her cheek. "I will return for you."

"Momma said the same thing of Da, but I never saw him."

"You know my life is in God's hands?"

The girl nodded through a hiccupped sniffle.

"I have prayed, Father Bartholomew has prayed, now you must pray too. Pray God will let me keep my word to you and return quickly." He cupped her chin and raised her face until their eyes met. "Know this, I leave my heart here with you, sweet girl. I love you ever so much, I think I will burst from it." He kissed her forehead.

Car pulled from his grasp and slid her arms around his neck, burying her tears in his collar. "I love you too."

The child ran off, and Shane moved to the chopping stump. Plopping down, he stared at the back door.

*Lord, what am I to do? My heart is bound to Margaret.* His head hung low as he stared at the dirt between his feet. *I love her.* The confession made his heart tumble. He lifted his head with great difficultly and dared look toward the door that would lead him to the one thing he desired more than anything in all his life. Again his head dropped. *Lord, it is likely I will not survive this mission. My wasted days have left me bereft of any sizable skill with the sword.* He swallowed the clump of tears rising in his throat. *Is it best that the words are never spoken? Would it be better for her? Would I save her unwanted pain when I never return?*

The weight of his heart threatened to pull him down into the very earth never to be heard from again. Could he leave and never tell her how he felt? Would she welcome his confession of love or scorn him for a loathsome wretch without two coins to rub together. Shane struggled to his feet and trudged toward the door. *I will never have anything to provide for her or Carling. Best make my leave and allow them to make a better life without me.*

Shane eased into the empty tavern. Margg glared at him from

where she cleaned a table. "I would speak with you."

"Speak."

"I am leaving to join in the search for Princess Milana."

She hurled a tankard—still with a little ale in it—at him with a grunt.

He ducked and wiped the drops from his tunic as it rolled back to his feet after hitting the wall. He picked it up and set it on the bar. "I have only a few words, and then I will be out from under foot, Lady Margaret."

She flung another cup at him, "Don't call me that!" She raised a wooden trencher to throw next. "Fine, leave—you never wanted to be here. This place has always been beneath you. Daily I have seen the disdain on your ugly face."

Shane clenched his fists but kept his voice flat. "'Tis not truth, as well you know."

The trencher flew, hit the wall behind him, and snapped in half. "What do you want? My blessings?"

"I would most heartedly accept blessings from your lips, Miss Margg." He said in a pleading tone. "But I did not come seeking any more from you. I came to tell you I will return when the princess has been found."

She snorted, "You needn't worry yourself."

"Well, if it is all the same to you, Miss Margg, I will cover you daily in prayer and return when I may to repay the debt I still owe."

She paused and stared at him through slits that hid her sparkling hazel eyes. When he did not say more and did not leave, one fist landed on her hip, and her toes took up an annoyed rhythm against the reed-covered floor.

Shane closed his eyes and fought the urge to charge across the room, capture Margg up in his arms, and kiss her soundly. He surely might die in this quest never tasting of those sweet lips. His stomach knotted at the injustice.

She cleared her throat. "You have voiced your promises—for all their good. Is there yet more you require?"

Shane bowed his head and groaned, "Might I be allowed to take my sword?"

Her angry yelp made him duck the item he figured she threw next, but nothing hurled passed him. "Get out! You and your detestable weapon."

Sleep would not come. Shane wrapped John's cloak more tightly about him. Not the heavy wool nor the bright fire could keep the tremor within him at bay. He leaned back his head and let his mind wander. He vaguely recalled the ride on the peddler's wagon that had brought him to Kinglet taking about three days from the city below the castle mount. On foot it would take him a good deal longer. Mayhaps five days.

He had risen well before the sun and walked all day and well past it setting without finding sight of another soul. He rolled his neck.

*Snap.*

Shane searched the surrounding darkness. Someone or something followed him—he'd felt it all day. Nothing moved among the shadows.

He laid back his head once more and begged sleep to come. *I should have stayed to the road. Surely I would have met someone, mayhaps even secured transport.* He scolded himself yet again, but he had thought a direct route through the forest would have brought him to Sheepshire, or Far Bend in good order.

*Snap. Pop. Scratch.*

Shane shot to his feet. His hand went to the hilt of his sword.

Shuffling in the underbrush came from many different directions —but whatever made them stayed beyond the reach of his fire's light.

Shane drew his weapon and walked the perimeter around his camp. The forest fell silent. He made several circuits, but not another sound filled the evening except his own steps. He made his way back to the log he leaned against earlier. He settled, wrapped tight in John's cloak, pulling the hood to cover his face, and he tried to sleep.

He dared one last glance. Shane blinked and stared harder. Eyes—human eyes stared back at him from the edge of the light. *Lord, protect me.*

# Chapter 43

Shane rolled his shoulders and stretched his back as he sat on a rotten log at the edge of a clearing. Now midday on the Lord's Day, he still saw no signs of any habitation. Mayhaps he had passed them as he wound through the dense forest with large impassible areas of thick undergrowth.

His head shot up. Gooseflesh rose on his arms. Still Shane believed he was being followed. He saw no one, but he needed to know. He moved further into the shadows of the tree line.

*Snap. Crunch.* Surely those had to be human steps—steps that belonged to the eyes he had seen last night. Eyes that now haunted his waking hours. *Crunch.* This was no gentle forest creature.

A stumbled step was followed by a muttered curse.

Shane drew his sword, slow and silent. He moved, pressing his back against the nearest tree, waiting for the man to draw within reach.

The sounds ceased. Whoever followed him must have stopped.

Shane held his breath, his sword at the ready.

*Snap.* A twig beside him broke. He jumped out and leveled his sword at the man's throat.

The intruder froze without a sound.

Shane stared at his shadow's tall, dark leather boots, scanned up the baggy breeches to the closed short cloak and ended at the bowed, hood-covered head. He pressed the sword until it touched flesh.

Hands rose in surrender.

Light hit a scar on the right palm that ran down the side of the wrist. He clenched his teeth and used the sword tip to push the hood off. He sprang back. "Fie, Margg! By all the saints in heaven, I nearly ran you through, woman. What, by all that is holy, are you doing out here!"

"I came to assure you kept your promise …" She swallowed, but it did not chase the tremor from her words. "I can't bear to see Car hurt again."

Shane paced a few steps and threw his arms out in the air. His feet stomped through the undergrowth, and his words ground through his teeth. "Have I *ever* broken a promise to that dear child?" He marched back toward her and used his sword to point, though it remained several inches from touching her. "And speak truly, woman, have I ever broken a promise spoken to you?"

She shook her head, and it rose so she could glare at him. "Nay, but you have no love for me—that has always been clear."

"Arrrgh!" Shane rammed the sword back in the sheath and raked his hands through his hair. "Like you ever spared me even a kind word, woman. I have done naught to warrant your venom, and I hold no ill at all toward you. You saved my life."

"But you look at me with resentment and it only turned to disgust when you returned from Nara's that day. I know she told you the manner of woman I am."

Shane threw up his hands. "I have not one wit of a notion of what you are blathering on about. Nara voiced no ill against you and shared in no gossipmongering with me, Margg."

"Don't you lie to me again!" She pointed her finger. "You know what I did. It shows on your face, clear as the berries on that bush."

Shane's fists clenched tight until his nails bit into his palms. "I know naught of anything you have done other than care for a man not to your liking."

"Must I speak the words?"

"Aye. Say them now that I may at last discern what I am accused of knowing."

"I am a murderess!"

Shane staggered back several steps and braced himself on a tree. "What?" The word choked from his throat. "Who did you kill?"

Her head dropped and her arms wrapped around her. "My husband, Jarman. He beat me often. One day I woke covered in blood, and I never saw him again." Her words trembled over her lips as unshed tears shook her body.

Shane charged her and seized both her upper arms in a firm grasp. "Is this what you believe?" He shook her when she did not respond.

She looked up, tears pooled in her eyes. "Aye. 'Tis true."

He shook her again and tightened his hold until she winced. "Now you listen to me, Margaret of the Hart and Spoon, and you listen well. You never laid a hand on your foul man. Nara found you in that pool of blood—your blood and that of your unborn babe. Her and Willham carried you to your home where she and Hannah and a handful of other town women tended you for days. You nearly died. It was Nara's Willham who took your Jarman into the woods and saw justice done. He died rightly for his crimes, but Willham feared what would happen when others learned of his deed. There is no blood on your hands, Margaret."

Tears spilled down her cheeks. "Truly, I didn't kill him?"

"Nay."

She trembled. "I didn't murder, but I deprived Car of her father."

"Naught of this was your doing. Willham acted right in his handling of Jarman. Knowing what I do of the townsfolk of Kinglet, I think they would have touted him a hero, but he made his choice to leave. No blame rests on you."

"But there was a change in you when you returned from Nara's that day. I saw it."

"The words the dear woman said over me blessed me to my core and rattled my insides." He stared at her. Her hazel eyes were dark like the leaves around them. "If you saw any change in me toward you," he struggled past the longings he felt. "You saw a man fighting his desire to comfort a woman who had seen far too much of grief—while she yet remains pricklier than a hedgehog. I truly hold no ill—"

Margaret's lips pressed to his as she pushed against his hold and rose up on her toes.

Shane broke the touch and stared at her for the beat of a heart before he captured her lips again. His hand released an arm, and it wound into her plated hair to deepen the passion their lips shared. She tasted sweeter than he'd dreamed. His other hand encircled her waist and forced her body against his.

She answered his need by opening her mouth to him and burying her fingers in his hair.

Shane lifted her feet off the ground, ready to feast upon her.

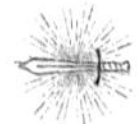

Shane's grip broke, and he dropped her back to her feet. He pushed her away, staggered several steps, and stood with his back to her, his arm braced against a tree as he panted for breath. Margg missed his warmth. She had been so wrong about the man. What she thought was disdain had been passion—as deep as her own.

She took a step toward him. She would be his.

He raised the flat of his palm to stop her. "Nay." He shook his head and gulped air. "Nay, I will not."

"But—"

He stood straight, fists clenched, muscles stretched taunt under his tunic. "Nay. I will not dishonor another woman! Never again will I treat a woman with such disrespect—especially you. Never you, Margaret."

He stepped further from her, crossed his arms against the tree, and leaned his head against them. "You need to return home, Margaret."

"You want me to go back? Alone? Through the woods in the coming night?"

"What of the tavern?" He spun and closed the distance between them. But his breaths quickened again and he stepped away. "What of Car? Who cares for her?"

"Matthew sees to the tavern. Told him I'd split the profits with him, and his father agreed to spare him. Car is with the priest. He did well in caring for you?"

Shane nodded, his fingers again forced through his hair.

Margg noted little remained of the warrior's knot as he turned from her again.

"I fear for your safety, Margaret. If anything were to happen to you …" He swallowed hard. "I may not be worthy of you, but I could not survive knowing you no longer took breath on God's earth."

"You are the chosen son of the king of all Veronia. I am a widowed tavern owner."

"You know well I have no name and no standing of my own. I have nothing to offer you."

"Yet I desire no other."

Shane leapt from her as she tried to lay her hand on his arm. His eyes closed as he fought for a steady breath with clenched fists.

"Should I live through this quest, and you still feel thus, I will seek your hand proper, Margaret."

"I accept. Now let us continue. Where do we head?"

Shane stared at her slack jawed and limp of arm.

"Well, don't stand there gaping at me, future husband. Where do we head?"

Shane pointed over the log she had seen him sitting on earlier.

She moved in the direction he indicated, and he fell into step behind her.

"I hoped to come to Far Bend or Sheepshire, and prayed God would—"

Margg whirled, and he stepped out of her way as she went back out into the clearing. Shielding her eyes, she found the sun not long into its descent. She pointed in a new direction and started walking. "This way, warrior. Continue there, and we'll find ourselves knee deep in Bottom's End Bog."

"Margaret," he raced after her. "I don't think—"

"Well, this is clear as always." She turned her head with a wicked smile. "If we left the thinking to you, I would be traipsing through the forest alone at night heartbroken to the point of taking my last breath. Let me do the thinking for a spell and we'll have this princess found and be on our way to the altar before the summer."

Shane's steps stumbled in the leaf litter. "Umm …"

"Come," she reached out her hand to him. "Together?" Hope filled her plea. His warm callused hand laced through her fingers and held tight.

As the sun painted the sky with flaming orange, they came out into a small clearing no more than a rod across. "We will sleep here."

Margaret turned and considered the space. She shrugged and set about collecting stones and forming a fire pit.

No words had passed between them as they walked through the afternoon. What did one say to a woman who had given every indication of hatred one moment, only to kiss him so soundly in the next, he nearly alighted in flames at the passion. Then she accepted a request for her hand that was never in fact spoken. He looked down at the hand she had held all day, now chilled from the absence of her touch. His head swam, and his thoughts puddled in an incoherent tangle. "I will collect some wood."

"Nay," Margaret stopped him and took off her cloak, revealing a bow and quiver slung across her body. "Scare us up some food, husband." She handed him the weapons, and their hands brushed. Heat surged up his arm and started his heart racing once more.

Leaving behind John's heavy cloak and the bedroll, Shane turned to the woods and prayed he would find a cold stream along the way.

When Shane returned, he carried two hares. As Margg dressed them, Shane still did not speak. He paced around the edge of the tiny area, as if looking for danger—but she worried he feared what was within their camp more than anything that might be lurking in the darkness beyond.

She'd acted impulsively when she kissed him earlier. So many times she'd wanted to kiss him but never dared. When she learned the truth—she had not murdered her husband—the look in Shane's eyes spoke of a depth of concern she never hoped possible. As if drawn by some unseen power between them, she'd pressed her lips to his.

Her heart lurched now remembering when he pulled away with such speed, but then—he captured her in his arms and kissed her with such hunger and passion she feared she would faint away. But again he fled from her.

Margg smiled as she laid the prepared hares over the fire. He respected her more then she knew. He was a man of honor. A man she loved more now than even at midday when she was discovered.

When the meat was done, she set them aside to cool a bit. "Will you come and eat, husband."

"No vows have been spoken, Lady Margaret." He circled around once more before sitting cross-legged a short distance from her.

"I trust they will be," she whispered.

"What can I give you?"

"Your love."

"You already have that."

"Then what more is there to say?"

He shook his head. "The rite must be performed by a priest. This is not a matter I will commit without the blessings of God Almighty."

She handed him a hare. "Then we shall find one in Sheepshire. Now eat."

Shane bowed his head. "After the blessing."

She lowered the roasted meat from her lips and waited for him.

"Lord God, I beseech You … bless this food … and on behalf of Princess Milana, protect her and comfort her wherever she may be." His thoughts seemed jumbled, as if he couldn't find the words he wished "Give her … strength to endure … grant those who search for her speed." He gulped air. "Let this food nourish our bodies and provide us strength in the coming days. Bless the efforts of those who search for the princess. Return her home with all due haste, Father."

Margaret caught him peeking at her when he paused. His eyes quickly closed again. "I also ask You to cover Carling with Your mighty hand … calm her tender heart. Let Your peace wash over her

even as we pray. Finally, Lord, I beg of You, protect Lady Margaret …
She has chosen to join me … on this quest, and my heart is consumed
… by fear, my Lord. Wrap her ever in Your mighty hands … shield
her from all harm. Amen."

"Amen," Margg whispered.

He took his meat and ate. "Thank you."

She smiled. "Might I ask you a question?"

He nodded.

"Why did you not pray for your own safety and success?"

"I fear God would strike me for asking after my own needs. I am a
sinner of the blackest heart. But in this quest, I had hoped to earn
some measure of forgiveness."

"You can't *earn* forgiveness."

A groan slipped past his lips. "As Father Bartholomew has
informed me. I am a man cursed then. A man unfit to be your
husband."

The meat dropped to her lap. "Now, Shane, I know little of the
Holy Words, but this I do know. Forgiveness is not earned. It is a gift
from the Most High. You but accept it."

Shane's head hung, "You know naught of the man I have been."

"I wouldn't think it mattered. If God can't forgive all evil deeds of
men, where is the hope in His resurrection?"

He looked at her for a long time, and a slim smile tugged at his
lips. "Thank you. I pray your words are true." He pointed to the items
he had dropped earlier. "Take the roll and the large cloak and get some
rest. We will start out before first light.

"We could share them …"

"Do not tempt me past what I am able to bear, Margaret. I have
made a vow to you before God. Do not see me add to my guilt any
shame against you."

They curled into their separate cloaks and drifted off to sleep.

*Shane!*

He bolted to his feet from a deep sleep. The fire was but coals—and Margaret was nowhere to be seen.

# Chapter 44

"Shane."

"Help. Shane I'm here. Help me."

"Shane, please."

Screams and shouts came from every direction, but none truly sounded like Margaret. "Lord, help me. You woke me to protect her. Lord, *please*."

A guttural curse found his ears and he raced toward it. Shane ran full speed through the brush, branches slapping his face. He tripped over roots straining to hear her again.

Another curse and a struggle; and he was nearly to her.

He burst through the brush and ran-through the first black form. It bellowed and crumpled to the ground. Freeing his blade, Shane removed the head of another. A third released its hold on Margaret's arm and lunged. Black nails sharp as hawk's claws lashed out. Shane blocked the first few swipes as the shriveled remains of the human consumed by evil screeched in frustration. Another lunge and the creature was relieved of a hand. As it bellowed in pain, Shane ran it through, and the last one scurried back into the night.

Shane steadied Margaret in his left arm, keeping his sword at the ready as he hurried them back to the camp. He sat her on the bedroll and loaded the fire with as much wood as the stone ring would hold.

When the flames leapt high, he went back to Margaret—kneeling before her.

"Where did they touch you?"

Her eyes rose to meet him. They were large, and the reflection of the flames danced in their watery depths as she stared.

He cradled her face. "Margaret, speak to me. Tell me where they touched you?"

"What were they?"

"The horde. Now, where did they touch you?"

"The horde? They don't exist except in mothers' tales to frighten their children into behaving."

"You forget I was raised by the woman who found the way to defeat the horde and their evil. Queen Mariamne was attacked on the way to her new home with King Edgar. She told the royal healer Carrington how to cure the infections. This evil is no child's nightmare—it is a real danger. Margaret, where did they touch you?"

"I'm not hurt …"

Shane gripped her shoulders and shook her soundly. "Tell me where they touched you!"

She flinched at his tone and volume but pointed toward her feet. "Two held my ankles."

He searched each in the light of the leaping flames. "No damage to the leather. Where else?"

She continued to stare at him.

"Tell me."

She lifted her arms and showed him where their hands had gripped her above her elbows.

Shane pushed up her left sleeve and found nothing. He turned her toward the light and noted the tear in her right sleeve. He rent the fabric, making it larger, and groaned.

"What? What have you found?" Margaret tried to retrieve her arm.

"Be still. There is a scratch. The poison has begun to spread. Two tendrils already snake toward your shoulder."

"Poison?" Her movements grew frantic.

Shane moved but did not release her. "Do not fear. I know what must be done. I will not allow this sickness to overtake you." He cradled her face in one hand, and drew closer until only a breath separated their lips. "Trust me, beloved. I will see you whole."

She blinked and swallowed. "Poison?" Her eyes widened, and her breath came in shallow puffs. "Those shriveled-up things—those black screeching bodies—they were human? They infected me? I'm going to turn into one of them?"

He held her firm as she thrashed in panic. "You will never become one of the horde." He removed the dagger from her waist and stuck the blade in the hottest part of the fire. "The puncture is small. 'Twill be easy to rid you of it."

Her gaze shifted from him to the dagger and back. She struggling to get free. She started shaking her head. "No."

Shane took her other arm, holding her firm. He spoke with soft words. "Margaret, hear me. It will be quick. A single touch of the blade."

She squirmed and fought to free herself.

"Let me do this. If you do not, the poison will overtake you, and I will lose you to the evil. You will become one of them."

She became stone in his hands.

"If the queen spoke true, the burning is not terrible. It kills the spawn within but leaves the host untouched and without scar." He considered her carefully. "Will you allow me to do this to save you, please?"

Shane's heart held still, but at last she offered him a single nod. He inclined his head as well and loosened his grip. She didn't jerk away, and he released her.

He removed the short cape he wore and placed it backwards over her so the hood covered her face. Her hands rose to remove it, but he captured them and held them still. Kissing them each in turn, he whispered. "Nay, beloved. The spawn is released in the burning, and it can enter your lungs and re-infest you. We could never free you of it then."

Her hands dropped, and she remained unmoving.

Shane cut a corner from John's cloak that she still wore, wet it and tied it around his nose and mouth. He drew the white-hot blade from the fire and pressed it to her arm.

Margaret yelped, but the burning was quickly complete, and Shane removed the cloth from his face and pressed the coolness against her skin. "'Tis done, my love."

She removed the hood and buried her face in Shane's chest.

He wrapped her in his arms and held her as she drifted off to sleep and through the remainder of the night.

As dawn light crept into the sky, he tried to leave her sleeping as he tended the fire. The need to circle their clearing looking for danger and reciting prayers also pulled at him. He remembered the stories of Sir Halton praying as he walked circuits around Mariamne and his men. The queen had told of the holy light that had surrounded them because of those prayers.

Every time he tried to leave, however, Margaret clung tighter and snuggled closer. He prayed for her continued safety trapped in her embrace and begged God to cool the fire burning within from her nearness.

She woke well rested and hale with the sun.

Shane prayed for strength and alertness after two nights with little rest. His thoughts rolled and pitched like a ship tossed in a storm. Where else had the horde returned? Where they again under the thumb of the Black Knight? How could he face those people he had left behind? How would Princess Milana feel should he be the one to rescue her? Would she even come with him? Would he find redemption or more shame? Could he keep Margaret safe?

His stomach tumbled as the swells of anxiety grew, and he struggled to put one foot in front of the other. But Margaret strolled off, and he was forced to keep pace.

# *Chapter 45*

As the sun descended toward the western horizon, Sheepshire appeared in flashes between the trees. For the first time, Shane took the lead. He made sure Margaret remained within reach. He wanted her near but not in harm's way. *Lord, watch over her.*

The local inn hummed with noise, which spilled out the doors and tumbled down the street. "It may be safer for you to remain here at the Sheep's Inn than to continue with me."

She propped her fist on her hip and stopped. Her mouth opened ready for a retort. Her gaze locked with his.

She nodded and took a step forward as her arm swung free of its perch. "As you wish," she huffed. "I will do as you think best, husband."

Shane fought to keep his feet moving smoothly beneath him.

They entered to a cacophony of voices. Shane noted the many men clad in royal guard tunics. These were men he knew—had trained with. A familiar laugh drew his attention. Snatching up Margaret's hand, he pulled her to the far side of the room.

"Ethan, my brother. Oh, good it is to see you," Shane called out over the ruckus.

Ethan, son of King Edgar's thane and his childhood friend, turned slowly on his heel to face him. A scowl marred his face.

Shane withdrew his arm offered in greeting, too late remembering his current status. He bowed deep at the waist. "Forgive me, my lord. I know not my proper place." Shane turned to leave.

"So it is the wayward imposter heir, come to seek his glory in the search for the missing princess."

"I seek no honor nor fame. I only pray Princess Milana may be returned home safe and in all due haste. I pray you find her soon."

"So you do not intend to help?" Ethan's voice was incredulous.

"I will do all to find her." Shane glanced around the room. An odd sensation strummed his heart to a furious beat. "With so many of the king's guard under your leadership, who protects King Edgar and Queen Mariamne?"

Ethan scoffed at him, "Protects the king and queen? They are walled up in the impenetrable castle. The castle has never fallen."

"It near did the year I was born—in an attack by the horde."

A full laugh rumbled from Ethan now. "The horde was vanquished in that battle and the Black Knight run far from Veronia."

"The horde has returned."

Laughter—ignited by Ethan—spread throughout the inn until it roared like a wildfire.

Shane stood straighter and looked Ethan directly in the eyes. "Four attacked us this very morning before the sunrise." He waved his hand out toward Margaret, and Ethan's gaze shifted to her.

"And who is this wench? Another of your conquests?"

Shane stepped forward and words ground through his clenched teeth. "You will not insult Lady Margaret. I deserve your ire, but she has done naught to warrant your shameful behavior."

"Lady?" Ethan looked about him with a smirk, and many around called out crude comments to, and about, her. "I hardly think her a lady dressed in men's breeches."

Shane pulled her closer.

"Well, I believe you would know best whether my behavior is shameful or not. You were the king of all such behavior as I remember."

Shane tightened his grip on Margaret's hand and moved her toward the door.

"That's right, you spoiled boy. You never stood and fought a good fight in your life. Run off now."

Shane turned on him. "I have implored the Almighty to redeem me of my former ways. I am not the man I once was, old friend. I am appalled to see you took up the rogue's call in my absence. Turn now. Do not walk the path I once did. It will destroy your soul."

They slipped back out into the night in the wake of the laughter that filled the inn beyond capacity.

Shane drew Margaret close pressing his forehead against hers. "Forgive them, I beg you. They are good men—far better than me. Their shameful behavior is a reflection on me and not you. I sore regret that it has spilled over upon your fine character."

She shrugged. "'Tis not like I have never heard such things said about me."

Shane dared lay his hand upon her cheek. "Well, it shall never be said again, lest the man wish to see his throat slit."

She laid her hand over his and smiled at him. "Forget their words. I would rather have a husband who does not believe any truth in them at my side than my honor fought over." She removed his hand and laced her fingers with his. "Now, what are we to do?"

Shane started walking. "Have you any coin?"

"A little."

"Mayhaps it will be enough to purchase the use of a horse. We have at least a full day's walk to the castle. I know the horde is there. I feel it deep within me. We need to hurry or all will be lost."

"Master Shane," a youthful voice greeted them in the stables. "Didn't think we would ever see you again."

"Squire, might there be a horse for sale or even rent here in Sheepshire?"

The young man's chin rose, and a flash of something colored his face, but it vanished before Shane could name it. "All the horses belong to the king's guard."

"A mule? Plow horses and a wagon? Anything?"

The lad shook his head.

"We have a little coin."

"It does not change the ownership of the mounts housed here, Sire."

"I am a man of lower birth than you, sir, please only call me Shane."

The youth smiled and turned to one of the stalls, leading out a large blond warhorse. "Here, take this one, Shane. Could carry you both."

"I will not take Lord Ethan's mount."

"But you seem most insistent to be on your way. I won't tell a soul. Here, take him."

Shane raised his hands and backed toward the door. "I will not add thieving to my long list of sins."

The lad's voice dropped, and words dripped with hatred. "You could honey and feather me and take him. 'Tis not like you haven't done it before."

Realization dawned, and Shane gasped. "Rand. Oh, I do remember the evil I did you, lad. Glad I am to see you elevated to squire and are stable hand no longer. Mayhaps, God willing, you will find it in your heart to forgive an arrogant reprobate for his cruel behavior, for I sore regret every moment of it."

Rand rocked back on his heels as if Shane had struck him. His jaw hung limp.

Shane bowed. "Forgive me, Rand, for all I have done. I call God's great blessing upon you." He turned and led Margaret out of the stables.

Looking toward the rising moon, he asked, "How fair you?"

"Well, husband."

"I intend to walk until I reach the castle."

"Then I intend to walk at your side."

He turned to her in wonder. "How is it God has chosen such a fine woman to love such a lowly sinner?"

She slipped her arm in his with a gentle smile. "'Tis God's good favor to show love to His children and give them every good thing. Then again, mayhaps you are merely my gift from my Heavenly Father."

He could not find the words to respond. The storm of doubt whipped into a gale force, and he feared he would never find redemption in the days to come. Mayhaps it would be better to die in battle with the horde than face all who knew him and remember his ill deeds toward them. Had he not just experienced their bitterness of him?

Margaret tugged on his arm until his feet started moving. "Come, husband. You have a castle—and a princess—to save."

*Could it be so easy?*

# *Chapter 46*

As the sun warmed their backs in the early evening of the next day, Shane and Margaret crept out onto the last rise overlooking the wide valley below. They lay on their bellies and looked toward the castle mount.

Margaret gasped and gripped his forearm with a fierceness that caused his fingers to tingle. "What are we to do? There are so many."

A ring of the horde encircled the castle mount. Their black shriveled forms stood in disorganized lines three deep.

"Indeed, my brother, what do you intend to do?"

Shane's head snapped around at the familiar voice on his other side to find Ethan lying with them.

"What…?" Words fled from Shane's lips like a deer from a hunter's arrow.

Ethan's hand rested on his shoulder, and a slim smile turned his lips. "Forgive me, brother. I had to know it was true."

Still no words came to Shane's tongue.

Ethan waved him to follow as he crawled back behind an outcrop of large boulders out of sight.

Shane looked back toward Margaret on his far side and stared at her for a long moment, before he followed. When they rounded the rocks and stood, Shane came face to face with the entire royal guard.

Ethan threw out his hand, and Shane took it without conscious thought. Ethan grasped his forearm and pulled Shane into a tight embrace. "I praise God to know you have truly chosen to follow Him, my brother." Ethan released him with a thump on the back. His familiar smile spread across his face. "I am sorry for my behavior, but I had to know. I heard you were changed, but I admit I did not believe you had it in you to alter your course so profoundly."

Shane continued to stare.

"You could not be provoked to defend your own pride. You could not be goaded into an argument. You could not be enticed to steal even when you had great need." Ethan inclined his head toward Margaret. "But you fought for the honor of a lady."

Ethan bowed deep. "Forgive my men and me, my lady. We truly meant you no disrespect and do not besmirch your honor."

She looked to Shane and then back to Ethan. "Think no more of it, my lord."

Ethan straightened, offering her a gentle incline of his head. "Please, call me Ethan. We are all friends here."

Turning his attention once more toward Shane, Ethan crossed his arms. "So what are you going to do about the horde, and how can we assist you?"

Shane tried to catch his scattered thoughts, but it was like snatching a fly in mid-flight. He looked at those assembled with his old friend. "You are the royal guard. Should you not come up with the plan?"

Ethan shook his head and moved to a flat rock nearby. He sat and invited Shane to join him.

Shane now shook his head. "We have walked all night and day. Lady Margaret is exhausted and in need of sustenance. I must see—"

Ethan waved over a muscled young knight, and Shane recognized him immediately. "Oswin, see Lady Margaret is provided with a comfortable place to rest and as much food and water as she requires."

"Oswin," Shane faltered, remembering the humiliation he heaped on the man in the training corral. "Forgive—"

Oswin raised his hand. "'Tis done, my friend. Think no more on the matter. I assure you your lady will be well cared for, and I will protect her with my life."

"We all will," the men nearest the conversation echoed as though one man. They bowed to her, and Shane nodded that she could follow Oswin.

"She is a beauty," Ethan said as she disappeared around another bend.

"She believes God has called us to marry." Shane shook his head. "I still fear I am no good for her."

Ethan again offered the space on the rock next to him for Shane to sit. "Just hearing you say such tells me you are the man she needs. You will never take her love and think nothing of it. Again I say, you are not the man you were, my friend."

Shane slumped to the rock and leaned forward, resting his forearms on his thighs. "You do not know the power your friendship has on my spirit."

Ethan's slap on the back almost propelled his weary body off the rock. "Sight of you has restored my spirit as well. Now what do you wish us to do about the horde?"

Shane's head hung low, shaking just above his hands. "I am a man of no standing, Ethan. And insufficient in my training—as well you know. I will do as you command."

"Nay, it must be you."

Shane's head jolted up. His mouth opened, but he was given no time to protest.

"Do you think it a mere coincidence to be found at such a time as this? My men and I have traveled the woods between the castle mount and Sheepshire at all hours of the day and night and never seen a hint of the enspelled ones. Yet you, Shane were attacked as you came to lend aid in the hunt for Princess Milana."

"We know more followed us throughout the night, waiting for us to stop or for our vigilance to falter. But in truth, Margaret was attacked—not I."

Ethan cleared his throat. "You could have easily defeated them. But they took your love—for in putting her life in danger—they would prevent you from fulfilling your God-ordained destiny."

Shane continued to stare.

Ethan pointed in the direction of the castle mount. "Even if I had seen one of the horde, I would never have concluded they had laid siege to the castle. But when you spoke the words, I knew the utter truth of them. This is your battle to win, Shane."

"If you believed me, why did you tarry? You should have arrived long before us as we were on foot and you astride your mighty war horses."

"We used the time to send word in every direction of the kingdom for all our fighting men to return to the castle valley and await instructions." Ethan waved out a hand to a mule among the grazing warhorses, four crates with wide slits were strapped to its sides. "We have carrier birds to deliver your orders. I but need know what missive to strap to their legs."

Again Shane's head hung. "I know not."

Ethan's hand lay on his back. "God has already given you the answer, my brother. You have but to speak the words and it will be done."

He closed his eyes, clasped his hands that hung between his knees, searching for the answer. *Lord, Your servant Nara spoke a destiny over me. Now here Ethan too says it is my destiny to rid our kingdom of this horde. But I cannot do it, Lord. I have not the wisdom nor the skill to see Your will be done. Lord, I beg You, let this pass to another more worthy.*

The clink of tack on the grazing horses danced on his ears. The swish of men's boots through the tall grass clumps sprouting up amongst the rocks added to its cadence. Hushed voices added rich harmony. A band of crickets hiding in the dark cracks joined the symphony.

Shane's breaths slowed as the music around him caressed his weary spirit. His heartbeat, deep and steady, became the bass. He never wanted to lose this peace. Here he could thrive—but in the turmoil of the moment around him, he could be the cause of great ruin. Here he could breathe and never fail. And he knew, *God is here.*

*Lord, help us.*

A vision came. The castle valley lay before him. The sun painted the eastern sky with pinks and oranges. The horde stood in neat rows, black swords raised for battle. And surrounding them was a single ring of Veronian Knights—filled with God's holy light.

The revelation faded, and Shane propelled to his feet. "Holy light."

Ethan stood beside him. "Yes, the horde are no match for it, but how do we assure they are all vanquished?"

No trace of the weariness from but moments before remained. Shane's heart beat a strong and sure tempo. "We surround them at daybreak with every man who carries the Spirit within him. There will be no escape."

# Chapter 47

"But I cannot go with you," Shane protested yet again though in hushed tones.

Ethan seized hold of his arm and pulled him away from the other men. "*You* received the vision of how we are to vanquish this enemy. *You* gave the instructions that were sent to each of the surrounding villages to share with the men gathered there. *You* must lead us, brother. The Lord Himself has ordained it."

Shane shifted the weight back and forth on his feet. He turned and took two steps away, raking both hands through his hair. "I do not possess the light," he confessed.

"Of course you do."

He turned to look Ethan in the eyes. "No, I do not. I never have."

"You speak of another time—a time before you surrendered fully to His will. But now—"

"I do not possess—"

Ethan stepped nose to nose with him. "When was the last time you attempted to call it forth?"

Shane's gaze wandered as he scoured his memories.

"See! It is as I said. Now—try."

Shane opened his mouth.

"Try it Shane, or so help me, I will knock you senseless."

Mirth tugged at the corner of Shane's lips at the thought of the many times the two of them had wrangled together as lads. Ethan never took him down, being that Shane had been the heir, but now—now Shane knew many things were different.

Shane turned his back on his friend and drew his sword. He closed his eyes and tried to steady his erratic breathing. *How did one even call up the Light of God?*

"Invite Him to fight for you," Ethan whispered behind him. "Have faith that He is with you—within you. He will never fail you."

Shane did as instructed. A brilliant glow filled Shane's blade as Ethan's hand pummeled his back. "See, you are not the man you once were. Now you are a servant of the Most High."

Shane turned and gazed at his friend as wonder and gratitude flooded his heart like a swollen river after a heavy rain.

"Well, do not just stand there with a fool's grin on your face. There is a battle to be won, and we have to get to our position before the sun rises." Ethan's gaze shifted to the skyline. "Even now the sky colors with dawn. Make haste, man." He strode away with brisk steps.

"Thank You, Lord," Shane whispered as he sheathed his weapon. "Thank You for allowing one such as I to be counted among the number of men who fight for Your glory and honor this day."

The camp hummed with activity as Margg stirred from her slumber. She stretched and worked at the knots held tight in every muscle. Never had she been so sore or so tired. She watched as Shane and the blond man called Ethan exchanged heated words before Ethan ushered Shane away from the others.

Ethan returned with purposeful strides a few moments later. "Prepare to take your places, men. I lead my men to secure the area around the town, closest to the road up to the castle. We are to meet with men from Hill Crest who cover south of the mount."

He turned to a slender man with unruly brown locks. "Gamel leads his men directly at the foot of this rise to join with us."

Shane returned at that moment, a look of awe on his face unlike anything Margg had ever seen. "Gamel's men will span the distance between us and Shane and his men. Shane takes up the span along the royal hunting grounds at the foot of the Kestron Ridge. They will be joined on the east by men from Crooks' Bend." Ethan turned and waved Shane forward. "Give us the word, brother."

Shane looked at each man gathered around him, and bowed his head. "You, gathered here, know me. You know well the man I once was and the damage I left in my wake. I do not stand before you as a leader, a knight, or a lord, but as a mere man who wishes only two things: to follow the will of my Lord and Savior, and to rid the land of the evil standing at our door."

"Huzzah!" the men shouted, startling Margg as she sat behind them listening.

Through the gaps between those gathered around, she could see Shane smile. "Huzzah indeed. Faithful men of Veronia, draw near to our God. Call upon His name. Let Him fight through you, and let all glory be His alone when the enemy is defeated." They shouted again as Shane took a knee.

Every man knelt with him.

"Lord, we give You our lives and the coming battle. Let no man stand in the way of Your perfect will and plan for this day. Go before us. Fight for us. And if it be Your will, save us this day."

"Amen." The men stood, moved toward their mounts, and started off in three groups.

Shane came and knelt before Margg as she worked to get her

swollen and blistered feet back into her boots. "Oh, Margaret," he groaned, cradling one foot in his hand. "I am so very sorry."

"'Tis not your fault, Shane."

His head rose at his name, and she tried to remember if she had ever used it before. It felt welcome and familiar on her tongue, much like her favorite treat.

He tried to grab a rag and wash her foot.

She pulled it from his grasp and wiggled it into the boot, ignoring the sting. "There is not time for such healing ministrations."

Shane looked about him as all left but those of the royal guard assigned to his care. "Margaret, no men can be spared to see to your safety here."

She reached out to get his aid to stand. He pulled her to her feet, and she hobbled for a few tentative steps before finding a position she could tolerate with less pain. "I go with you."

"Margaret, we go to battle."

"'Tis not safe for me here. There's nowhere for me to go to find safety with the horde out there." She stepped close, placed her hand on his arm, and gazed up. "I go with you, husband. If we're to die, we'll do so together. If we are to be parted by death, I'd spend my last moments with you."

Rand led two horses to them. "My lord."

"Rand, I asked you call me Shane."

"Aye, my lord. I heard." He smiled and rose into his own saddle.

"See, I have a horse. Fear not over me." Margg moved to the smaller of the two beasts.

Shane helped her onto her mount, handing up her bow and arrow. "Are you skilled in the use of these?"

"I can shoot well enough."

He took to his saddle. They turned their horses toward the trail. "I remember stories from my youth of some who could use the Holy Light even in their arrows."

"I am not a woman of deep faith," she confessed.

"Do you believe Christ is the Son of God?"

"Yes."

"And that He died to pay the penalty for your sins?"

"Yes."

They came to a wider part of the trail, and his horse dropped back to come alongside hers. He turned and considered her for a long moment before he asked his next question. "And, beloved, do you accept what He has done for you and repent of your sins?"

"Yes."

His smile grew. "Then you carry the Lord within you, as do all these men. Ask, and He will fight for you as He fights for us. Trust in Him, and you will be safe."

She nodded and turned to gaze on their route as they wound in among the trees, trying to stay out of sight of the horde. *Would God fight for her, through her, as He did these soldiers—as He had for the queen all those years ago?* Margg wondered if she had the depth of belief needed. She dared a glance at Shane. He surveyed the shadows of the predawn forest around them, alert to any danger. *What if he dies today? Can I go back to my tavern and raise Car alone? What if I die?*

Her stomach knotted until she feared she might wretch. She closed her eyes and tried to imagine such a future. But God had brought them together. They never should have met. They never should have fallen in love—yet here they were. She took one final deep breath and released all that might transpire in the coming moments of battle. *Lord, it is not my regular practice to pray, but here I am. I give myself to You, and trust You with whatever may come.*

# Chapter 48

Shane took the middle position among the dozen men with him. They spread out about two rods a part. A signal would be passed from either end to him when they were linked with the two adjoining divisions of Gamel and Crooks' Bend.

A flash of light behind them caught his eye as he turned to Margaret, who remained close to his left. He stared into the darkness of the deeper forest, searching for it. But it did not appear again. His gaze shifted again to Margaret. Her bow lay notched with an arrow resting on her right thigh. She met his stare. No apprehension hovered about her. She considered him as though it were any other morning at any task needing to be done.

Shane swallowed the fear threatening to choke him. "I do not know what the next hours may hold for us—"

"God will see us through."

Her response came so swift and sure it stole his breath. "How can you know?"

She shrugged and turned back to stare through the trees at the enemy lines materializing in the dawn light. "Seems an odd thing for God to drop you in my pig pen, cause you to steal my heart, and then allow either of us to die here to these vermin. Though I will not question the Almighty if He sees fit to do so—but it'd seem wholly unfair."

Shane could not contain the smile tugging at his lips. He eased his mount nearer to hers and placed his hand over hers. "I believe you are mistaken, my lady. For, in fact, it was you who stole my heart."

She gazed at him for several moments before she leaned over and captured his lips with her own. She withdrew with a smile. "Do you well, husband, to care for my heart you carry, as I will for yours. I wish not to be a widow before the marriage vows are spoken."

She pulled back and sat straight once more. Her command was spoken with a tightness that revealed the fear he had not seen on her face or in her eyes. Her kiss set his body aflame and his thoughts to flight, but the veiled fear in her chilled him to stone.

The flash of light to the rear once more drew his attention.

The circle complete around the black enspelled enemy before them, Shane bowed his head once more. *Lord, I again give this battle to You. Let no manner of pride or thought of my own glory hinder me.* He dared a stolen glance at Margaret. His heart shuttered. *Protect Lady Margaret, please Lord. See her safely back to Carling.* His stomach knotted painfully. *I cannot bare the thought—*

He felt as if someone had shoved him forward. Shane opened his eyes and scanned the area around, but no one sat near enough to touch him. His pulse quickened, and his breathing turned to shallow puffs.

*Lord, I—*

Again a pressure against his back propelled him over this horse's mane. Shane put his hand on his sword and slowly drew it from its home. The blade shone in the deep shadows. He raised it high above his head, pointing the tip at the heavens. Every man within sight of him did likewise, and the forest filled with holy light. Margaret raised her bow as well, and the arrow glowed.

Shane forced himself to inhale a single slow breath and released it with a shout. "For the Lord and your king!"

Horses snorted as they were spurred forward.

Mail clattered.

Men shouted the call all along the line in either direction.

Hooves drummed the earth.

Veronian warriors burst from their cover and charged at the shriveled enemy before them. Lowering their glowing swords, they closed the distance.

The neat lines of the gathered horde turned to face the threat with murderous shouts and terrifying wails.

Shane came to his first enemy and ran him through while his horse never slowed. The creature on his lit sword screeched and evaporated into a puff of black smoke. The next fell, and the next, with little effort. Shane took his attention off the battle ahead to look for Margaret. She loosed three arrows in quick succession, dissolving an equal number of black creatures.

A bolt of pain tore through his right thigh. Shane's hand loosened its grip on his sword and it started to slip from his fingertips. He bellowed at the heat coursing through his leg as the limb trembled. He snatched the hilt tight in his grasp once more and turned to see the blood soaking his breeches through the gash rent in them. His sword filled with holy power once more, and he swung it back, beheading the creature that had wounded him.

Shane lashed out at three more in haphazard swings, trying to clear a path before him.

The enemy whirled away and came at him again.

He bellowed in rage and reared back his horse to keep the beastly vermin at bay. One scampered away, but four more joined in their attack against him. Lashing out to his furthest reach from the saddle, Shane managed to cut one across its naked chest. It writhed and squealed on the ground for a moment as Shane removed the head of another that ventured too close.

Whirling his mount, Shane struck down two more as they tried to form a circle around him. But in the turn, Shane didn't see Margaret. She no longer fought at his left.

Taking his eyes off the enemy at his feet, Shane scanned the field for her. His heart pounded until it was the only thing he could hear.

Enemies bunched up in small clumps and attacked the Veronian men in force.

Blazing swords slashed through the air.

Battle cries mixed with death shrieks, but Shane struggled to comprehend any of it. Margaret was not anywhere in the fray.

Hands grabbed at his bleeding thigh, and a howl tore from deep within Shane's body. Other hands jerked him from his saddle. He hit the ground on his right side. The sword dropped from his grasp. His arm tingled like he slept on it and it now tried to wake once more. His head throbbed, and he fought to recapture breath in his aching lungs.

Pain burst through his back once and then again. He rolled onto his back, hoping to block the coming attack with his arms.

Four of the horde hovered over him. Three kicked at him, and the last launched himself onto Shane, landing on his chest and stopping any air from entering his body. As the black creature atop him raised his hands, the dawn light gleamed off the dagger in its grip.

White teeth shone out between the ebony lips as the weapon flew toward Shane's throat.

He threw his arms before his face in a vain attempt to protect himself. "Lord, please."

## Chapter 49

Air rushed back into Shane's burning lungs as the weight atop him vanished. He dared move his hands from his face and saw the last of the creatures towering over him disappear in a puff as the arrow that vanquished him dropped to the ground beside him.

Margaret drew her horse between him and the charging horde. She loosed another glowing arrow as she shouted at him. "You fool man! Stop looking for me, pick up your sword and fight! So help me, Shane of the royal family—" Two more arrows flew, and she stole a quick glance at him. "If you get yourself run through on some fool notion of protecting me, I will—"

Advancing enemy drew her attention, and she charged at them cutting off the bite of her threat.

As Shane rose from his back, his head spun. His stomach churned, and he tossed his head aside to wretch—but nothing came. His entire body trembled, and he turned his gaze toward the battle once more. Light from atop the battlements high above caught his attention. There several of the horde were trying to scale up the sheer face of the castle mount. The light above came not from blades filled with holy light, but soldiers' bodies.

Memories of how Mariamne showed the soldiers how to allow God's power to flow through their entire beings flooded his mind.

Shane scanned the battlefield around, noting others must have seen the men above too as they dropped their swords and surrendered fully to allow God to work through them.

He allowed himself one last glance at Margaret as she let fly the last of her arrows and clamped his eyes shut. *Lord, I give Lady Margaret and little Carling fully into Your care. I offer myself as Your instrument. Use me as You will.*

Warmth flooded his body. A sweet fragrance filled is nostrils as his lungs worked with ease. The dizziness vanished along with the ache in his leg.

Shane opened his eyes. He stood, light pouring from his body. The holy light emanating from him joined first with the light streaming from Margaret, then with the other soldiers on the field near him. Their light mingled with others around the enemy until it joined with the light from those up on the battlements.

Shane scrunched his eyes shut against the light of God flowing from all of them, which outshone the sun itself.

Silence.

The shrieking and waling ceased.

Not a clang of sword remained.

No bird called out from the trees.

Not even the wind whispered.

Shane peeked through one creaked lid. Both opened, and he looked out on a field containing only Veronia's warriors. Not a single enspelled creature remained.

"Huzzah!" The shout rang out and filled the valley below the castle. Soldiers greeted one another with hearty thumps on the back and cheers to God.

Margaret ran to him but stopped short of leaping into his arms.

He reached out to her and drew her to himself. "The Lord be

praised."

She tightened her grip on him. "The Almighty has been good to us."

As he released her, Shane again was caught by a flash of light at the corner of his vision. He looked once more into the deep woods behind them.

Hooves pounded, drawing his attention back toward the valley. Soldiers greeted one another all over the field. Revelry filled all the land between the forest and the castle mount—but Shane could not bring himself to join in their merrymaking. Laughter assaulted him, and he cringed as others came to honor his leadership in the day's victory. For Shane, the battle was not yet over.

Ethan's mount rumbled near as he leapt from the saddle and seized Shane in a fierce embrace, pounding him on the back. "'Tis done!"

"The Lord has won a great victory here this day, but the war is not over."

"Indeed, brother?" Ethan released him and took a step away. "We will praise His name forever, and the story of this day will never leave our lips." He looked Shane up and down. "Are you well, man?"

Shane glanced down at his leg and pulled open the rent fabric. Within lay a perfectly healed leg—not even a scar remained. "Aye. It would seem the good Lord worked many a miracle this day." He glanced back at Ethan as awe and gratitude flooded his spirit.

"God be praised!" Ethan shouted. He continued to stare at Shane. "Why do you not celebrate with our men?"

"As I said, brother, this battle is won but the war is not over. We have yet to find Princess Milana. Until she is safe in her mother's arms and celebrates her union with Lord Robert, I will not make merry."

Ethan nodded and called his men. The word spread from one clump of revelers to another until a large group gathered around. All looked to Shane.

"Faithful men of Veronia, you have fought well today—but as Lord Shane has reminded me, we still have not completed our mission. Princess Milana has yet to be returned to us."

Men grunted as their moods sobered.

Ethan turned again to Shane and called out for all to hear, "What would you command of us next, brother?"

Shane took a moment to look about. He moved to a nearby boulder and stepped atop it to address them. "The weapons of the horde should be collected."

A group of men shouted out, "Aye, my lord," and moved off to see to the task.

"A large band of warriors should make haste into the royal hunting grounds and the forests about and bring down as much game as they can carry. We do not know how long the castle and town have been under siege. They could be in great need."

"Gamel, Rand—I and our men will see to it." Ethan turned to leave, but Shane caught him by the shoulder.

Shane's volume lowered so only those nearest could hear. "Ethan, my friend, I have a special request of you."

Ethan's head cocked to the side.

"Would you do me the greatest kindness and see Lady Margaret safely to the castle."

"Why are you not—"

"I go in search of Princess Milana, brother."

Ethan inclined his head. "Where will you look for her?"

Shane turned to the forest, remembering the flashes of light he had seen throughout the morning. "I think the Lord has shown me the way."

"I will send a group of men with you." Ethan raised his hand to call over some of the men.

"Nay, brother. The townspeople and castle must be cared for first. If two could be spared, I would welcome their company."

With a nod, Ethan called over Oswin and Joshua. They went to gather Shane's horse as Margaret approached. In her hands she carried his sword.

"I give you the same charge husband. Take care to return to me."

He pressed his lips to her forehead. "I shall return to you with all due haste, my lady. Then we shall see what future the good Lord would have for us." He helped her into her saddle, and he watched her ride away at Ethan's side. The field around him grew quiet, and he turned his attention once more to the deep woods below the mighty Kestron Ridge.

# Chapter 50

"Mayhaps we should split up," Oswin offered.

"Or return and collect more warriors for the search," Joshua said.

Shane's attempted rescue of Princess Milana did not proceed as planned. He had covered much ground during the battle, making locating the source of the flashing light nearly impossible. He reined in his horse and released an exasperated sigh. Could be he was not the man God chose for this task. *I should have returned to the castle, and Ethan should be completing the mission assigned to him.* He rolled his shoulders and looked to either man who flanked him. *What is best for Milana?*

Shane turned and looked back through the trees but could no longer see the base of the castle mount. The woods in this area were several leagues deep.

"My lord?" Oswin said.

"Aye, Oswin, we must go about this in a more methodical fashion. The day is over half spent and we have done little more than wander in circles."

"You know she is here, my lord?" Joshua asked.

Shane shook his head. "Nay, I know naught of anything other than I saw light coming from somewhere deeper in the woods. I felt in my spirit if I found the light, I would find the princess."

Oswin looked out at the dense trees surrounding them. "There are no dwellings in this area of the forest."

"Where could she have been held for all this time here?" Joshua asked.

As if someone had created a painting and hung it before his eyes, a view exploded before him. "A cave."

Oswin turned, his brows arched high. "The Kestron Rigde is riddled with niches and hollows. How do we find which one?"

Shane spurred his horse. "Oswin, you head to the east toward Crook's Bend. At the foot of the mountains work back toward me surveying any opening large enough to hold the princess and her captors." Shane pointed to better direct the knight. Turning to the other knight. "Joshua, you do likewise to the west. I will continue straight, and we shall meet up before nightfall. God willing, Milana will be with one of us."

The men acknowledged and headed off.

Shane jerked upright, preventing him from falling from the saddle. Two nights—or had it been three—without adequate sleep? He struggled to stay awake.

Again he jolted awake moments before falling. It had taken Shane another hour to pick his way through the close-growing trees to reach the foot of the mountain. He first turned east and traveled near a mile, stopping often to investigate possible caves. He found naught to aid him. No niche lay deep enough to be of use and there were no human tracks anywhere he traveled.

He turned and worked his way back the other direction. Without regularly dismounting to check those places he had already passed, he moved more quickly. But without leaving the saddle, he struggled to remain alert. Sleep wrestled with him like a gigantic ogre.

He came back to the small strip of his trouser he rent and tied to a thin branch. Now he would search new ground and look to meet with Joshua in short order, as the sun already hung low in the sky. Sunset would not be far behind. He hoped he would not be sleeping under the stars yet another night, but that seemed like a possibility the longer the search went on.

Shane's head lulled forward, and his eyes drooped once more. He stepped from his mount and stretched out his back. He took hold of the reins and started walking. His feet scraped across the forest floor, and his toes caught on several roots. After a half dozen times, he lost his balance completely and dropped to his knees.

He sat there, head hanging low, trying to summon enough strength to stand. *I cannot do this, Lord. I am not strong enough. I am not worthy.*

The forest lay quiet. No birds chirped, no animals scurried between the trees. Then a breeze wound among the branches and stirred the leaves surrounding his knees. It brushed his cheek, and Shane looked up. He glanced to the heavens through a web of multiple tangled branches but saw little. *Lord, I need You. You know where Milana is this very moment. Let her be already found.*

The strength of the stirring wind increased. Shane dropped his head and a tumbling large yellow leaf caught his attention. It rolled and flipped, dancing along before him, while no other leaves moved at all. Shane watched, mesmerized as the bit of sunlight danced away from him until it disappeared around a section of rock jutting out from the base of the mountain.

Shane pushed to his feet and followed the rambling leaf. As he came around the outcropping, a dull glow emanated from an opening in the rock ahead. The leaf disappeared inside. He looped the reins of his mount over a low branch, drew his sword, and moved inside.

He paused in the opening to allow his eyes to adjust before following the dim light much deeper within the cave.

*Scrape!*

Shane raised his sword and called forth the holy light.

A black enspelled creature sprang at him. He slashed at it.

It leapt back, staying out of reach.

Shane moved forward, with slow, deliberate steps. He drove the creature into a niche in a dark corner.

It snarled and wailed, slashing out with its sharp claws.

Shane came within reach, and then a step nearer yet. "I had better find Milana alive within this cave—but I still send you to hell now." He thrust, running the black form through until his blade hit rock.

It vanished with a screech.

Shane turned and moved to a narrow opening leading further into the cave. Beyond the first opening lay another, but the light came from further still. The holy light glowing from his sword lit on several pairs of white eyes. A low rumble filled the cavern.

"Lord, hel—"

# Chapter 51

Shane woke flat on his belly, face in the dust of the cave floor. Light came from before him and behind him. He felt around for his sword and found it with ease. Filling it with holy light, he made a careful examination of the cavern where he found himself. Six or more swords lay scattered about the floor around him. Near his feet, lay a rock with a dark smudge. He knelt and held the light close to it. Blood. He touched the back of his head—no wound could be found, but some of his hair was sticky. If the holy light that filled his body before had healed his leg completely, mayhaps the same had happened again. He remembered calling out for the Lord. "He must have saved me again," Shane whispered to the stonewalls.

Seeing no other enemy or danger, Shane glanced back at the first cavern he had come through. Bright sunlight shone through the opening. *Must be well into the day already.* He turned back to the other opening. Making his way with slow steps, he scanned every dark crevice for anymore of the horde. He stepped into the last opening. His eyes were immediately drawn to the source of the light.

Milana lay on a shelf carved from the cave wall. She rested shrouded in holy light, her dress soiled and tattered.

Shane dropped the blade and raced to her side. Falling to his knees, he reached out to take her hands. "Princess Milana."

She pulled weakly to free herself of him.

"Princess Milana, 'tis Shane."

Her eyes remained closed. Her face was thin and drawn, her lips cracked. Her voice came in huffed gasps. "No, I know your tricks. You cannot fool me."

Shane dared place his hands on the sides of her face. His heart thundered in his ears. "Milana, 'tis me, Shane. Truly. Open your eyes and see for yourself, my little princes, bright and shining."

Milana stilled and one eye cracked open. "Shane?"

"Truly, 'tis me, Your Highness."

Her cracked lips tried to form a smile, but blood broke through in several spots. "Oh, Shane," her eyes closed, and she relaxed into him.

The Spirit slipped back within her, and the light emanating from her flesh went out, leaving them in utter darkness.

Shane groped along the cave floor until he found his sword, called forth the Spirit, and carefully scooped Milana into his arms. He carried her outside and knelt near his horse. Still cradling her in one arm, Shane swung the blade out to fight whatever crunched through the leaves, announcing its approach from the far side of the outcropping.

Oswin came into view a stuttered breath later, and Shane lowered his blade. "Throw down your skin."

The water skin fell quickly. "Is she—"

"The princess is alive—weak, but she yet breathes."

Milana coughed and sputtered at the liquid poured into her mouth. Shane allowed her to catch her breath before offering her more. She drank her fill, before she opened her eyes. "Shane," she sighed as she gazed up at him. "I feared I might be dreaming."

"'Tis me, Princess, a no good dream."

She drew her tongue over her lips and ventured a small smile again. "Shane, glad I am to see you. I have prayed for you every day."

"For me, Princess?"

"Oh, aye, I begged the good Lord not to take my spirit until I was given the chance to ask for your forgiveness."

Shane shook his head and soothed back her mussed hair. "I fear your confinement has left you quite unwell, Your Highness. You have nothing to be forgiven for, 'twas I who did you wrong."

"But you turned from your old ways and surrendered to our precious Lord. I did not believe you and took my wrath out upon you. I know it was because of me that you left. I am so sorry, Shane."

"No, Highness, I needed to go and find a way to redeem myself." A smile sprang to his lips. "Turns out God had already done the work of redemption in and for me. I but needed to receive it."

Milana's smile grew. "Indeed."

She nestled back into his arms.

Oswin moved forward, drawing his sword at the sound of something approaching from the west. Shane also picked up his blade again.

Joshua appeared at a distance through the trees, and Oswin called out to him.

Shane rose to his feet, cradling Milana in his arms as Joshua joined them. "One of you should ride ahead at all possible haste and alert the castle of Milana's return. She will need the ministrations of Carrington, and Queen Mariamne, King Edgar, and Lord Richard will want to greet her.

"Aye, my lord. I will see to it." Joshua turned his mount and moved away between the trees before anyone could stop him.

With Oswin's help, Shane mounted, Milana wrapped in a blanket and nestled in his arms. Turning toward the castle, Milana placed it on Shane's shirt. She pulled herself up and pressed her scratchy lips against his jaw. "I love you, brother, and thank God He brought you back to me." She settled back against his chest and slept.

Shane swallowed the gratitude clumping in his throat and threatening to leak out is eyes.

"I too thank God He brought you back to us, Lord Shane."

"I am no lord, sir."

Oswin laughed. Mayhaps we should dispense with the titles?"

"After all we have seen together, it does sound as though we wish to put on airs."

"Brother?"

Shane nodded at the man riding easily next to him. "It would be my honor."

"The honor is mine, friend."

They fell into a comfortable silence as they picked their way along the smoothest trail through the deep woods.

# Chapter 52

Shane and Oswin rode out of the forest as the sun painted the sky in deep oranges. Milana never stirred during the entire journey.

"Do you think Joshua has delivered the good news?"

Oswin's gaze rose to the heights of the castle mount. "Look," he raised his chin. "They line the battlement looking for you."

Shane spurred his horse into a gentle trot. "They look for their lost princess."

Oswin drew alongside, "And the kingdom's hero who rescued her."

As the sky turned to deep pink, Shane led the way through the castle's outer gate. Cheers atop the battlements and more within the bailey filled his ears until they rang. He worked his way toward the royal healer's home. Lord Richard came forward, his brows furrowed, his lips pursed tight together.

"She lives, sir. God has sustained her." Shane handed Milana down into Lord Richard's waiting arms.

"Thank you, Lord Shane. Thank you for bringing her back to us. God bless you."

Shane did not have time to respond as Richard rushed his love to receive the healer's ministrations. He turned, and his eyes took in all those gathered around chanting his name or shouting huzzah. Hands reached up to him, welcoming him home and calling out blessings upon him. An excitement stirred, which he did not expect. He thought he would never see his childhood home again, or if he did ever return, it would not be to joyful shouts and God's well-wishes upon him.

A deep need stirred. Shane's eyes drifted past the cheerful throngs to the imposing building standing in the middle of the bailey behind the crowd. The chapel. The one place he had most avoided while growing up within these high and familiar walls now called to his heart. He stepped down from his horse and passed the reins to the first pair of willing hands. He greeted hands as he managed slow progress to the sacred house.

"Shane!" A voice cheered above the den.

Before he could fully turn and respond, arms encircled his neck and held him so tight it forced the air from his lungs.

"Son of my heart, oh how I have missed you."

"My queen," Shane stammered.

Queen Mariamne pulled from him and placed her warm, soft hands on either side of his face, fixing him with a scrutinizing stare. A smile graced greeted him.

Shane noted a few more wrinkles and grey hairs, but she was still a beauty, and he floated in the reminder of how much she loved him—and he her.

"You look well, my son. God has been gracious to you." Her smile grew as she leaned in and lowered her voice. "And I very much approve of your fine lady."

A hand pummeled his back and nearly drove him into the queen. "Shane, my son!" Mariamne disappeared into the healer's home, and Shane was engulfed in a bear hug that again drove all breath from him. "I could not be prouder of you, son." The pounding on his back continued. "Well done. Well done indeed!"

King Edgar released him, and he inhaled a deep gulp. He hoped to capture an even breath to speak with this man who still loved him as a son, but Edgar pounded twice more before following his wife into Carrington's home.

Shane watched him go and turned back to the chapel. The crowd had now dispersed, but his eyes caught on a deep royal-blue gown. His breath again fled his lungs. Margaret stood a few feet away. The satin hugged her curvaceous form, and his blood ran hot. She did not come closer, forcing Shane to stagger toward her.

When he was almost within arm's reach, he found a whisper of a voice that strangled out of his throat. "Lady Margaret … you look … you are a—"

Her hands shook as they brushed over the skirt. "Queen Mariamne insisted I take it. It is one of her own."

Shane nodded. "Well I know. It was always my favorite. You are a vision."

Margaret remained quiet just out of his reach and avoided looking to him.

"Shane!"

Shane barely had time to turn toward the squeal before Carling slammed into him. He stepped back trying to keep from toppling over. She leapt into his arms the moment he reached down to her. Her arms wrapped around his neck and nearly strangled him.

"Beautiful girl, what are you doing here?"

She loosened her grip and sat back on his arms. "Father Barfar… Barfar-o-m …"

"Bartholomew."

"Ah-huh! Him. He brought me the day after ya and Margg left."

"I thought the good Father was going to take care of that

troublesome priest?"

She giggled. "Oh, he did. He sat way in the back and when the priest asked for money, he stomped forward and yanked the moneybag from his hands and pushed him to his knees and called him a thief. Father gave out some of the money and," her eyes grew big and her voice took on a breathy awe, "the king's guards, they came and they took the priest away in sackles."

"You mean shackles?"

"Ah-huh. Then Father told us how much God loved us." She wiggled from his grasp and slid to the ground. She twirled in a bright yellow dress. "The queen let me wear it. Isn't it the prettiest thin' ya ever did see? It used to be Princess Milana's when she were little."

Shane knelt. "I remember this dress." He brushed his finger over a dark streak along the scooped collar.

"I didn't do that, Shane, I promise."

He stroked her arm. "I know, little one. I caused that stain."

Her head tilted.

"I was unkind to Milana and tripped her as we played. She split her lip, and a few drops of blood landed there."

"That wasn't nice."

Shane shook his head and chuckled. "It most certainly was not. Did I not tell you that you would not like me if you knew me?"

She stepped forward, slipped her arms around his neck again, and laid her head on his shoulder. "But yar nice now, and I love ya."

Shane tightened his arms around the child and scanned the bailey for Margaret, "I love you too, precious girl."

Carling popped from his arms and ran toward the queen, who was exiting the healer's. "Is it time to help with the meal?"

Mariamne put out her hand for the bouncing girl, "Nearly so, little one, nearly so."

Carling turned back to Shane as she went off. " I get to help serve the meal with the queen."

"Aye, and Lord Shane needs to clean himself or the meal will be delayed," she said to the child. Mariamne looked toward him, a smile mirroring the brightness of the sun. "Your room is as you left it, a bath has been drawn, and Alden awaits to assist you."

"I wish but a moment to express my gratitude," he pointed to the chapel behind him as he rose to his feet. "I bear a great load to be grateful for."

Mariamne's smile grew (though it did not seem possible) as she made her way to the inner ward.

At last Shane was alone and turned toward the chapel, climbed the steps, and pushed open one of the massive oak doors.

# *Chapter 53*

Shane's boots disturbed the reverent silence as he made his way eagerly to the altar. He knelt and was about to lay prostrate when Father Bartholomew entered from his chamber to the left.

"Shane, my son, good it is to see you. I heard the cheers of your triumphant return with the princess."

"And I heard you had a priest arrested by royal guards." Shane sat back on his heels with a smirk.

"If I could have the man flogged, I would do it myself." The Father plopped down on the first pew near him. "That wretched man. The guards escorted him back to his home and seized his extensive property and the remaining money he was robbing from the good people he was supposed to be shepherding. They are distributing it equally among his parishes. The monk has been delivered to the holy house on Egret Isle. They have promised to work the man until his gluttonous spirit is once again chastened before God."

"Then all is well in Kinglet Hill?"

Father Bartholomew's gaze shifted back to Shane, and his continence softened. "Yes, my son. Several young priests, who have been well trained in the Word of the Lord, have stepped forward to attend to full-time service in each of the villages formerly overseen by Jonah. They will be fed on the Word daily."

"Thank you, Father."

The Father stood. "It was you who brought the need into the light. You have done well to vanquish much evil in our land, my son." He turned toward his chambers. "I will leave you to your prayers."

"I came to thank God for all He has done for me, but I find I do not have adequate words to express the depth of my heart, Father."

Father Bartholomew continued walking but called out over his shoulder, "But the Spirit itself maketh request for us with sighs, which cannot be expressed."

Shane smiled and lay prostrate. *Lord, hear my heart as it overflows with gratitude for all the works of Your hand.* Shane lay there in quiet humility, thinking of all God had done for him— restoring him, choosing him, using one such as him. He thought on Milana, Margaret, and Carling, Mariamne, Edgar, and Ethan. Tears filled his eyes as he counted the many blessings that overwhelmed his soul. He could lay here until his hair turned gray but he would never be able to express his gratitude satisfactorily.

The bells, announcing supper would begin in half of an hour, rang overhead, drawing him from the holy moment. He rose blanketed in peace and bursting with joy.

*It is time to properly ask Lady Margaret for her hand.*

He bounded up the stairs and came to his door. Part of him thought to knock, as he knew he truly did not belong, but he was welcome here. He pushed open the door and stepped inside his old chambers.

Alden rose to his feet and bent in a deep bow. "Welcome home, Highness."

Shane stepped quickly to the man and embraced him. "Well you know, old friend, I am not royalty. It is only Shane now."

The elderly gentleman shook, and sputtered, "Oh, my. My lord, I don't know what to say."

Shane released him and looked him over. "Tell me you are hale and God has been good to you."

"I am most well, my lord, as God has returned ye and Princess Milana to us, so He has been exceedingly good to us."

"Good, good." Shane moved to his inner chamber and pulled off his tattered and filthy shirt. "I don't have much time to bathe and redress. Will you assist me, Alden?" His eyes caught for a moment on the elements of his knighting. His cloak, shield, sword, belt, and spurs were all displayed neatly in the corner. His breath caught in his throat.

"Of course, my lord." Alden shuffled into the room behind him and gasped. "My lord!"

Shane ran a hand across his back, feeling the scars and the badly set rib. "Aye, I had many lessons to learn, my old friend. But I have finally learned them well." Shane moved into the bathing chamber and shed the rest of his borrowed clothes. The water was the perfect temperature, and he sank into it with a sigh. "Oh, how I have missed this luxury."

Alden entered and handed him the things he required. "Will ye speak of yer journeys, my lord?"

As he worked to clean his hair and scrub his body, Shane told of all God had done for him.

Alden handed him a towel. "God be praised. He has done great things." He hobbled into the bedchamber to select some clothes. He looked through the various possibilities and scowled. "I fear, my lord, ye have amassed an array of muscles that have outgrown yer former wardrobe."

"I have spent much of my time away at physical labor." Shane strolled into the bedchamber with a towel around his waist and another that he worked over his hair. "What about the blue shirt? The one with the toggles? It always fit too loose to my liking."

Alden found it, and he donned it, checking the fit in the mirror. "It now appears too snug, my lord."

"But it will serve for this night." He tried several trousers before a pair could be found he trusted to sit in without bursting the seams. A doublet left unbuttoned and a tall pair of boots finished his attire for the evening.

As Shane worked his hair into his favored knot, Alden scooped up several of the unwearable items and shuffled toward the outer chamber. "I will take these to the tailor at once. He will have at least two pairs altered by morning."

"'Tis late, Alden. Allow the man to eat and join the celebration. These garments will do me a day or so."

Alden nearly tripped over his own feet. A grin spread across his face, "God be praised, but if it is not good to have ye home, sir." He continued on his way with the clothes. "I will tell Samuel what ye have said."

By the time Shane returned to the hall below, most were gathered at the boards, and the women had already laid many of the tables. He paused for a moment as he noted that women not helping this evening were seated with their men, at the same tables. Shane smiled and moved to a bench just left of where the king sat at the high table on the dais. He hoped there would be enough room for him, Margaret, and Carling.

King Edgar waved him up onto the dais beside him once more. Shane bowed and pointed to Carling as she bounded passed with a tray of cheeses and then to the spot he was headed. Edgar lifted his cup to him and inclined his head, granting him leave.

When Shane sat at the long board, several knights moved to be nearer to him. They shook his hand and thanked him for leading the battle.

"The glory is God's alone. I am blessed He allowed me to be a part of it at all."

Margaret laid the last of her trays and moved to sit with the servants at the far side of the room. Shane called her over.

She stopped but did not turn toward him.

He started to stand to retrieve her, "Lady Margaret, please join me."

Finally she turned and came to sit beside him.

"Good evening, Lady Margaret."

Her lip disappeared between her teeth.

"Here, Car, sit and eat now." She took the last tray from the girl and delivered it herself. When Margaret returned, she slid Carling over using the child as a barrier between them.

Shane reached around the girl and brushed Margaret's arm.

She shied from him.

"Are you hale, my lady?" he whispered as he leaned near.

She only nodded and snatched up a brown roll, picking at it but eating little.

Shane seemed to lose his appetite as well. *Something is very wrong.*

As he sat listening to all the things Carling could tell him about her few hours in the castle, a lord came and wiggled his way into a place directly across from him. His white hair was cut short, and his clean-shaven face showed the ravages of time in deep wrinkles and small dark blotches. He inclined his head to Shane but didn't say anything as Carling once again captured Shane's attention.

A few moments, later the king rose, hefting his tankard high in the air.

Every head turned toward the doors to see whom he saluted. There, clinging to Lord Richard's arm, stood Princess Milana. Her clean deep-green gown made her look pale, but her hair was done, and she walked of her own—though Richard was her support.

Eating daggers pounded on the boards, and shouts and whistles rang out. The room erupted in cheers. "Long live Princess Milana. Long may God bless her."

She smiled and dipped a small curtsy. Lord Richard led her toward the dais, but she stopped him when her gaze met Shane's and directed Richard toward where he stood.

Shane made his way to her so she wouldn't have to maneuver between the close tables, and she laid her hand on one cheek and kissed the other. "Thank you again, brother."

"It was my privilege, sister." He kissed her forehead as he had when she was a baby, and again peace enveloped him.

She continued on her way to sit beside her mother at the high table, Lord Richard on her right.

Edgar again raised his tankard.

The hall hushed.

"We praise the Lord Most High for the return of Princess Milana and Lord Shane."

Dagger thumping echoed again.

"We praise our Lord Almighty for the victory over the horde."

"Huzzah!" rang off the walls.

"We praise our mighty heavenly Father for all the blessings He has showered upon us."

Cheers shook the ceiling beams.

"Princess Milana, we welcome you home with all joy and look forward to celebrating your wedding ceremony within the week. Lord Shane, we are most grateful for your return and your help in the harrowing events of these last months. I will never cease to praise my God for Milana's return, and your own. I welcome you and the Lady Margaret, and Mistress Carling. May you soon also know wedded bliss."

Shane raised his cup to the king and bowed low. "Thank you, Majesty, for all you have done for me."

Margaret's head hung. She wouldn't look at Shane or the king. *Does she tremble?*

"Eat, my friends, enjoy this day the Lord has provided for us and share in our great joy."

The eating continued, but Shane kept a close eye on Margaret as she picked at the little food she moved to her plate.

# Chapter 54

Shane rolled from his side to his back in his overstuffed bed. It would be hard to return to the skin-covered cot in Margaret's tavern, but he did not see a place for him here. He was not the king's son—though he was loved as one—and he feared his own nature. He stared up at the fabric encasing his bed. *If I remain, I will become that greedy, unkind, thoughtless wretch once more. Better to live with naught with Margaret than become that man once more.*

He pulled the curtain aside and light streamed through the window. "Alden?"

Shuffled steps came toward him as he flung his feet over the side of the bed and sat up. "Aye, sir?"

"What time is it?"

"The bells for breaking the fast have just rung, my lord."

"But 'tis late. The sun is well up."

"Aye." One side of Alden's mouth rose in a smirk. "But much of the castle was up celebrating well into the wee hours of the morn. They could not be roused to leave the hall to see to the laying of the boards until a short while ago."

"I retired too early to notice." Shane raked his hands through his hair.

"Ye have had a hard few days. But all should be better now, sir. Ye are home." Alden laid out a newly altered shirt and pair of trousers.

Shane washed his face and brushed through his hair. His mind turned again to Margaret. She had disappeared from the celebration, though when, Shane was not sure. Carling captured his attention as she marveled at the minstrels, jesters, jugglers, and other performers hired to celebrate the evening. When next he looked up, Margaret was nowhere to be seen.

"Is Lady Margaret well?" he had asked Carling.

One of her small shoulders had shrugged as she sat enraptured unable to pull her gaze from the juggler as he added yet another ball into the air.

Shane asked after her, but no one knew where Margaret had gone. His own weariness had proved too powerful at that point, and he left Carling in Queen Mariamne's care and retired.

Now as he finished dressing, an urgency driven by a need to find Margaret pushed him to move with haste. He charged from the room.

"My lord?"

"Alden, I must find Lady Margaret."

He had his hand on the outer door when Alden called out again. "Mighten ye be needin' shoes to speak with yer lady fair?"

Shane's gaze dropped to his hose covered toes. His shoulders sagged. "Aye, my friend. With my fate, I would slip on the castle tile and land on my arse." Shane chuckled as he took his boots from the man.

Down in the hall, all was prepared but few had yet gathered for the meal. Margaret swept out of the kitchen, carrying trays laden with food. Today dressed in a green overdress, she seemed both more beautiful and deeper within herself. She almost ran into him before she took notice of his presence.

"Good morn to you, my lady."

She dipped a curtsy and stepped around him.

He gently took her upper arm and pulled her to a stop. "Margaret, you are unwell? What is it that vexes you so, my lady? Tell me, that I might put your mind at ease."

Her head rose, and tears pooled in her eyes. "'Tis naught ye can do for me, my lord." She pulled from his grasp. "There is but little I can provide my feeble aid to, please let me see to it." A tremor flavored her words.

"Margaret?"

"Oh Shane, there you are, son of my heart. It does me good to see you here." Mariamne came and embraced him. "Might you sit with me a moment before everyone arrives and tell me of your time away?"

Shane watched Margaret disappear into the kitchen once more. He stifled the desire in his heart to chase after her and sat beside the queen talking for a short while before the hall filled.

Shane managed to get Margaret to sit with him and Carling again, though she still ate little. The same lord took his place across the table. Shane ate with undue haste. He needed to spend time with Margaret. Mayhaps they should even leave for home. *Does she worry over how it goes with the tavern? Could it be the bustle of life in the king's castle overwhelms her? Has someone treated her unkindly?* A million possibilities bombarded his thoughts, but until he could get her to a place she could speak freely, her unease disquieted him as well.

An idea struck him. "Carling, have you seen much of the castle?"

She shook her head, eyes dancing, and mouth stuffed full.

He reached past her and touched Margaret's arm. "I would be honored to show you about my former home."

Again Margaret pulled away. "There is the cleaning to see to, my lord."

"Please, Margg, won't ya come? I want ya to come with us."

"As do I."

A slow breath slid from her, and her shoulders fell. "Very well."

They walked out of the hall, across the ward, and into the bailey. Margaret's steps were heavy, and she stood off from them.

"I think we shall start at the outer gate and work our way back to the hall. I can show you where I was suppose to take my training with the sword, and the many things we have here. Mayhaps, Lady Margaret would like to visit our tiny tavern?"

She didn't respond.

A chorus of barks erupted as they passed the hounds. One yap rose above the others. Shrill and insistent.

Shane stopped and considered the mongrel, scruffy with wiry hair. "Scruff? Is that you, boy?"

The dog leapt wildly at the end of his tether. His tail flew at a frantic pace. His yaps turned to yowls and from there to howls punctuated by loud barks.

Shane approached the near-grown pup. He tried to pet the erratically moving head, but Scruff bathed his hand in kisses instead.

"He remembers you, my lord," the huntsman said from the doorway of the kennels.

"Is he really yar dog, Shane?" Carling asked, giggling at the dog's antics.

Shane stroked the dog, who still had not settled. "Every creature loves the one who saved him."

Carling's laughter increased as Scruff knocked into her, trying to get closer to Shane.

"Mayhaps we could take him home with us?" Shane looked up to see Margaret's reaction.

She stood with her back to him, head hanging low.

"My lord? Might I have a moment of your time?"

Shane's attention was drawn to the gray-haired lord, who had made a point to dine across from him twice now. He stood with his hands behind is back, shifting his weight between his feet. "I am spending some time with my family, my lord."

"I would speak to you about your future, sir."

Shane considered the man and then glanced down at Carling. She sat playing with Scruff. "Carling, I will be back in a few moments."

She nodded but didn't look up.

Shane walked past the man and snatched hold of Margaret's hand.

"I would speak to you alone—"

"If this matter concerns my future, sir, it concerns Lady Margaret. If what needs saying cannot be said in her presence, I need not hear it."

The man tensed, looked from one to the other, and pursed his lips. At last he nodded and they moved away.

# *Chapter 55*

As the lord led the way up the nearest tower to the battlements, Margaret tried to pull from his hand, but Shane locked their entwined fingers together and held firm.

Moving some distance from the guards on duty, the man stopped and turned to face them. He paced a couple of times, his hands going from behind his back to his sides to clinched in front of him to back behind him once more.

"Will you speak, my lord, or nay?"

"What must be said is no easy thing for me, Lord Shane." He made one more small circuit across the battlement and back. "I am your father, Shane."

Shane almost lost his grip on Margaret's hand, but her trembling tightened it. "Lord La …"

"Lawson."

"Aye, Lord Lawson. I was led to believe Lord Averill to be …"

Lawson nodded. "Aye, many did believe so when Lucsa threw herself at him before she died. In truth, it was I who took her as lover." His cheeks colored as his gaze shifted to Margaret. "Lord Averill was one I shared confidence with, and it was he who advised I put Lucsa off."

Lawson turned away from them, fussed with his hands again, and looked over the wall to the south. "Lucsa worked in our kitchen. She smiled at me whenever our paths crossed." A wry chuckle blurted from him. "When my wife forbid me sweets, Lucsa sneaked them to me."

He sighed as his shoulders slumped low. "I spent more time with her after my son turned two. My wife doted on the boy. I told myself my flirtations with the woman were nothing, but then I found myself in her bed. It soon became a place I frequented. She came to me the following year, saying she was with child. I could not face my own sin. I eagerly took Averill's advice and sent her out of my home, refusing to acknowledge the child could be mine. I cut her off from all aid, all contact, all mercy."

Now Lawson turned and looked at Shane. "God saw my sin. He knew my heartlessness, and like David, I could not hide from the consequences of what I had done. My boy died of the fever before he saw five winters. But unlike David, I refused to acknowledge my sin. God would not let me hide. My wife carried, and lost, six more children before she too died. Still I would not bend my knee."

He shook. "Then I came to the council of the lords. She stood before me again and pointed her finger. It was as though God Himself put my sin in the light for all to see. But you … you Shane." He whispered the next words. "My son." He stood a little taller. "You—flesh of my flesh—you refused to take the crown, and the glory she tried to ply you with. You chose the right, when for so many years I clung to the wrong."

"I confessed my sin that very day and came to claim you as my blood and rightful heir, but you left the castle before I could seek you out. I have long looked for you, Shane." He stepped nearer, offering Shane his hand. "I claim you as heir, Shane. You shall be lord of Clophill Manor at any time of your choosing. I welcome you and your family." He smiled at Margaret, whose head hung so low she never saw his offer of friendship.

Shane did not take his hand outright. "Sir, I find I am at a loss as to what to say."

Lawson nodded, and his hand disappeared behind his back. "It is much to take in all at once, my lord."

"I will speak with Lady Margaret. She owns a tavern in Kinglet Hill. She may not wish to give up her independence to be a lady of nobility." Shane did his best to suppress any smile.

Lawson nodded. "Of course, my lord. I know too that King Edgar and Queen Mariamne wish you to remain here. You have much to consider. But I had to speak."

Shane now extended his hand. "And glad I am you did, sir. Thank you for giving me a name, and a title of some standing."

The men exchanged an awkward handshake, and Lawson left Shane and Margaret on the battlement to continue the discussion.

Shane's heart soared. He did indeed have a title and could now provide well for Margaret, Carling, and the future children born to him. He turned to her, but again she shied from him. He snatched up her hands and pulled her nearer.

"My sweet lady, I can now properly ask—"

"Nay, my lord. Don't speak the words. I am not the woman for you." She again tried to pull from him.

"I will have no other as my wife."

"You are a lord—true, and legitimate. I am of lowly birth." Her attempts to free herself became more frantic.

"I am the son of a nobleman and a witch, my lady. Saying I am legitimate is far beyond my status. I am grateful for Lord Lawson's offer, but I spoke true. I go where you go—manor, tavern, hovel, cave. Where you lay your head, I desire to be."

Her tears tumbled and her voice broke. "I be no good for you, my lord." The more her anxiety grew, the more frantic sounding her words became.

Shane tightened his hold on her wrists, and frustration gave his words a bite. "Margaret, speak woman. Whatever vexes you, I will hear the words. Did you not yourself say, God brought us together and it would be a cruel thing indeed to not let us be as one?"

At last her gaze rose to his, her cheeks wet and eyes swollen. "I heard what you said—of what my husband did to me. I spoke of it to the royal healer as he tended my feet. He examined me." Her voice broke, and she cried her next words. "I can never bear you children, sir. As a lord, you must have an heir." Her tears increased.

Shane placed his hands on either side of her face and held it tenderly, wiping her tears with his thumbs. "Margaret, my love." He smiled at saying those words. "We have Carling. When it comes time, I will see she is married to a good man, and if need be, announce him as my heir. But my dear lady, a physician knows not all. Heavens, King Edgar believed he could sire no children—yet God blessed them with two."

Joy bubbled up in him until he thought he would explode from it. "What of Hannah in the Bible, who prayed at the tabernacle before Eli for a child. She bore Samuel and many other children. Sarah was childless until she gave Abraham a son at ninety. And the holy Mary. She had never lain with any man, and yet bore the Savior. Whether we are blessed with children is all in God's hands, Margaret. Now, woman, will you wed me?"

She stared at him, her breathing reduced to stuttered gasps.

"I love you, Margaret of the Hart and Spoon, and wish only to live each day at your side as we raise Carling. What say you?"

She nodded and slipped into his arms, nestling her head under his chin. She clung to him, and the tears started again.

He kissed the top of her head. "I care not what Carrington told you. I believe God will bless us with children."

She tightened her hold—and he burned.

# *Chapter 56*

Shane stepped from his horse in the village square of Kinglet Hill and tossed the reins to one of the knights who now pledged him loyalty.

"My Lord Shane, good it is to see you again, hale and fitting of your title." Hannah stepped forward with a quick observance and tried to loop her arm in his.

Shane stepped from her. "Mistress Hannah."

"Have you come to reward the kindnesses shown you here? Or mayhaps you seek something more?"

"I returned to speak with my friend John."

A pout grew on her slim lips as she tilted her head and batted her lashes at him. "Oh, my dear lord. Are you quite sure you did not come for someone else?"

Shane reached out his arm toward those now joining his party of travelers. "Hannah, have you met my wife, Lady Margaret?" He wrapped his arm tightly about her and placed his hand on Carling's shoulder as she stood before them. "And our daughter, Mistress Carling?"

Hannah stood agape for several moments before sputtering, "My ladies, it is good to see you again. Fate seems to have smiled upon you."

Nestled in his embrace, Margaret spoke softly. "Hannah, might I offer you some advice, dear?"

The woman kept her gaze lowered but gave a single nod.

"Be yourself—without claims or pretense. Honor God, and allow Him to lift you if He should see fit to do so."

"Thank you, my lady. You are most kind." Hannah turned and disappeared in the growing crowd.

"So it is Lord Shane, the missing heir?" one man said, giving him a bow.

"I am no true heir of the king, though he loves me as his own—as does our queen. I have come to learn I do carry a bit of the nobility in me, but I would request you just call me Shane—and friend." Shane offered the man his hand. It was taken quickly as others around offered theirs as well.

"I heard we had royal visitors," a voice boomed above the others.

Shane started to turn at the same moment a mighty palm landed on his back. He stumbled forward, knocking into Carling. "John, my friend." Shane reached out and embraced the man. "How is your family?"

John nodded to Margaret and Carling, dressed in their finery. "Not as well as yers, I would wager, friend." He gave them a deep bow. "M'ladies." Straightening, he leaned into Shane, "Have ye made an honest woman of her?"

Shane turned to defend his beloved's honor, but he only had time to open his mouth before John threw up his hands in surrender and a boisterous laugh filled the air.

"Peace, friend. I meant not to besmirch the woman's character. I wished only to know if ye married her. Couldn't rightly understand why ye waited so long pinin' after her as powerful as ye did."

Shane swallowed the anger and nodded his head. "Aye, we were wed last week."

"And we received word the princess is safe by your hand."

"By God's hand, John."

"Oh yes, our Mighty and Loving God. Thank ye kindly for sending us a proper priest to see to our spiritual growth."

"The brother has been good?"

"That he has, that he has. Learned as much from him as from ye." John crossed his arms and considered him for a moment. "So what brings ye back to our tiny hamlet? Can't see ye as a man to gloat over yer good fortu—over yer blessin's."

Shane shook his head, took Margaret's hand, and—after a quick glance at her—turned back to John. "We had some business we wished to discuss with you."

John swept out his hand toward his home, and they followed him. Carling and Scruff played with his children outside while Margaret and Shane moved inside. Sitting across the table from John and his wife, their newest babe cradled in her arms, Shane turned to Margaret.

"I have decided to join my husband in his father's estate and help him there," she said with quiet grace. "I therefore have no need for the Hart and Spoon. You have," she cleared her throat and started again. "You have always treated me with kindness, offering aid even when I couldn't repay you. I would like to honor that gratitude by offering you the tavern."

John rubbed his chin. "Don't think I can rightly afford to buy it off you, Margg, and there is me own business to see to as well."

They both shook their heads. "No, brother," Shane said. "She wants to give it to you."

"Matthew has done a fine job of running the place, and he said his sister Katherine has been a big help. Let them run the tavern. The money the tavern brings in can be used to support your family, and you can gift it to Matthew when he marries—or Katherine." Margaret smiled.

"I don't know how to thank ye for such a gift."

"Allow me to return in a month and help you add those rooms to the tavern we discussed. With a proper inn here in Kinglet, everyone's business will grow."

John threw back his head with a laugh. "A fine lord come and help throw up mud walls?"

"I know myself well, John. 'He also that is slothful in his work, is even the brother of him that is a great waster.' I have lived far too long as that man. My hands will always find good to work at, and I would work with you, my friend."

John's hand shot across the table. "I will never see you become a laze-about, Shane. Ye have me word on it."

As the men shook hands, John's wife came and embraced Margaret. "Ye don't know what this means to us."

"I do know. I have been in great need before. God has been gracious."

"Thank you, m'lady. God bless you and Lord Shane with many children."

Margaret slipped her hand in Shane's. She stole a look from him.

"Thank you kindly," Shane said. "We are trusting God for all His hands will provide us in the future." Shane led Margaret outside. "Carling, are you ready to continue our journey."

"Yes, Daddy."

Shane loved to hear her call him that. He squeezed Margaret's hand, knowing God would bless them with more children to fill his every moment with joy. Back in the village center, they remounted their horses and met Lord Lawson outside the tavern.

"Is your business here concluded, son?"

"For now, Lord Lawson. I will return once my family is settled and see to building the inn for my friend."

"You intend to continue to labor?"

Shane kicked his horse to draw between Carling and Margaret. "Every day of my life, sir."

# *Afterword*

Shane rode to the crest of the ridge, joining Carling and Lawson. Little over a week had passed since he learned Lawson was his sire, but he could not bring himself to call the man father. King Edgar had raised him and taught him to be a man of honor—a man after God's heart. Lawson had shirked his responsibilities until left with no other options. Mayhaps in time …

Margaret, his beautiful bride, reined in her horse beside him, making his heart beat harder.

Scruff jumped and barked around them.

In the distance, the sun glinted off the ocean as Carling looked down into the town spread across the valley. "What's that place?"

"The town of Clop Valley," Lawson said.

"That is only one town? It has more houses than a whole bunch of Kinglet Hills."

"Kinglet is a very small hamlet, my girl," Shane said.

She turned and smiled up at him, and he returned the gesture.

Looking back at the valley, she pointed to the large manor house surrounded by a mighty wall on the hill beyond the town. "What's that?"

"That," Lawson said with pride, "is Clophill."

Carling stared at him, her head tipped to the side.

"It is your home, sweet girl," Lawson said.

"We are going to live there?" Her jaw hung open for a moment. "'Tis bigger than the king's castle."

"Well, my girl," Shane explained. "the royal palace is limited by the size of the rock it is built upon. Had the castle mount been larger, the kings of old would have built more grand."

Carling turned back to Lawson. "Which room is mine?"

The lord laughed. "There are a few rooms already used by servants, and my captain and his wife have a few rooms, so other than mine, you will have your choice."

"And you will not have a single room," Shane added. "You will have a bedchamber with a bathing chamber, an outer sitting chamber, and a playroom."

"Four rooms? Just for me?" Her eyes were as big as goose eggs. "And I can pick any I wish?"

"Well, don't go too far from us, little one," Margaret said.

Carling's head swiveled around toward Lawson. "Can we go right now?" She didn't wait for anyone to give her leave but spurred her horse forward.

Lawson's knights followed her and moved to surround her as she urged her mount into a cantor.

"It will be a joy to have children in the house," Lawson called as he moved to follow.

Shane turned to Margaret. Her lip disappeared between her teeth. He reached his hand out, and she took it. "Fret not, my love. God has our days in His hands."

She nodded, and they moved down the hill, followed by more knights who had fought the horde with him and chose to serve Shane.

Shane and Margaret made their home in Clophill. He never forgot how God saved him from himself. He regularly worked in the fields with those who served on his lands. He taught the three sons Margaret gave to him to value hard work of their own hands, to render aid no matter the social status of the one in need, and to follow God with their whole heart. And God blessed all his labors.

Glossary of Terms

**Ale-washed** – drunk

**Bairn** – a child; son or daughter.

**Bit by a barn weasel** - Tavern term, 1670 – 1700 for being drunk

**Braies** – underpants, fairly loose drawers

**Crenel** – any of the open spaces between the merlons of a battlement

**Dais** – a raised platform, as at the front of a room, for a lectern, throne, seats of honor, etc.

**Divan** – a long cushioned seat, usually without arms or back, placed against a wall

**Fief** – a piece of land, formerly granted by a feudal lord to somebody in return of service

**Fremd** – Old English for alien or strange

**Hart** – an adult male red deer

**Ill-liver** – old Scottish slang for an immoral person

**Kirtle** – a woman's loose gown, worn in the Middle Ages.

**League** – a unit of distance, in English-speaking countries usually estimated roughly at 3 miles

**Merlon** – (in a battlement) the solid part between the two crenels

**Night rail** – a woman's loose garment

**Pace** – fine feet

**Palled** – Totally drunk. From word for "sated." Late 1600s.

**Rod** – a distance equal to 5.5 yard

**Sandesman** – old English for "man who was sent," a messenger

**Snood** – a netlike hat or part of a hat or fabric that holds or covers the back of a woman's hair.

**Soapwort** – a plant, of the pink family, whose leaves are used for

**Thane** – originally meaning a military companion to the king, a thane was a man holding administrative office

# About the Author

Michelle Janene (Murray) the office manager/secretary/go-to-gal her her church by day
and writes Christian fantasy and historical fiction in all her free time.
She lives in Northern California with two crazy dogs and the characters of her imagination.

If you enjoyed *Rebel's Son* please review it on your favorite site.

Join Michelle's email list and get a free novelette at
MichelleJanene.com
You can also connect with Michelle:
Facebook: Michelle Janene-Author or Strong Tower Press
Twitter: @MichelleJaneneM
Instagram: michellejanene_author
Pinterest: www.pinterest.com/michellejanene
Goodreads: Michelle Janene
StrongTowerPress.com

# Other Books

Check out these books also by Michelle

*Mission: Mistaken Identity*

The Changed Heart Series:
*God's Rebel*
*<u>Rebel's Son</u>*
*Hidden Rebel*

*Seer of Windmere*

*Barbarian Hero*

*Guardians of Truth*

*Culling a Miracle*

*Lost Stones*

*The Last Good King*

*The King's Vengeance*

*Thice a Bride*

*Dragon Fire*

www.ingramcontent.com/pod-product-compliance
Lightning Source LLC
Chambersburg PA
CBHW051640180726
48284CB00006B/1801